DISPLACED PERSONS

"These stories are somehow both tender and tough: while never sentimental, they have a clear-eyed vision of those who have been displaced, unhoused, and dispossessed. Though often wry and witty, they recognize the cost of anybody's personal history— Israeli, Jewish American, European—and those who must pay when the bill comes due. Joan Leegant writes eloquently about families, and she has a genius for portraying children and young adults. This book is beautiful and wonderfully readable. I loved it."

—CHARLES BAXTER, author of *The Sun Collective* and *The Feast of Love*

"In the funny and harrowing short stories of Joan Leegant's excellent collection *Displaced Persons*, characters navigate myriad forms of displacement, from putting a new life together after divorce to finding their place in an adopted country.... The short stories in *Displaced Persons* address difficult issues of Jewish identity and social expectations about marriage and family with complexity."

—FOREWORD REVIEWS

"What does it mean to be unsettled, to be neither here nor there? This is the question that animates Joan Leegant's uncannily sharp-eyed story collection *Displaced Persons*; caught between cultures, generations, geographies, and realities, her protagonists stumble into danger and emerge with desperate insight. The ground underneath this phenomenal book is both unsteady—moving in every sense of the word—and richly fertile."

—DAVID EBENBACH, author of *Miss Portland* and *The Guy We Didn't Invite to the Orgy and Other Stories*

"Moving, riveting, masterful—these stories, exploring the many ways human beings can be displaced, take the reader on a most profound journey. With impressive courage and beauty, they reveal how people can not only be displaced from their original homelands by the violent sweeps of history, but also how individuals can be exiled, through the loss of love or health or innocence, from their neighbors, their families, and their past selves. This collection forms an expansive and gorgeous tribute to the resilience people show when they manage, while still haunted by all that was endured or lost, to make homes in new and foreign realities."

— **JESSAMYN HOPE**, author of *Safekeeping*

"Joan Leegant's stories of women and men grappling with displacement (sometimes in their own homes) shimmer with wit and compassion. Few writers see so deeply into their characters' lives. Prepare to feel a shock of recognition."

— **DAWN RAFFEL**, author of *Boundless as the Sky* and *The Strange Case of Dr. Couney*

DISPLACED PERSONS

~

Joan Leegant

newamericanpress

Milwaukee, Wisconsin

newamericanpress
✧
Milwaukee, Wisconsin

Some of the stories in this collection were originally published, in slightly different
form, as follows: "The Baghdadi" in *The Normal School* (Spring 2012) and in *The
New Diaspora: The Changing Landscape of American Jewish Fiction*, Victoria Aarons,
Avinoam J. Patt, Mark Schechner, Editors, Wayne State University Press, 2015; "The
Eleventh Happiest Country" in *New England Review* (2018) and in *Moment Magazine*
(September/October 2019); "Beautiful Souls" in *Colorado Review* (Fall/Winter 2011);
"Displaced Persons" in *The Literarian* (March 2012); "Remittances" in *Promised Lands:
New Jewish American Fiction on Longing and Belonging*, Derek Rubin, Editor, Brandeis
University Press, 2010; "Bus" in *Bellevue Literary Review* (Spring 2013); "Hunters and
Gatherers" in *Salamander* (Spring/Summer 2015); "Wild Animals" in *New England
Review* (2023); "The Innocent" in *JewishFiction.Net* (2014); "The Book of Splendor" in
Ascent (March 2017); "Roots" in *Moment Magazine* (November/December 2012).

Printed in the United States of America
ISBN 978-1-941561-32-4

Cover + Book Design by Angelo Maneage

For ordering information, please contact:
INGRAM BOOK GROUP
ONE INGRAM BLVD.
LA VERGNE, TN 37086
(800) 937-8000
ORDERS@INGRAMBOOK.COM

For media and event inquiries, please visit:
WWW.NEWAMERICANPRESS.COM

PROUD MEMBER

DISPLACED PERSONS

— PART ONE: EAST —

— PART TWO: WEST —

Much has been said about being in the present.
It's the place to be, according to the gurus,
like the latest club on the downtown scene,
but no one, it seems, is able to give you directions.

— **BILLY COLLINS**, "THE PRESENT"
from *The Rain in Portugal: Poems*

— PART ONE —

East

THE BAGHDADI

· ◊ ·

HE WAS BORN IN BAGHDAD and had come to Israel in
1962. But he was not one of those gung-ho Israelis who
thought all Jews should live there, he said. Only those who
had nowhere else to go. This was the second thing he told
me after giving his name, which was Murad. We were in a
parched courtyard at the university sipping lemonade, the
steamy afternoon closing in on us like a cloak, the boxy
apartment buildings of the Tel Aviv suburbs looming just
beyond like so many Soviet era rockets. An obscure novel-

ist from Oxford had been invited to speak—experimental, unreadable—and I'd felt obligated to attend. A foreigner, I did what was necessary to keep the job. Refreshments were being served beforehand to fortify us.

"I teach physics," he said, fishing in his wallet and pulling out a business card. "I did my M.A. in the States. Michigan. I come to these lectures to keep up my English."

I read the card. Hebrew and English. Murad Shemtov, Faculty of Sciences, Ben-Gurion University. "You drove all the way up from Beersheba for this talk?" I said. I had to find something to say. I wasn't interested in him but I had nobody else to talk to. The lecture was scheduled to start in a few minutes.

He tipped his head in the direction of the apartments. "I live over there. In Ramat Gan. I read about the talk in the newspaper. I like to meet Americans. It gets boring here."

I slipped the card into my bag where it would sink to the bottom with the linty tissues and broken pencils. I was a part-time lecturer in the English department filling in for someone who'd become ill. A lucky break. There were few positions for someone like me, a foreigner with an underused PhD. "Would you like to have a coffee after the talk?" the Baghdadi said.

I looked up. He was not attractive. Short, stocky, sixty-three, sixty-five. I hadn't come to the country for encounters with novel and picturesque fellow Jews from all over the world whose wrenching life stories—persecution, months-long treks across continents—would raise the hair on my arms. I was there because I needed a break from the

16

dreaded winter in Boston and because my husband had left in July to take up with a dancer from Moldova who was twenty-six years younger than him. Than me. And because I hated the pitying looks I was getting from our friends at home, as if I'd contracted polio.

"I don't think so," I said. I looked him square in the face. He had a thick mustache that made him look like Saddam Hussein.

"All right," he said, no trace of a smile. I paused, waiting for him to walk away or say something more, but he didn't, and before I could muster the courage to walk off myself, someone came along and shepherded us into the auditorium.

~

The lecture was long and tedious, the novelist reading from a prepared text that was excerpted from his forthcoming book of equally tedious criticism. The Baghdadi was waiting for me in the muggy October dusk. A full moon hung in the sky like a yellow coin. Construction machinery was silhouetted in the distance. New buildings were going up everywhere.

"Last month," he said, falling into step with me on my way to the bus, picking up the conversation as if it had never been interrupted, "the Americans brought the oldest Jew in Baghdad to Israel. Your soldiers accompanied him. I read about it in the newspaper. Fifteen Jews remaining in all of Baghdad, and they brought him. Eighty-nine years old. Did you know that Iraq is the oldest Jewish community in the world outside of here? In existence since the exile

17

in 586 B.C. to Babylon. Which is of course now modern Iraq."

"No, I didn't know that," I said. I also didn't know why I hadn't told him to go away except that all the other people at the lecture had quickly dispersed and I'd been left alone. I didn't really know anyone in the department; my only acquaintance, the person who'd told me about the position, was on sabbatical abroad. Most of the other faculty wasn't aware I was even there. I came to the university twice a week to teach my classes and left. No meetings, no committees, no other responsibilities.

"It's true," the Baghdadi said. "So now this man is stuck in an old folks home. He was taken from his house, his neighborhood, his friends, all Muslim but they treated him like one of their own. Therefore I telephone him and call on him. Because he is by himself, and the unpleasant facility in which he has been placed is not far from my flat." He made a *tsk tsk* sound. He carried a leather shoulder bag, like a woman, or an Italian. "These Americans. So impulsive. Or perhaps suffering from an excess of enthusiasm. They thought they were doing him a favor."

"It was a PR opportunity," I found myself saying. I hadn't meant to get involved in the conversation but there it was, pulling me in. "A photo-op," I said. "Probably some dumb government reporter's idea of good press. One of those embedded types trying to shore up public confidence in a tragically misbegotten war begun by our former Texas cowboy president."

"I think this is so. Do you love your government? I do not think you do."

18

We were nearing the bus stop. It was deserted. I'd feared as much. I rode a special line that was attached to the university and ran only during daytime hours. Now I'd have to walk to the other side of the campus and hope for a cab.

He said, "I loved the American government when I was in Michigan. I couldn't believe it. No censorship. Separation of religion and state. A civilized parliament. In Israel they shout at one another in the Knesset and poke fingers in each other's faces. The military until this day can censor newspaper articles. We did not have television until 1967. Ben-Gurion did not want it. He said it would make the population foolish and passive."

"Smart man." I made a show of looking at the schedule posted in the bus shelter, though it was obvious nothing was coming.

"Such a pity," the Iraqi said.

I glanced over at him. "What is?"

"Your war. The old man from Baghdad. The Israelis encouraged his removal, I'm sure. A big coup for Jerusalem." He took a handkerchief and wiped his forehead, which had been glistening slightly. A faint scent of mint emanated from his person. Maybe he used a minty detergent for his handkerchiefs, or kept gum in his pocket. Or a private supply of leaves for tea.

I took a long look at him as he wiped his face. He was not appealing. But he was attentive. Ramat Gan was ten minutes away. There was no bus, no one was waiting for me at my apartment, my one child on junior year abroad in Athens and my forty-eight-year-old husband in Paris strolling by the Seine and making French teenage love on satin sheets. "I'll take that coffee after all," I said to the Baghdadi.

He tucked away the damp handkerchief. "Very good," he said as if he'd been expecting me to change my mind all along.

~

He called me two days later. I wasn't surprised. The coffee had been brief and chaste—some talk about the construction boom in Tel Aviv, his recollection of winters in Michigan—and then he'd driven me home and asked for my number. He liked to use his English with native speakers, he said. When Israelis spoke it, he found the accent grating. My English was pure, he told me. Melodic, like the sound of a waterfall, or bells at a chapel. I must not be from New York, he added, where the tone is irritatingly nasal. Or Chicago, where it's flat like the landscape. He said this without smiling, without flattering; it was merely a fact, in his view. He was an amateur musician, a violinist who played in a chamber group in his apartment complex and had an ear for such things.

"I thought you might want to meet the old man," he said on the phone. "Why not? You have time, and you would find him interesting."

I said I didn't see how I would find him interesting since I spoke neither Arabic nor enough Hebrew to sustain a conversation. Nor did I want to view the man as a spectacle, a side show: The Oldest Living Jew from Baghdad. The Oldest Living Jew From the Oldest Jewish Community. It sounded like one of those coffee table books boys receive from distant relatives for their bar mitzvahs, the kind you don't know what to do with for the next thirty years and keep packing and unpacking every time you move house. My husband had several. *Famous American Jews in Baseball. A Pictorial History of the Jewish People. Jews of Many Lands.* He had brought them to the marriage along with his stamp collection and volumes of Blake and Coleridge and a terror of deep middle age with its inevitable closing of doors.

"I believe he speaks some English," the Baghdadi said to me. "The British were in Iraq for some time, you surely know. He told me he also once studied French. An educated man."

I glanced around my apartment, deciding. The owner was originally from London, working for the year in Toronto. We'd communicated only by email and she had left me extensive notes. The washing machine had a tendency to get *chuffy*. The building's *lift* didn't work reliably. Some of the cafes on the block had lovely *take-away*. I pictured Maggie Smith or Judy Dench or some other grande dame of the English theater, and it made me feel crude and childish, as if we Americans had never grown up or learned any manners.

"Well, then, what do you say? Are you terribly busy, or could you come along?"

He had my number, as my husband used to say. *That salesman really had your number. Like you were going to turn down an offer like that.* Of course I wasn't busy; no one would mistake me for overbooked. I wore my idleness on my sleeve.

"All right, I'll join you," I said, though I knew he knew that would be my answer. I didn't particularly like him, but there was something about him. He seemed to see through me. This made me slightly uneasy, men who presume, who think they have you pegged, but I went along with it. It's not like I thought there would be any danger.

~

Who hasn't seen such places? The warehoused elderly lining the lobby in wheelchairs, the faint urine smell, the bored-looking aides. The old man sat erect and alert in a small common room off the lobby. Someone had tried to cheer up the place with flowers. A radio played piano sonatas. The Baghdadi said something in Arabic to the old man, who nodded, glanced in my direction. His eyes were a surprising bright blue, and he was clean-shaven, though he bore a strong resemblance to the mustached Baghdadi nonetheless. Or perhaps he didn't; perhaps it was my inability to tell the difference. Israelis often told me how much I resembled other Americans. Our body language, clothing, posture: we looked alike to them.

The Baghdadi gestured to a chair: I should sit. We had brought a box of pastries. The old man looked in the box, looked away. Later we would have coffee, the Baghdadi told me. They would show me how they drank it in Iraq. Demitasse espresso, with a small spoon, a cube of sugar between the teeth.

Someone turned off the radio. The sonatas melted into the air. The old man looked at me, sizing me up. He wore gray sweatpants with a Castro logo, a stylish brand of

Israeli sportswear I'd seen in the shops.

"Please tell him I'm not your wife."

"My wife? This is not what he thinks."

"I've seen this look before. Please inform him."

A shrug, then a cascade of Arabic. Apparently the old man had forgotten his English—if he'd ever had any. The old man laughed and the Baghdadi smiled and chuckled. I hadn't seen him smile before, and his teeth were shockingly white, as if he'd had them recently replaced or refinished, like formica kitchen cabinets.

"What's so funny?"

"Pardon?"

"Why are you laughing? The two of you, you're laughing."

"We aren't laughing."

"Yes, you are."

The old man watched us through the volley.

"He says you ought to have been my wife. Perhaps then you wouldn't have left me for another man, like my actual wife did."

So. A kindred spirit. Had he sniffed me out? Like finding like? He gave the old man a French newspaper. French Jews were buying up real estate in Israel like there was no tomorrow. A decade of antisemitic violence had made them nervous; they wanted insurance policies. A place to run to, just in case.

The man glanced down at the pages. Within a minute his eyes had closed.

"Let's get a coffee," the Baghdadi said.

"Now? We've only just arrived."

"Soon they will take him to his room and bring him his medications, help him change his clothes. He has occasional accidents. We should give him privacy." He saw my reluctance. "Don't worry. He knows I am coming back."

In the café across the street he told me about his wife. They'd met in the Israeli army. She had come from Moroccan stock. "They're unreliable, the Moroccan women. They are too beautiful, so they cannot remain faithful. They and the Yemenites. Next it will be the Ethiopians. Have you noticed? Their women are magnificent. Like the Queen of Sheba, every one of them." He sipped his espresso. "And your husband? Where is he?"

"Paris," I said. "On a fling. A long fling." He nodded as if it were nothing; as if a fling were part of marriage as usual. Business trips. Lecture tours. Flings. "With a dancer from Moldova. You know where that is? I looked it up. Eastern Europe. Between Romania and Ukraine. She's a year older than our daughter. How transparent is that, chasing a woman the age of your children."

"And your daughter?"

"Abroad for the year. Athens. Seven hundred and fifty miles from Tel Aviv. A two hour plane flight." I picked up my coffee. "I couldn't bear the thought of sitting home alone in my cold house in Boston, but I couldn't very well follow her to Greece. So I came here. I visit her, she visits me, it works out." His expression was unchanged and I wondered if he thought I was rich, a spoiled American who could hop countries just like that, on a whim. "The university position here was quite serendipitous," I said. "Lucky," I added, in case he didn't know the word. "I ran into an Israeli colleague at a conference who told me about it. It's not like I don't need full-time work. I do. But my job was ending. Ordinarily I'm not idle. I'm actually a college administrator, not an academic. It's important for women to have satisfying careers, don't you agree? My daughter knows this."

"What does she think of her father's behavior? With the dancer?"

I watched him over the rim of my coffee cup. Why was I telling him about this? Since when did he deserve the truth when no one else—not my friends, not even my sister—did? "She's horrified. The dancer was her friend from university. That's how he met her. She was visiting us before returning to Moldova for the summer. They had sex in our guest room while my daughter and I were making strawberry shortcake for her farewell dinner."

An impassive nod. He reminded me of our accountant, a bland man who preferred to do the numbers in his head to using a calculator. It had taken me years to understand that the silences during our appointments meant only that he was running figures. I went on, unable to stop myself. "The girl's an unbridled opportunist, my daughter has since learned. Sleeps with everything in pants. She wants a visa or green card or whatever it is one needs in order to stay in the States after college. So this is how she tries to get it. My husband is the latest in a string of such opportunities. Though apparently a very receptive one."

"Most unpleasant."

"Most. Do you have children?"

"A son. He lives in Nice. He is married to a Gentile

who calls me to harp and harangue. She favors the Palestinians. It is very fashionable in France to favor the Palestinians. They don't see that the Arab leadership bears any responsibility for the situation here. Only Israel is to blame. I find it tiresome. I am not naïve about this government, but there are two sides. I have told my son not to come see me if they can't say anything good about this country."

The old man was sleeping when we arrived at his room. We left the pastries, and the Baghdadi left a note. "The Babylonian Empire was the cradle of civilization, you no doubt know," he told me as we walked to his car. "Literature, law, astronomy, mathematics: it had it all. Did you know that Babylon was the largest city in the world at one time? Two hundred thousand people lived there in 1700 BC. It was the center of Jewish life for a thousand years. The Talmud was completed there in the year 700. It took three hundred years to compile. " He opened the passenger door for me, then walked to the other side, let himself in. "But Iraqi Jews have always been in exile."

"I thought you said you were not that kind of gung-ho Israeli. The kind who says all Jews should live here," I said.

"I'm not. Jews should feel free to live wherever they please." He started the ignition. "That doesn't mean some are not still in exile."

~

Three days later he was waiting for me on the concrete plaza outside my building at the university. It was during the half-time break for my first class; what was supposed to

26

be fifteen minutes to stretch or use the facilities routinely bled into half an hour. Students here were not concerned with the rules; they were not cowed by authority.

"The old man is very sick. I need your help," he said before I could even open my mouth. I had wanted to express some indignation over his aggressiveness, showing up in the middle of my workday, but I couldn't work up a sufficient froth. "The doctors don't know what is wrong with him. Surely you must be acquainted with American physicians here who can diagnose the problem."

"How would I know any American doctors? I've been here two months, I hardly know anyone at all."

"You must think. I can pay for a private consultation. The physicians at his facility are the worst in the system. They don't care about the residents. They treat them like cattle. Worse than cattle. They are happy to let them die."

One of my students was smoking a cigarette and watching us. I turned to her but she kept staring. I tipped my head, hinting that she should move off, but she stayed put. I wasn't good with these young people; they were different from students at home. They required a bluntness, a directness I didn't have and couldn't appropriate. They found me vague and indecisive, overly polite; I allowed too many competing opinions in class and praised anyone who contributed. They wanted someone who was more forceful, someone with strong views. They thought I had no backbone.

"I'm very sorry," I said when the smoker hadn't moved, "but I can't help you."

"The Americans are to blame," he said. "They brought

him here. In Iraq he wasn't sick. In Iraq his neighbors cared for him. You have a responsibility."

"*I* have a responsibility?" It was ridiculous. I wasn't the U.S. government, the U.S. military. I didn't authorize the airlift of the Oldest Living Jew in Baghdad. "Look, I appreciate that you're concerned, but I have nothing to offer you. Why don't you call your colleagues at Ben-Gurion? Or ask your chamber music friends. You've lived here for fifty years, you must know a million people. Why are you asking me?"

He looked stunned, even—for the first time—silenced. As if no one had ever posed such a question. "Why wouldn't I ask you?" he said. "I would ask everybody. That is what one does. You ask everyone. Then maybe you will get to the person who can help. Why are you Americans so afraid to ask for help, or to offer it? I remember this from Michigan. People told me: Murad, no one wants to get involved. I do not understand this."

I looked away, exhausted. My daughter had emailed that morning. Her father, my husband, wanted to fly to Athens this weekend to see her. She was furious and didn't want him to come. She wanted to know what to do. I had limited patience at the moment.

"Here is what you can do," he said, and I turned back. "Call the American embassy and get a list of American physicians. They will give it to you. They will not give it to me."

His face was deeply lined and he looked like he hadn't slept. I would need my passport, he instructed, when I called the embassy. Then he handed me his cell phone and a slip of paper with a number. We moved to a stone bench in the shade. The plaza had filled with students milling about between classes, lighting up and sipping from plastic water bottles. Two girls in tight jeans squeezed onto the bench beside us and unwrapped pungent-smelling cheese and tomato sandwiches. I took out my passport and dialed the number. With each name the clerk read to me, I repeated the information aloud while the Iraqi wrote it down in tiny precise script on a small pad, the girls listening attentively. When I was done, I closed the phone and handed it to him. He hurried off in the direction of the parking lots, the girls calling out to wish him good luck.

~

I phoned him that evening to ask about the old man. "Were you able to reach any of the doctors?"

"I beseeched many answering machines. Now I am waiting for the physicians to ring me back."

"Then I won't keep you. You must leave the line free."

"This is no problem," he said. "It will beep if a call comes in."

I didn't know what else to say. Yet I'd wanted to call. "My husband is asking to visit my daughter in Athens. She doesn't want him to come."

"Tell her she must allow it. He is her father."

"But why? His behavior has been disgraceful. She's entitled to be furious. Apparently he's told this irresistible dancer that he was cornered into marriage and trapped into parenthood. Trapped. This is what my daughter now has to hear. Can you imagine? I can cope with the part about being cornered; the marriage has had problems, some of it my fault. But for my daughter? All her college friends know what's going on. It's humiliating."

"She must agree to see him. You must tell her."

"But that would be a complete denial of her feelings. Which is not how my daughter and I operate. I don't dictate what she should do; I encourage her to make her own decisions." I glanced around the British woman's living room, agitated. It was arranged too carefully, too perfectly; I was afraid to move anything. There were crystal vases on the bookshelves and a set of gold-rimmed bone china teacups on display. Everything seemed perilously close to breaking. One scream, and it would all come crashing to the floor. "This isn't Afghanistan, where girls have to obey the patriarchal hierarchy. Or ancient Babylonia, for that matter."

"Those are not relevant. She is his daughter, she must let him visit her."

"But you told your own son not to visit you," I said.

"That was political. This is personal. It is different."

"That's baloney." Silence on the other end. "That means garbage in English. Bullshit, if you'll pardon my crudeness."

Another pause. An elaborately framed painting of pears in a bowl that hung behind the couch was slightly askew. I wondered if I could bring myself to adjust it. Touching anything seemed fraught with the possibility of wreckage.

"In 1900," he said, "there were fifty thousand Jews in Baghdad, a quarter of the city's population. Judges, professors, doctors. Then came the 1930's; the government sided with the Nazis. Anti-Jewish riots, a bloody pogrom. In 1948, when Israel was established, things got worse. Boycotts of Jewish businesses, destruction of property, arrests. One hundred and twenty thousand Jews were airlifted to Israel in 1951. The Israelis arranged it. It was very important to get out."

"You've changed the subject."

"I haven't. You will see."

"All right. 1951. You told me you didn't leave until 1962."

"Correct. My family was not ready in 1951. But ten years later I was a teenager. They were hanging Jews in the public squares, claiming they were Israeli spies. It was dangerous either way, staying or leaving. Escaping Jews were shot or kidnapped; if you succeeded in getting out, you would never be able to return. I made my escape plans with a friend whose father was so angry he was leaving that he could hardly speak to him the entire two weeks it took to make our preparations. Baghdad was his home, this boy's father insisted. Our home. Jews had lived there for two thousand years. Things would improve, he said. We just had to wait it out. Israel was a backwater, a primitive wasteland for illiterates and farmers and the useless religious who prayed all day, and he wanted no part of it."

"So what happened?"

"The boy and his father had words. Terrible words. My friend said vicious things, accusing his father of being too attached to his business and his possessions. He called his father a coward and a selfish bourgeois. He told him he was blind to the lessons of history and to the opportunity

31

to be a free man. The father called my friend naïve and starry-eyed, unprepared for real life and influenced by Israeli agents pushing emigration just to have more bodies to populate Israel's unlivable perimeter and fight its wars. Words hurled on both sides, like spears."

"And then what happened?"

"The boy left and never saw or spoke to his father again."

"Never? Not even a phone call?"

"Nothing. He was bitter and angry. So was his father. They held to their positions. Righteous indignation, I think is the term. And then it was too late to rectify matters. History conspired to keep them apart." A beeping came on the line. "I must go. Please excuse me. Someone is trying to call."

~

I composed an email to my daughter. *Your father is a narcissistic child. He has no idea how hard this is for you. Forget about Sofia, she's not worth a nanosecond of your attention. Do you want to come here for the weekend? We can have drinks at a café on the sand and then go to a museum so you will feel like it's educational.*

I read it twice, then deleted it and stared at the empty screen before turning to the pile of student papers next to me. I didn't want to tell my daughter to let her father visit. She shouldn't have to allow it. I thumbed through the pile. *Romantic Love in the Early Sonnets of Elizabeth B. Browning. E.B. Browning: Poetess of Love or Loss? How Do I Love Thee, Mrs. Browning Counts the Ways.*

32

I didn't want to read these papers. I had stopped crying over my husband and didn't want to think about love. Love made you miserable. It made you scream and smash things and leave your home and friends and everything familiar just to get away. It made you run off to Paris for what you foolishly thought was a second chance, and arrange a career-killing transfer to your company's European office so you could do it. It made you conduct hours-long phone calls from Athens with your mother, trying to figure out how you could have missed it, how the happily married life you thought was going on around you turned out not to have been so happy. I leafed through the pages beside me, reading a sentence here, a sentence there. *Elizabeth Browning is a good poet who gets very often sick. Elizabeth Brown was invalid, writing poems in bed. Elizabeth Barrett married Robert Browning who wrote romantic letters which her father did not approve, he did not want any of his children to be marry, so they are running off to Italy, no wonder she writes such strong love poems of feeling.* I flipped through each one, checking to make sure there were no blank sheets inside, a nasty new trick sweeping American campuses perpetrated by bloodthirsty students eager to ferret out lazy professors, and when I was satisfied that their Israeli counterparts had no such cruel intentions, I gave everyone a B+, for trying.

~

The old man, it turned out, had undiagnosed diabetes. This was why he had been so lethargic and sleepy, the Baghdadi told me over coffee on the patio of the university cafeteria, triumphant. The American doctor had diag-

33

nosed it in a snap, he said, raising his fingers in the air to demonstrate: *snap!* Just like that, the American physician knew.

"How could it have gone undetected for so long?" I asked.

"It was mistaken for exhaustion, old age. In Iraq it was less noticeable. He ate better there. More frequent meals with his neighbors. Food he was familiar with. So it was naturally controlled. But when he came here"—he waved around, drawing in the whole country with a sweep of his arm—"everything was disrupted. The condition became aggravated." He picked up his coffee cup. "Now the American has saved the day. He will have medication and he will be all right."

"Who is this wizard doctor?" I asked, in case I might need one sometime.

He withdrew a folded piece of paper from the leather shoulder bag and handed it to me. Steven O. Goldstein, M.D., an address on Hayarkon Street, Tel Aviv. Near the big hotels. And the embassy. Convenient to diplomats and tourists.

I read down to the diagnosis and recommendations. Everything was neatly typed in Hebrew and English. The old man's age was listed as eighty-nine with a question mark. His name was Sasson Shemtov. Shemtov. *Good name* in Hebrew. As in good reputation. It was a name I would not have forgotten.

I handed back the paper. "He's your father, isn't he," I said.

The Baghdadi carefully put the paper into his pocketbook. "Why would you say that? Shemtov is a common name among Iraqi Jews. It's like Smith in America." He looked up at me, his expression fastidiously neutral. "Half of Babylonian Jewry carries this appellation. Shemtov. It means He of a Good Name. Jews in Iraq, you must understand, did not have formal second names until my grandparents' day. Before that, it was simply So-and-So son of So-and-So. You carried your father's given name. It was a form of respect. When the authorities gave them the list of choices, everyone chose this because it was closest to what they were used to."

But I knew I was right. And I knew that he knew it. It was his life he'd been narrating, he who had fled and could never go back, who had had words with a father he would not see or speak to for fifty years. But now all that had changed.

"Has your daughter decided what she will do?" he said, folding his hands, composing himself. "About your husband's visit?"

"No."

"Then you must tell her."

"I will tell her she doesn't have to see him. That she should listen to her feelings."

"I think you are wrong."

"I didn't ask for your opinion thank you."

"But it is her father."

"Exactly. And that doesn't give him a free pass. He needs to bear the consequences of his deeds. Actually, he needs to learn that there *are* consequences. This is not something he has in his repertoire."

He refolded his hands, his accountant face immovable. Light perspiration had gathered above the thick mustache.

"You are making a mistake."

"You're one to talk. What about your son?"

"This is different."

"No, it isn't." I'd had enough. I was tired of his bull-headed insistence. I took my briefcase and got up to go to the bus. "I don't understand you. You're doing the same thing with your son that you did with your father. Repeating your own toxic history. Righteous indignation, I think you called it." I stopped and looked at him a long minute. "And now you're just projecting that onto me, trying to get me to do what you aren't able to do yourself." I turned and started to walk off.

"Why is that wrong?" he called after me, but I pretended I didn't hear.

~

Their photo appeared in the weekend edition of *Ha'aretz*. In the English-language version the article was titled "Father-Son Reunion: the Oldest Jew in Baghdad Comes Home." The old man sat in a straight-backed chair in the common room at the senior residence, the Baghdadi posed stiffly behind him. They had been separated half a century ago, the article said, and had been brought together courtesy of the U.S. Central Command in Iraq. According to the reporter, the son, Murad, hadn't passed a day in Israel without thinking of his father.

And the father? the reporter asked. Fewer than fifteen Jews were said to still be living in Baghdad, not enough men for even a minyan. Was the father happy to be settled in Israel, finally among his people?

Of course, his son answered for him. For his father, every day in Baghdad had been as the psalmist wrote: *We sat by the rivers of Babylon and wept as we remembered Zion.*

And now? the reporter asked.

Now we are both here, nobody in exile anymore. Not him, not me.

You? the reporter asked. *You've been here fifty years.*

There are many kinds of exile.

That night, I closed my eyes but couldn't sleep. I kept seeing the two of them, the old man in the chair, the weepy son with his hand on his father's bony shoulder. I got up and turned on my computer and pulled up my daughter's email.

You have to let him come see you, I wrote. *Do it soon, as soon as you can. You need to listen to me, I know I am right.*

I read it twice, then hit Send. Later, when my daughter next came to visit, I would explain.

THE ELEVENTH
HAPPIEST COUNTRY

· ◊ ·

Roi's old friend from the army, Tal, had been an actor before he got religious and now he wanted to make another film and wanted Roi to do it. An action flick. Tal checked with his rebbe in B'nai Brak and it was all right.

"Whoa, man. Looking like that?" said Roi, waving at Tal's face—the beard, the peyis spiraling down over his ears, the black kippa. They were at a café in downtown Tel Aviv on Sheinkin. It wasn't certified kosher but you couldn't traife up espresso beans.

Tal had an answer ready right away. He said the movie would be about a former con man who'd found God but was dragged back into crime by his former con man buddies to do one last heist. So he does. It goes wrong and he goes to jail. Or maybe it goes right and he makes off with a pile of stolen cash. Tal hadn't figured that part out yet.

"How can you make a flick like that?" Roi said. "It would have to have some cheesy ending where the guy sees the light again and gives it all back and comes to his knees in repentance. It'll be terrible. Shit. I can't direct shit like that."

"No, no," Tal said. His eyebrows were thickly bunched in concentration. Roi hadn't noticed before how hairy Tal's eyebrows were. Maybe because now there was so much additional hair in the same neighborhood. "It'll be a real heist movie with a real heist movie ending. Prison or victory. The fact that the guy's religious will have nothing to do with it. He'll just be like all the other scumbags and thieves, only with"—he waved at his face—"this." He paused. "What?" His dark eyes looked hard into Roi's. "I'm not asking to film my life questions. No deep meaning here. I promise."

~

Roi didn't believe him but he didn't have much else going on and Tal was a good friend. Also a good actor. Really good. The Americans were about to recruit him and make him into a star but then Tal disappeared into some yeshiva or other. But before that, you could tell Tal was onto something. When everyone else in workshops were protecting themselves and not wanting to get in touch with their inner murderers or thugs, Tal, with no acting classes at all, threw himself into it whole hog. A woman, a dog, a Nazi, a prissy British schoolmaster, he was totally there. So there it practically killed him. He felt everything. And was everything. He could be an eggplant or your conniving uncle or psychotic cousin. It got to be too much. Totally permeable. Eight, nine films. It was after that that he got religious. He said if he was going to feel everything in the universe, maybe he should try feeling God. Roi wasn't crazy about religion but he thought Tal had a point. It didn't cost him anything and was better than drugs or another trip to India or a psychiatrist. The only side effects were the dark clothes and the hair.

Also, Roi had to admit, Tal looked much better these days. He'd put on needed weight and the little flecks of gray in his beard gave him some nice dignity. Though removing the tattoo had hurt. Roi was there and saw. It had been on Tal's upper arm, a small anchor with a coiling rope, like in American sailor movies. Very popular. Which is what the guy in Goa told them when he sold Tal the design, the two of them decompressing in India after the army like all the other hollowed out Israelis looking for a shred of bliss. About Tal's tattoo Roi liked to say that he was there for both the installation and the teardown.

~

Roi called up a couple of producers he knew in north Tel Aviv where the money lived and said he had an amazing project but couldn't say who was attached but that when they found out it would blow their minds. Everyone

41

in Europe would be jumping all over this one. He was giving the Israelis a heads-up because he loved them and there
was loyalty and it felt only right to give them first dibs before he went to the French or the Germans or the Austra-
lians. Is it Tal, is it Tal Geffen, they wanted to know, but
Roi played coy. I can't say. Soon. I promise. Soon. They
were all immediately on board, Roi's past flops forgiven.
Roi was a good salesman. He knew it, they knew it. Nobody minded a little manipulation. It's how the game was
played. They played it in T.A. the same way it was played
in L.A. and that made the Israelis feel good: they were as
pro as Hollywood. Except in Israel they all knew each other for a hundred years and went to school together and the
army and to each other's kids' bar mitzvahs. Which had
its drawbacks. They drove each other crazy. Nobody was
polite. They loved each other like brothers, which could
make them all want to kill each other until they made up
and all went out for beers on the beach.

~

After India, where Tal's brain got wrecked on E and
raves and too much inward gazing because after the army
nobody could bear to revisit that experience even in their
best nightmares, Roi and Tal went together to New Jersey.
They worked the Dead Sea products pushcarts in the malls
and then Roi went to film school in Manhattan while Tal
recuperated on Roi's couch from the strain of employ-
ment and made the hummus. Roi got his tuition paid by
an eighty-five-year-old Jewish philanthropist in New York
who wanted Israeli film to stop being only about trauma-

tized Holocaust survivors finding redemption on kibbutz or the Mossad chasing down ex-Nazis in South America. That's all Americans ever saw, the philanthropist, Len, said. Could Roi learn to make movies that showed ordinary Israeli life? Len had read somewhere that Israel was one of the happiest countries in the world, according to surveys. Why was that? Could Roi make movies to show that?

He could, Roi said, and Len shook his hand and paid two years' tuition and invited him and Tal to his and his wife Ruth's boat in the Hamptons whenever they wanted. Roi dedicated his first film to Len, who died before it was released but not before arranging distribution, and for a while Roi was a hot property.

~

The heist, Tal told Roi the next time they met, which was at a kosher joint on Tchernikovsky because Tal was hungry, would involve diamonds. Which Roi immediately said posed a problem because a) no diamond dealer would let them near the goods to film and b) Jewish diamond dealers were a hackneyed stereotype. Roi wanted Tal to come up with something original, something not involving jewelry or gems since the genre had been thoroughly saturated, starting with the mother ship Hitchcock heist about jewels and gems in the fifties starring Gary Grant.

Paintings? Tal wanted to know, working his cheese toast. A treasure map? An ancient codex? Coins?

Done done and overdone, Roi told Tal, watching him eat. The cheese looked like the old government issue yellow cheese, which surprised Roi as he hadn't thought about that in a long time. It wasn't the actual government brand because that didn't exist anymore, but this was just like it, bland yellow squares, and seeing it gave Roi a puddly nostalgic feeling for his childhood when nobody in the country had any money and everyone felt heroic because there were more important things to worry about than gourmet food. Now all the places made trendy goat or sheep's cheese toast, which was tasty but not the same in terms of character building.

"How about Judaica?" Tal said, picking up his second half.

"No, no. Too kitschy, sentimental schlock, grandma's candlesticks hidden in her quilt while escaping a pogrom in the Pale. And anyway what kind of black market is there for that?"

"A big one! Don't you remember the display case at Len and Ruth's penthouse? Brass menorahs from the trash heaps in Spain? Handmade silver Torah pointers and twelfth century spice boxes? Who knows where Len got all that? He'd have gladly paid some shady middleman."

Roi said he didn't remember any of that stuff at Len and Ruth's. It had been sixteen years ago, after all.

"I remember," Tal said, plucking the olives off his plate and popping them into his mouth. They looked like very good olives. That was one thing the country was very skilled at. Some Israelis were now curing their own olives, like the Arabs did, instead of buying them at the super-market. It was a trend. Like getting a share of a vineyard if you lived in California. "The man was devoted to the Jewish people. Loved everything about them. Made a big impression on me. An inspiration."

Roi said he believed him. All Roi remembered was the yacht. Someone said Spielberg had one nearby so Roi went there often, hoping.

~

Tal's first acting role was in Roi's debut film. Honoring Len's wish to portray ordinary Israeli life, the story was about four post-army friends with nothing to do after India and were now in Tel Aviv filled with angst about their tormented country and their tormented tattooed selves. Roi couldn't afford to pay four professional actors so Tal took one of the parts for free because how hard could it be to play a guy lying on somebody's couch unable to move? He was amazing at it and the film was a hit. Tal became a celebrity. Women threw themselves at him. People stopped him on the street to say he was just like their brother or son or cousin and to ask how he ever got out of the funk and off the sofa.

They were asking about his character but it applied to the real Tal too. The answer of course was Shira, who had a bit part as the love interest of one of the other guys and had nothing to do with Tal's character. But though in real life Tal fell hard for Shira, Shira fell harder for Roi and became Roi's girlfriend and, not long after the film wrapped, his wife, so Tal didn't mention her when people asked about the cure. It was one of those things that could've destroyed the friendship but didn't. It took a while for Tal to recover, which he did on one of the other guy's couches. Roi and Tal still loved each other like brothers after that because what could they do, it was Shira's choice.

~

Tal's next idea was that the object of the heist would be a priceless antiquity, a clay statue of a Canaanite fertility goddess with pointy breasts and prominent genitals. Len had a couple of those in his display cabinet. Eight or ten inches tall, very valuable. They also made a big impression on Tal.

"Are you crazy?" Roi said. This time they were in Roi and Shira's apartment on Bograshov. Roi brought fried eggplant and chopped salad from the takeout place on Dizengoff to the coffee table. Shira was in Helsinki making money to support Roi's art because she was a crackerjack software developer and believed in him, but Roi worried that the spousal gravy train was going to dry up. He hadn't had a successful project in six years. Shira was thirty-nine and dropping hints about a baby. A little Roi. A little Shira. A little Shiroi. "How could your rebbe approve a movie about a pagan idol?"

Tal was stretched out on the sofa looking at the ceiling like it was psychoanalysis. Or the old days on Roi's couch in New Jersey. "Blank check, the rebbe said. I can make any film I want. Because I'm supposed to do whatever I need to fulfill my destiny as a human being." He pulled himself up and suddenly noticed the food. "Who is each of us in the image of the Creator? That's the essential question. The only sin is to fail to use the gifts you were given when your soul was being filled up for its earthly existence."

"You make it sound like you go to a pre-life gas station and then someone in charge decides whether you get diesel, hi-test, or regular."

46

"It's exactly like that! I'm personally limping along on regular."

"And this is your rebbe's philosophy?"

Tal heaped up a plate and passed it to Roi, then made a plate for himself. The fried eggplant was the takeout place's specialty. Nobody else's compared. "Yes and no. His and mine. Mine of course is adapted from sources more learned than myself."

~

After the debut four-Tel-Avivis-on-the-couch movie, Roi and Shira went on a three month honeymoon in the South Pacific and then came back and blew what was left of their money on a motorcycle and a down payment on the overpriced flat on Bograshov at the peak of the market. After that, to keep fulfilling Len's wish to make movies about ordinary life, Roi made two films about gorgeous post-army Israelis surfing and clubbing and driving around near the high-rise beachfront hotels in fancy cars they got from somewhere—it was the movies, so a little license was allowed. It was like *Hawaii 5-0* without a plot. The characters brooded about the meaning of life during the day and then went out at night and sucked it dry. Sex. Booze. Drugs. Jaunts to Berlin for the jazz. Jobs of no description. Mothers and fathers who fed them whenever they dropped in and didn't disapprove (again, it was the movies). Tal was in both of them. He was in great shape. The occasional pallor from the late-night lifestyle and excess weed was nothing a little makeup couldn't fix.

At first, audiences loved them. Look how cool we are! How free! But with the second one, people started to get depressed after the screenings. They'd leave the theatres feeling hopeless. There was too much aimlessness in the action, in the actors' faces, in their body posture; nobody could make a commitment to anything, not even breakfast. The films were trying too hard, people said. Emptiness infected them like an invisible plague. The Porsches and Maseratis—which were faked, Roi had a great mechanic in Holon who could fix up a Nissan to play the part— couldn't cover up the hole in the center of every scene and every character. This was no longer a happy country. Roi Fein was warped, Mr. Alon Know-It-All Tamir wrote in *Ha'aretz,* and his leading man Tal Geffen needed to get some sun and nutrition.

What a philistine! Roi fumed while they pored over the reviews at the late night beer joint at the port. But after that, Roi changed direction. He apologized to Len in his grave at the Gates of Eden in East Hampton and made a feature about a scarred Holocaust orphan who finds love in the arms of a beautiful Sabra in a settlement on Israel's perimeter on the eve of the War of Independence which wasn't called a kibbutz though everyone knew it was, including Alon Tamir, who called it a derivative mash-up of exhausted themes without a single original sentiment. This was quickly followed by a caper about a disgraced Mossad agent tracking an aging Nazi in Ohio in hopes of restoring his honor, which critics called tired and predictable despite the hunt taking place in the American Midwest instead of Argentina. Roi's next two projects were for a British children's network Shira connected him to through a London contact she had at work but neither aired due to changes in

48

THE ELEVENTH HAPPIEST COUNTRY

management, though Roi did get paid a small kill fee and was told they loved his style and would keep him in mind for the future.

~

Ditch the sexy Canaanite idol, Tal said at their next meeting. Even if his rebbe approved, there was a limit to what Tal could pretend to get excited about. He was, after all, a religious man. He had his principles.

"Let's come up with something fresh," Tal said, spreading tehina over his charred eggplant. They were in Jaffa near the water. The place was famous for roasting the vegetable to perfection. The only other place you could get eggplant this good was in the Druze villages up north on the Syrian border where they did it on charcoal in open pits. When Roi and Tal were in the army, they went to the villages regularly to eat; the men smoked hookah with them and brought them packages to smuggle through the strip of no-man's land to their relatives on the Syrian side— lace for wedding dresses, antibiotics, cell phone chargers. Roi and Tal and the rest of their unit did the smuggling during their regular forays to look for snipers. It was a cat and mouse game. The snipers were always there, waiting for the Israelis. Sometimes the cats won, sometimes the mice. You could keep score by the number of packages that got through. "Something with meaning," Tal said. "What do you say?"

Roi sipped Turkish coffee. He loved the stuff but lately it had been upsetting his stomach the way it did to old men who couldn't handle it anymore. Turkish was a tough guy's drink, *botz,* mud, it was called when his father was growing up and all they had was the lousy Nescafe powdered instant and *botz,* and now his father couldn't handle mud anymore either. The truth was, Roi's stomach had been giving him trouble for weeks, and he'd have preferred to meet at the apartment with a heating pad over his gut but Shira was back from Helsinki. She didn't mind Tal but she didn't like him hanging around their place. She was afraid he'd never leave. She always knew when he'd been there. She'd come home from work and plop down her two laptops and sniff the air like a tracker, and if she detected anything hinting at Tal's presence, she'd ask Roi. Roi didn't lie.

"I should go back to Len's wishes," Roi said. "Forget the high crime stuff and the other crap. Do regular life again. But not burned out post-army guys. Different regular life from what I did before."

Tal scooped up tehina with his pita. "What's regular life here? Women dragging their shopping carts to the vegetable man? Cats in the alley shrieking? Ten kinds of strudel in the bakery window? Fat old Russians at the beach?" He pushed the other eggplant half to Roi and passed him the bread basket.

Roi had already done fat old Russians at the beach but Tal didn't know that because he was at the yeshiva then and didn't go to movies. The film had been a series of artful moments, glimpses of intentionally composed Tel Aviv life meant to show the clash of the real and the surreal. Hare Krishnas in blazing orange dancing barefoot down the cluttered center aisle of the shuk. African refugees playing bridge in Levinsky Park. Prostitutes in leather skirts studying for the dental school admissions exam. All of it wrapped in a looping montage of big pasty Russians swimming in the sea during all seasons. The point was elusive, something about complacency and indifference, the interplay between tragedy and hope, reality and image, etcetera. The film was called *Irina and Boris On the Shore* after Haruki Murakami's *Kafka On the Shore*, which Roi admired but didn't entirely understand, but none of the critics got the reference and none of Roi's investors got their money. The film was panned as eye-rollingly pretentious, evidence of Roi Fein's complete professional floundering, plus it was insulting to Russians who'd been in the country too long to be a clichéd laughingstock anymore.

"What exactly did Len say again?" Tal asked, polishing off his eggplant half and another pita. He'd lost fifteen kilo during the army and India, and all these years later was still making up for it. But Tal never got fat. All that religious discipline kept him from going overboard. "About being a happy country."

"We're the eleventh happiest country in the world, according to surveys. Better than the U.S., the U.K., France. Self-reporting. A contented life."

Tal wiped his mouth with his napkin and nodded sagely. "Amazing. Great eggplant." He looked at his watch. "Gotta go. Mincha. I pop in at the shul over there whenever I can." He pointed with his chin to a crumbling archway crammed between a shoe store and an electrical supply, then took a fifty shekel note from his wallet and put it on the table, waved away Roi's objections. "On me, brother," Tal said.

Roi watched him go. His stomach hurt. He shouldn't have had the Turkish. One night, when he and Tal were posted on the Syrian border, the snipers crossed over no-man's land and killed everyone in their unit except them. They were standing on a rise thirty meters away looking for a meteor shower that never happened.

~

The sixth movie Roi made, after the four zoned-out Tel Avivis on the couch and the *Hawaii Five-O* imitations and the derivative mash-ups, gave everybody multiple lovers because he figured that's why Israel was one of the happiest countries: a lot of sex. Sex enhanced by the great weather and the beach and the fear of death hanging perpetually over everyone's heads. The new film had a cast of eight, including Tal and not including Shira, who by then had given up acting and was at university learning computer programming, and in it, everyone hopped in and out of each other's beds, women and men, men and men, women and women, and nobody was ever possessive or jealous or hurt and instead were cool with all that. In addition to having great sex—which wasn't shown on-screen but was artfully implied—the characters cooked great meals together and read great passages of novels aloud to each other and went out en masse to restaurants to eat big plates of schnitzel and eggplant and salad and have beer and wear sunglasses. The movie had some minimal commercial success because of young audiences who thought it presented a better ideal than the slickly packaged American sex-and-the-city genre and—a surprise demographic—the old So-

cialist pioneers who were reminded of the early days of the
state when people on the kibbutz refused to bend to the
bourgeois conventions of marriage. Alon Tamir came out
of retirement to offer his condolences and pronounce it a
regressive step back to Roi's first cinematic failures. Tal,
who'd sat out Roi's other disasters, busy on projects directed by a pair of Canadians trying to get into the artsy
Tel Aviv scene, was the star of this one. The tattoo was especially prominent and credited, or blamed, depending on
your point of view, with starting the Israeli craze for body
ink, which previously had been taboo because of Jewish
law and also Auschwitz. Despite the reviews, Tal retained
his status as a celebrity. Hollywood came calling. His agent
claimed he was dating models.

But soon after the film came out, Roi saw worrisome
signs in his friend. Tal had thought all the freewheeling
sex alluded to in the movie and practiced for real after
hours was great, but he'd fallen hard for Mor, one of the
actresses, and again it wasn't reciprocated and Roi felt really bad about that. Weren't actors supposed to fall in love
with each other on set? It happened all the time; mythic
romances had blossomed that way. Paul Newman and Jo-
anne Woodward. Humphrey Bogart and Lauren Bacall.
Gene Wilder and Gilda Radner. Instead of flipping head
over heels for Tal, Mor let herself be seduced by the French
noir experimental cinema because of her dark sultry looks
and expert facility with the language—her family was Moroccan—and promptly moved to Paris, and Tal retreated
once again to Roi's couch, this time in Tel Aviv where
the couch also belonged to Shira. The funk lasted a year,

during which time Tal never left the apartment, which was also as long as it took for Roi to get backing for his next feature, a low-budget flick about a jolly fishmonger in Jaffa who made everyone happy because of the superb quality of his goods. Tal, who'd been ducking Hollywood's calls and was barely able to get himself to leave Roi and Shira's living room, played the fishmonger's son who didn't want to inherit the family business and instead wanted to surf and drive around in big cars near the high-rise hotels and meet girls. The movie tanked but it wasn't Tal's fault. It was because it was a ridiculous idea. There were fishmongers in Jaffa but none were especially jolly. Or if they were, nobody would make a movie about them.

Tal hung in for what Roi later called his minimalist Tel Aviv Luxe period. Luxe because they were filmed at nice clubs that let Roi use them for free for the exposure and minimalist because they were shorts and had no budget except for what Roi pulled out of his and Shira's overdraft. Tal played a series of lovesick men intoxicated by sultry female singers. After the fourth and final Luxe, and falling for Idit who played a smoky chanteuse with a nicotine voice whose turf was the piano bar at one of the high-rise hotels and who in real life was scooped up by a German director intent on making her into the next Marlene Dietrich, Tal had had enough. After listening to Roi fume over too many beers at a pub on Allenby over a review by the successor to Know-It-All Tamir who called the star-crossed lovers' chemistry as hard on the eye as that between Marge and Homer Simpson, Tal got up from the table and walked out and disappeared into the humming

54

incantations of black-hatted B'nei Brak and didn't come out for a very long time.

~

They met at an outdoor vegan place on Rothschild that was emphasizing the raw and fermented. Tal thought it would be good for Roi's sensitive gut. He urged the sauerkraut salad and keeping an open mind.

"Look, I know we haven't nailed the story yet but whatever it is, I'm sorry to say I can't do it," Tal said, tucking into a pizza he couldn't believe wasn't cooked. The cheese was made of cashews, the crust of flax seeds. "I realized that if there's a love interest in the movie, and there's got to be a love interest, she'd have to be my real wife. Because, you know—" Tal waved in the general direction of his person—"I can only have physical contact with a female who's my wife."

"But you're not married."

"Exactly. Though I'm being fixed up by my rebbe with a woman this Saturday night. Used to be a singer before she got religious. Divorced. A couple kids. Gives piano lessons. She might be the one. I'm thinking I'm ready."

Roi drank a seaweed cocktail and Tal ate the pizza and they talked about their old army buddies and Shira's punishing work schedule and the insane new Defense Minister and Tal's sister Gili who was moving back from New York because she wanted her kids to be Israeli, and then they gave each other a hug and Tal went on his way. His rebbe was encouraging him to think about becoming a welder. He'd liked that in high school and dabbled in it before he became an actor, and manual work was good for the soul. Tal was looking into it. Roi sipped his seaweed and watched him walking slowly up Rothschild. Maybe the pizza was slowing him down. Or the new career idea. Or he was thinking about the date. That it was time to settle down. Wife. Kids. At some point you had to grow up and face mortality. Not the mortality of death by sniper fire or explosions or war. The other mortality. The one that went by the clock. The regular one that the rest of the world lived by, if they were lucky.

The waiter came and asked if he should clear Roi's friend's plate. Tal had left the olives that came with his pizza, which was a shame because the olives, whatever else might be wrong with the country, were always very, very good. It was one of the reasons people were so happy. He told the waiter to leave them and the waiter nodded and told him to take his time. The waiter wouldn't want to throw the olives away either.

Roi's phone buzzed. A text from Shira. Shira had asked him last night: hypothetically, which did he prefer— Oren or Omri for a boy, Liat or Lilat for a girl. He said he had no preference. Well, you need to have one, she said. He was thirty-nine years old and he needed to choose.

He finished his drink and ate an olive and watched Tal walk up Rothschild. He watched for a full five minutes, watching him go from being a regular sized figure to a tiny speck to nothing, vanishing seamlessly into the crowds at Allenby.

He had his film.

Tal wouldn't be in it because you should never play

someone who's too much like yourself. In fact Tal would probably never see it because where he was going, you didn't see movies. And Roi wouldn't be in it either. For the same reason. Not that he was an actor, but there were times he was tempted.

But that was for later. For now, if he hurried, he could get home before it all slipped away. Turn on his computer and get it down, begin while he still had time—before Shira gave up on him and Len rolled over at the Gates of Eden and his investors changed their minds and his own clock ran down and Tal came back out again, still searching for the thing that would make them happy.

BEAUTIFUL SOULS

· ◊ ·

THEY WERE TWO AMERICAN GIRLS, Abby and Jennifer, best friends, sixteen and not entirely naïve, wandering in the Arab shuk in Jerusalem's Old City. Good girls, not rebellious types, they had left the hotel early that morning with their earnest parents, Lisa and Dan, Karen and Mike, to sit through the interminable Saturday morning services at a crumbling ancient synagogue off a winding alley, just as they had dutifully trailed along to all the tourist sites the entire week, and now this, an afternoon alone in the shuk, was their reward. No adults, just the two of them. They could go, the parents said, as long as they promised to stay together and be back at the hotel by four. Because at four-thirty it would be almost dark.

Now it was three, and they were hungry. Starving. They had fled the hotel as soon as allowed, skipping the buffet lunch, walking down King George Street to the Jaffa Gate exactly as their fathers had shown them on the map. Their mothers, in the lobby, waved them off. *Buy something special! For the holiday!* Because, yes, their school vacation coincided this year with—amazingly—Hanukkah! They would be in Jerusalem for Hanukkah! their parents had exulted months before, in Cambridge, showing Abby and Jen the glossy photos of enormous clay pots of burning oil on top of the Old City walls—no ordinary menorahs there!—just like the pots from thousands of years ago! The parental gushing was startling, weird, finally annoying. Because despite how the six of them looked tromping around Mount Herzl in the rain or staring at the terrible pictures of the concentration camps at Yad Vashem—and Jen and Abby knew exactly how they looked, four wide-eyed adults and two gum-chewing teenagers—the trip wasn't an attempt to instill ethnic pride in the two girls. Rather, it was because Lisa and Dan and Karen and Mike, friends since college, suddenly wanted to get into the Jewish thing for themselves. A *hole* in their endlessly re-examined lives, they told their daughters when selling them on the travel plans. *Hole?* Abby thought, rolling her eyes at Jen in Jen's parents' living room, a fire going in the fireplace, the first crisp days of autumn upon them. What were they talking about, these flaky quasi-grown-ups who had decided to investigate yet another potentially life-altering *ism*, just like their prior love affairs with shamanism and veganism and humanism and feminism and who knew what else? Jewishness—or Juda*ism*, as Dan and Mike, who knew a little more about it than their wives, corrected—had occupied a zero place in either family's existence, though the girls received the usual holiday cards from the grandparents in Florida and had managed to attend a couple of friends' bat mitzvahs, kids whose families had given up on their heroic attempts at urban child-rearing in virtuously peeling triple deckers in Somerville or Central Square and had slunk out under cover of darkness to the embarrassing suburbs. But that was it for tradition, religion—any religion—deemed collectively and unanimously by the four adults to be primitive, regressive, lethally divisive, the scourge of humanity. It was a tenet by which they'd all lived, Abby and Jen had been told ad nauseum. Which made the recent turnaround irritating, to say the least. They were exhausting and confusing, these parents. Abby, for one, wished they would just lighten up and be more concerned with their daughters' PSAT scores and insufficient wardrobes instead of their eco-conscious, human-potential, progressive, egalitarian, spiritual health.

But now, regardless of the grown-ups' starry-eyed wonder—Lisa and Dan and Karen and Mike planned to spend the afternoon reveling in the transcendence of their first ever fully observed Jewish sabbath—Jen and Abby would have their reward. Once inside the shuk, they'd moved with the tourist crowds down the labyrinthine al-

leys past the spice vendors and trays of sticky pastries, past
the silver shops and the men selling carved olive wood tables and nargilahs. At one stall, Jen had made Abby stop
so she could examine a wide-necked peasant blouse with
embroidery, but within seconds a middle-aged man with a
thick mustache appeared from the back and began pressing them in accented English. Only one hundred shekel.
One hundred. How much did Jen want to pay? Ninety?
Eighty-five? He'd give it to her for eighty. Or dollar, did
she want to pay dollar? For her, a special rate. Twenty dollar. Eighteen. Take. Try. See how nice it goes on you. He
swept the blouse off the hanger and held it up against Jen,
brushing her breast. Abby saw the hand touching Jen,
keeping it there too long. Was he really doing that? Putting
his hand on Jen's breast? Jen quickly mumbled she wasn't
interested thank you and pulled Abby out to the alley, and
neither said anything because they were supposed to not
be afraid of the Arabs or think poorly of them. All week
their parents had talked with them about the plight of the
Palestinians and the failed leadership on both sides and the
irrational hatred of the Other that was everywhere in this
world, responsible for so much suffering. They'd met with
nice reasonable Palestinians who wanted peace, and nice
reasonable Israelis who wanted peace, meetings arranged
by their guide where the parents were given envelopes in
which to mail checks, and where Jen and Abby were given
tea and cake and were ignored.

And so neither girl said anything after the experience
with the man with the mustache. Maybe he hadn't touched
Jen on purpose or maybe Jen looked pale and stricken be-

cause lately being around any males, Abby couldn't help but notice, seemed to make Jen uneasy. Like she was turning into some kind of prude. She didn't used to be that way but Abby had been noticing. So they said nothing but anyway didn't have to; they knew each other so well they could read each other's minds. That's how they'd been since they were four years old. Best friends who knew each other's thoughts. They walked fast and turned a corner and fell in behind a large German couple, tall blond people with wide shoulders who could have been Alpine hikers from an energy drink ad. When the couple turned into a shop, the girls followed and bought six tiny painted tea cups for hardly anything, three dollars apiece, which is what the Germans paid.

And now they were ravenous. And cold. They'd refused to wear their winter parkas, the coats so ridiculously *American,* they told their mothers at the hotel; they were from *Massachusetts,* for goodness sake, a little brisk weather never bothered them. But it turned out that sweaters weren't enough. The city shivered under a constant damp chill, December, the stone buildings barely heated. Even two sweaters weren't enough. Over identical white turtlenecks Abby wore Jen's borrowed black wool pullover, and Jen had on Abby's powder blue. It was the powder blue that the man with the mustache had touched.

They spotted the restaurant at the same time. It was down an alley, out of the way, next to a bakery; later, they would say the bakery smells had lured them over. That even though it was past three and they knew they should head back to the hotel, the yeasty sugary scent had enticed them. That's how they would explain it. They turned into the dark entry, the place on closer inspection more a bar or café than a restaurant. They knew it would be patronized by Arabs. In particular, Arab men. Their fathers had warned them, quietly, on the side, while showing them the route on the map so that Lisa and Karen wouldn't hear and get over-protective and retract the agreement to let the girls go. *When you go to the shuk you have to be careful around the men. It's not because they're Arab. Of course not. It's because in some places in the world men are different from what you're used to. It's a cultural thing. When they see young women alone they might think they're available. Their daughters don't go out by themselves like ours do.*

And so, yes, there were men in the café. The girls waited at the door and looked in. A handful of tables, all suffused in smoke, two or three men at each. Which, if Abby thought about it, was a little thrilling. If she were going to be totally honest. The mustached shopkeeper had shaken up Jen, but the men in this café, as far as Abby could tell in the shadowy dark, were a whole lot younger and a whole lot more attractive than the man in that shop. And there was something else: she didn't want to go back to the hotel. Didn't want to listen to their suddenly worshipful parents who were replaying every moment of the trip, going on about the amazing resilience of the Jews, and the holy aura of the city, and the miraculous building of the country, all of it so inspiring, how could they have ignored their heritage all these years, not just ignored but—dared they say it?—been ashamed of it, what had been going on with them, had they been sucked in by simplistic politics or rebelling against their parents? Was that what it was? How free were they, really, when their so-called liberation was prescribed in advance by developmental psychology or the rigid agenda of the left? Endless talk, hours of it, over every meal, at every tourist site, during every ride in the tour guide's van. The parents processed and processed, and every now and then one of them would toss Jen and Abby a sincere look and a probing question. *How are you finding this experience, girls?* To which neither of them would answer. So no; no parents right now, please. Abby looked into the dim café with its smoky low-hanging haze and knew she didn't want to go back to the hotel.

A man slowly got up from one of the tables, came their way.

"Yes, mademoiselles?" he said, and Abby felt herself blushing. *Mademoiselles.*

"Is it possible to get something to eat?" Abby said, taking charge, because Jen was still too upset to talk and anyway she was shy, and Abby heard herself sounding different. Sophisticated. Like she was acting in a play. *Is it possible.*

"Possible?" the man said, smiling, waving toward the back, toward a curtain of beads. "Of course. It would always be possible for such lovely mademoiselles."

They followed him deeper into the room. At the table nearest the front, two Israeli soldiers in olive drab smoked and sipped from tiny cups like the ones they'd just bought. Except for the uniforms the Israelis looked no different from everyone else in the cafe, black-haired men also sipping, smoking, watching them pass. The girls moved down the narrow center aisle. Their fathers had been right; there were no women. But it would have been rude and awkward to change their minds and ask to leave, even if they'd wanted to. Later, Jen would say she didn't want to go in, that Abby was the one who started it, but now neither of them protested, and they took seats where the man directed them, at a table for four in front of the curtain. Then the man vanished behind the beads.

They put their purchases on the empty chairs. Then they folded their hands. They pretended not to notice the half dozen men openly staring. They were young, these men, twenties, early thirties. And handsome, Abby thought. All the men she'd seen on this vacation were handsome. Sort of tough, tight jeans, sunglasses, or in cool bomber jackets like the soldiers. Some were even close to her age. They were nothing like the boys at home, nice sensitive Cambridge boys who were too polite to ever try anything with Abby or Jen or their friends, afraid of offending. Afraid of their own shadows.

Someone lit a pipe; a musky scent filled the room. That was another thing: neither Jen nor Abby looked over, but it certainly could have been hashish. The whole café could have been filled with hashish. Because this was, after all, the Middle East. They weren't that sheltered. They weren't totally naïve.

"I'm glad we got those tea cups," Abby said, clasping her hands, pretending no one else was listening.

Jen nodded morosely, mumbled she was glad too.

Were their parents crazy or what, with this whole Jewish thing, Abby said, lowering her voice, not wanting to say the word too loud, just in case. *Jewish*. Well, they had only a few more days of this, and boy, would she be glad to get home. Jen murmured that she would be glad too, and Abby said at least this was better than sitting around their apartments in Cambridge the whole school vacation, plus dealing with New Year's Eve, wasn't it lame that Caitlin's parents wanted Caitlin to have a girls' sleepover at her house so they wouldn't be tempted by the drunken brawls in Harvard Square, Abby said, but the talk between them was just air, meaningless words skittering on the surface, because both of them were wondering what they were supposed to do now. No one had come to take their order, and no one was eating at any of the other tables; they were just watching. And listening. Sipping and smoking and listening.

And then suddenly the man who had seated them came back from behind the curtain, beads swinging, with a tray he began to unload. Plates of hummus and chopped tomato salad and olives. Little bowls of oily red peppers and cauliflower and beets and other vegetables they didn't recognize, dense with lemon and garlic, a plastic basket of puffy hot pita, two glasses of steaming tea.

"For you," said the man. He swept his hand across the table. A minty scent rose up from the hot glasses. "Please to enjoy," he said, and walked away.

They looked at the plates. They hadn't ordered it. Still, they weren't stupid, they'd learned a few things in their lives, including that restaurants here might do things differently from what they were used to. They both knew this without saying. Maybe you didn't always order; may-

DISPLACED PERSONS ◊ EAST

be it was like eating at someone's house: you ate what they put in front of you. They had done this on the eighth grade class trip to Washington, D.C. where they stayed in people's homes. Jen and Abby were paired up, of course, and for three days they stayed with an African-American family named Jefferson—*after the President*—that served them grits and black-eyed peas and collard greens and cuts of pork they'd never heard of, let alone tasted, traditional foods in their family, the hosts said, and they had politely eaten it all without question because that's what you did. You were sensitive to the culture of others, which was the point of the class trip, and besides, you were their guest. But here Abby wondered: how much would this cost? They had with them American dollars and some shekels, but what if the man kept bringing dishes and they didn't have enough to pay for it?

"This looks great," Abby said, trying, and Jen murmured a mostly inaudible yes, probably worried about the hour, three-thirty already, but what could they do, it was too late to make it to the hotel in time. Their parents wanted them back by four so they could all stand outside in a circle and hold hands and wait for three stars to appear in the sky, signifying the end of the sabbath. *Separating the sacred from the profane, isn't that beautiful?* Their mothers had heard there was a special dance or song for this, they were going to learn it that afternoon. The men at the other tables were still watching as the girls began to serve themselves, small helpings, tentative. Abby broke apart the soft bread. They didn't talk, probably the first time they'd ever had a meal together where they didn't speak, because everything would be overheard. They couldn't even switch to a foreign language because Abby knew Spanish and Jen was taking French. Anyway, maybe people always watched the customers eat there. Maybe they wanted to see if the customers liked it. The truth was, Abby didn't mind. So what if some good-looking men were watching them? She ate carefully, tipping her head just so, flexing an ankle. It wasn't the kind of thing she ever did in Cambridge.

After a minute, one of the men got up and came over to their table. He pulled up an empty chair and sat down next to Jen, opposite Abby.

"You like this food? The food here is good, no?"

He was maybe twenty, twenty-one, slim and dark, in a black leather jacket. A gold chain glittered on his neck. "Yes, very good," Abby said.

"You come back again. Bring your husbands, your boyfriends."

Abby blushed, went for the tea. Jen stopped eating.

"What, not here with husbands? Boyfriends? I don't believe, such pretty girls like you." He inched up on his chair. Jen looked like the air was going out of her. She looked frozen. The man was sitting very close to her, and Abby guessed his knee was probably one inch from Jen's leg. His hair was slicked back, too wet, but he was good-looking. Except for his teeth. They were yellowed and crooked. Still, he wasn't afraid to smile. "Where you girls from?" he said. "New York? California?" The way he said California, he emphasized the *for* and separated the *nia*, so it came out Cali-*FOR-neeya*, which for some reason made Abby a little weak in the knees. Jen kept her eyes on the table. Or maybe they were from Philadelphia? *PhilaDELfeeya.*

"No. Boston," Abby said. She could feel the other men watching. Maybe they were jealous; maybe they wished they'd gotten up first and beaten this one to it.

"Ah, Boston." A yellowy grin. "Paul Revere and the Freedom Trail, yes?" He inched up closer and from the way Jen was shifting in her seat, Abby was pretty sure his knee was now against Jen's thigh. It was hard for it not to be. "You know this film *The Verdict*? Paul Newman? Is made in Boston. Great film. You see this film?"

Abby shook her head. Jen stared at the table.

"No? Maybe you want to come to a film with me and my friend. Very many good films here. You like movies? Ice cream and movies?"

"I like movies," Abby said. She glanced at Jen, but Jen wouldn't look at her. "And ice cream."

"We're here with our fathers," Jen said, her eyes fixed on the plates.

Abby stared at her. Their fathers? What was she talking about?

"They're right outside," Jen said to the plates. "Waiting for us."

Abby kept looking at Jen, but Jen wouldn't look up. Abby knew exactly what Jen was doing. She was hoping it would frighten this guy off if he thought their fathers were outside. Or he'd take pity on them, girls with strict parents who watched their every move, like the daughters in his family. Their fathers had told them at the hotel. *Girls in Arab families are supervised very closely. It's a conservative*

70

culture, very traditional. Not that we're criticizing. Just comparing.

A chuckle erupted somewhere in the shadowy room. The man smiled again, showing his bad teeth. "So where are such fathers that they let two beautiful girls eat by themselves? They don't come join you?"

"They're not hungry," Jen murmured to the table. "But they're right outside, a few steps away."

Abby kept looking at Jen. It was a stupid lie. Any one of them listening—and they were all listening—could just get up and open the door and see there were no Americans loitering out there, no middle-aged men waiting in the alley for their reckless stupid daughters.

"Such pretty girls, I don't blame a father for standing guard." The man had moved his hand, was resting it next to Jen's tea. He had on a big flashy ring, a blue stone set in gold. His nails were cut square across.

"I think we're finished now," Jen said, glancing around the room as if the waiter—as if there even was a waiter— might instantly appear. She was pale and wouldn't look at Abby, which wasn't right, that's not how they operated. They always checked in with each other, even if they couldn't talk. They'd do it with their eyes. Jen scanned the room and said, "We need the check. How do we get the check?"

"The check?" The man waved the ringed hand. His jacket shone a little in the dim light. "There is no check here. This is not America, not Boston. Here we take our time. Here everyone is like family. You eat, you drink, you make new friends, and then later, when it's time to go, you worry about paying. But not now." He pushed the plates closer to Jen. "You haven't touched the salads. What, you don't like this food?"

"We have to go," Jen said, still looking for a waiter, for anyone. "I'm not feeling well." Abby kept looking at her, but Jen refused to make eye contact. Maybe she really was feeling sick. Maybe she'd gotten so scared she was physically ill. She looked bad enough. But it irritated Abby. Jen was becoming a real Miss Priss. What was the big deal? A handsome guy comes and talks to you, what's so terrible about that?

The man clucked his tongue, *tsk tsk*, and opened a pack of cigarettes and lit one. "Such a pity," he said. "Afraid to talk to a friendly stranger. You should have a coffee. Tell me about yourselves."

Somewhere a chair scraped tile. Abby had never seen Jen like this. Did she truly not like boys anymore? She used to like boys. She used to be fun. A tall man in sunglasses walked by, lightly rapping the table as he passed. The man at their table glanced up, waved the other man away, dismissive, then took a long pull on his cigarette. The sunglasses man disappeared behind the bead curtain.

"Well, I suppose we're kind of late," Abby said, deflated, because what else could she do? Jen looked like she might get up and walk out, and she couldn't let her do that. "I guess we should go," Abby said. She watched the man slowly inhale, then make an O with his lips to let out the smoke. No one at home smoked. It was practically illegal in Cambridge. Smokers there were treated like criminals. Her friends would be shocked to hear she sat at a table with an older guy, a foreigner, who was smoking. It made Abby want to take a puff.

Jen wrapped her arms around herself, hugging herself in the blue sweater, and stared at the untouched salads.

"You're cold," the man said, looking at Jen.

Jen shook her head, but then she shivered, a real shiver, like she had the flu. Another chair scraped the tile.

"Yes, yes, you're very cold." The man put the cigarette on the edge of the table and took off his jacket and put it over Jen's shoulders. He had on a tight black nylon shirt. The gold chain hung down like a perfect horseshoe. He was very muscled, and Abby thought that in another place, her high school, for instance, he'd be considered a real stud.

Jen shook her head. "Please, no, I don't need your jacket."

"Yes, you do, you're very cold." He moved his arm around Jen's shoulders to keep the jacket from slipping off, but then he left it there.

Jen shook her head again, more firmly now. "I'm fine. I don't want your jacket."

"Ma zeh?" A loud burst of staccato Hebrew. The two soldiers from the front, long guns hanging off their shoulders. They were standing at the table. *"Ma zeh?"* one of them spat out again. "What's going on? He is bothering you?" he said to Abby. "This man, he bothers you while you eating?"

Abby stared at the gun, a huge appendage like a burnt tree branch, then looked at the soldier. Nineteen, twenty, wearing a green army beret and rimless glasses. He kept a hand on the weapon, agitated. "He bothering you?" he said again, and didn't wait for an answer. "Get up!" he said to the man. "Now!"

The man got to his feet. He was shorter than the soldier and seemed to Abby smaller than when he was sitting, as if he'd suddenly shrunk. He was almost petite, despite the muscled neck. There was something even dainty about him. The tight shirt, the jewelry, the lacquered hair. The Israeli poked his gun into the leather jacket sleeve, which was still hanging off Jen. "This your coat? You put on the girl?"

"She was cold," the man said.

"Don't tell me cold! Don't give me this bullshit! I saw the girl shake her head!"

The other soldier grabbed the man by the arm, pulled him away from the table.

"We come in here to get a little tea," the soldier with the glasses said, "and we find you bothering the tourists! What's the matter with you?" He gestured with his chin for the man to go to the other side of the room. The other soldier pushed him toward the wall.

"You okay?" the soldier with the glasses said, turning to the table.

"He didn't hurt us or anything," Abby said, looking straight at him. She had seen a lot of these soldiers on this trip, and usually they were really attractive in their uniforms. But this one didn't seem attractive at all. She could tell he was good-looking, would be good-looking in another place, maybe her high school or sitting in her parents' living room. But not here, in this café. Here he looked ugly. Ugly and mean and not desirable at all. "He was only talking to us."

"Only talking? Only talking? What are you, exchange students? Kibbutz volunteer on chofesh? How long you in Jerusalem? Two month? Three?"

"Five days."

"Five days!" The Israeli laughed. He turned to his partner. "You hear that, Lior? They're in the city five days, and they know everything! They think this guy, he's a perfect gentleman! Tom Cruise!" He turned back to the table. "You think he's Tom Cruise? Leonardo DiCaprio? This is what you think?"

"I didn't say he was Tom Cruise. I just said he didn't do anything. He was only talking to us."

"If he was only talking, why your friend here look like she going to be sick? You want to tell me?"

"She's got a cold. She didn't feel well all day. That's why we came in here. We thought maybe she'd feel better with some tea."

"This isn't America. You understand?" the soldier said to her. He had lowered his voice, was trying to calm down. She could see he was trying to steady the situation. The other one, Lior, was on the other side of the room talking to the men there in another language. Arabic maybe. "You can't go around all the time with a *yafei nefesh*. You know what means this, *yafei nefesh*?"

"No."

"Beautiful soul." The soldier paused. "You know what this is?"

"No."

"Bleeding heart. In English you say bleeding heart." The soldier watched her. "You can't be like that here. Maybe in America. But not here."

Abby turned away. Jen was leaning over the table, her forehead in her hand. Abby didn't want to look at her. Abby never wanted to look at her again. She turned back to the soldier. "He was just talking to us. I don't know why you're making such a deal out of it. We don't need your protection. He was only being friendly."

"Friendly?" The soldier leaned toward her. Behind the glasses his eyes were very blue. Maybe he wasn't twenty; maybe he was eighteen, or seventeen, practically her own age. If she lived there, she'd have to go into the army, she'd have to go next year. The black gun was swinging by his side. It looked like it was made of plastic, like a toy. Though Abby knew it wasn't a toy. "Friendly?" the soldier repeated. "Why you think no one eats in this cafe? Why you think there are no customers except five guys drinking coffee all day? Thousands of tourists in the shuk and not a one in this place. Why you think?" He looked up, gestured with his chin at one of the men at the other tables. They were smoking and sipping and listening. "Hey, Mahmoud, you want to tell her why it's empty here? Where the owner is, your uncle? Your cousin Hassan?"

Silence. The other man blew smoke, looked away.

The soldier turned back to Abby. "Last week a bomb blows up fifteen people at a bus stop. You want to know who drives the bomber there? Who helps him blow himself up and fifteen more? Seven little kids on the way to school, all waiting for the bus? You want to know where

76

the owner of this place was last week, where his son was?"

He stopped. He was getting red in the face and was trying to control himself. He didn't want to be yelling at her. The room was a tomb. Jen wasn't moving.

"But do we shut them down?" the soldier said. "Close up his restaurant, burn it to the ground? No. Because the Americans will say we starving East Jerusalem. The Europeans will say we're criminals. Anyway nobody comes in here. Because the whole shuk knows. The whole East Jerusalem knows. So only the family comes in here." He waved at the smoking men. "Just them. And us. Because now we have to protect them from their new enemies. Because some people are not happy that we know all about it. They wonder who told."

The soldier straightened up. He seemed exhausted. He gestured for Lior to come get the leather jacket. It was still hanging off Jen's shoulders and looked to Abby like a person, a dead person hanging off Jen. Then he told the girls they needed to leave, that he would escort them out.

"We can't go yet," Abby murmured. "We haven't paid."

"Paid?" The Israeli laughed.

"I want to pay, it's not right." Abby stood, unzipped her fanny pack. Her hands were shaking. Had the owner really driven a suicide bomber to his target? Did all the men there know it? Were they glad? Jen had told her that Palestinians in Gaza danced in the streets when Israelis got blown up, she'd seen it on TV. Their parents would never tell them that, but it was true. And what about the man who came to their table? Was he glad? He was standing by the wall but she couldn't look at him. If the men knew she and Jen were Jewish, would they want to kill them too? Maybe they already did know. She rummaged through the pack, hands sweaty, unable to think. There were no shekels, where were the shekels, she couldn't find the shekels. Or dollars. She dug into an inside flap, pulled out an American fifty, her emergency money, and put it on the table.

"Fifty dollar?" the Israeli said. "Are you crazy?"

"That's all I have, I don't care."

The Israeli swept up the bill, shoved it into her pack. "Don't leave that."

Jen was getting herself to her feet. She looked like a ghost. Abby hated her. She was her best friend, and she hated her. Jen unzipped her fanny pack, pulled out three twenty-shekel notes, put them on the table.

"That's too much," the soldier said.

"I don't care. That's what we're paying," Abby said.

Lior waved them ahead of him with his gun. The soldiers would walk them to the Jaffa Gate, the one with the glasses said, and after that they would walk them to the hotel and explain to their parents that it was dangerous to let two young American girls wander alone in the shuk. That they had no idea what it was like in this country. Did they think it was Disneyland, some Middle Eastern theme park with cobblestone alleys and exotic foods? Did they think everyone was a colorful friendly native like from a tourist video or a Hollywood movie?

They were at the door. It was already dark. "The start of the holiday," the soldier with the glasses said, pointing

78

his weapon at the pots high up on the walls. "They're lighting now. The first one. Look."

Abby looked. Sixty feet up, a giant flame *whooshed!* into the sapphire sky. It licked the air, furious, the pot a fiery cauldron like something out of a nightmare, like what ancient civilizations threw babies into in order to appease their ferocious gods. Behind them stood the men from the café, watching the flames, but Abby couldn't turn around. Couldn't look at Jen or the man with the leather jacket or the other soldier or anyone. She could only stand there and watch as the flames rose higher and higher while somewhere across the city their parents whirled and sang and danced in the darkness, and wondrously counted the stars.

DISPLACED PERSONS

· ◊ ·

My neighbor's son wants to move to Germany. He's twenty-one and went four times on heal-the-wounds summer programs, young Germans in dialogue groups with young Israelis like him, and spent two years studying the language at the Goethe Institute on the other side of Tel Aviv. He's done with the army and is ready for university. College is free in Germany, he tells his parents, and Berlin is exciting. Progressive ideas, lots of new jazz, a hub of Europe now that there's the EU. Israel feels provincial, isolated. The Jewish piece has nothing to do with it, he says. His grandparents' history is just that: history.

"Can you picture me telling this to my mother?" Sigalit says over untouched tea at my kitchen table in her excellent college level English. I know her mother's story, she doesn't have to remind me. "She'll have a fit." Sigalit's voice is hoarse from I don't know what, crying or shouting, though she doesn't seem to be the shouting type. I'm the only person she can tell. Because I'm an American. A politician recently started a fire storm by urging in *Ha'aretz* that all Israelis eligible for German passports—offered to every descendant of German Jews stripped of their citizenship in the war—should apply. No border hassles traveling through Europe. Cheap higher education. Abundant opportunities for work. And the unsayable: a place to go if Israel is wiped off the map by Hamas or Hezbollah or Iran. Germany as a safe haven for Jews if their existence here is threatened. This, for even the most cosmopolitan, globe-trotting Israelis, is hard to swallow.

"What does Omer think?" I ask, inching the tea in her direction. I don't know Sigalit's husband well. I see him at the mailboxes talking to the other tenants about the goings-on in the Knesset and which parties will leave the government today and which threatened to leave yesterday. That and his motorcycle. It's from the 1980s, and he refuses to give it up though it makes Sigalit crazy. He's had two accidents in the last three months. Doesn't he want to stay alive for his sons? she says. Doesn't he want to live to see them get married or have children or graduate university?

Though if the university is in Germany it might be a

different story. "Omer says I'm over-reacting. That lots of Israelis are doing it. Which I know, I read the papers. Four thousand applied for German passports this year alone." Sigalit finally notices the cup, picks it up. "He says I'm being neurotic, that it's not 1939 anymore. And anyway all the kids get wanderlust after the army so who knows how long Gideon would stay."

She takes a sip. What do I know? I grew up in Connecticut. Nobody I knew ever had to go to an army. Nobody I knew survived the Holocaust. We didn't have people like that in our West Hartford temple. "Could it be some kind of rebellion?" I venture. Canned psychology; it sounds so American.

Sigalit takes out a tissue and wipes her eyes. She is constantly weepy. Her 88-year-old mother is hanging on in an old age home ten minutes from our building, which Sigalit visits for two hours every day when she's not bringing her mother to her apartment for meals. "It's not rebellion." She stuffs the tissue into her pocket. "He really likes German culture. And how can I argue with him? Look at what they produced. Bach. Beethoven. Thomas Mann. Not everyone was Goering and Himmler." She waves toward my window. "You want to hear the irony? Out there, Ben-Yehuda Street? My mother says they used to call it Ben-Yehudastrasse after the war. Little German-run shops, tea houses where people sat all day discussing Max Weber. It was schizophrenic. On the one hand, Germany was totally taboo—the first Israeli passports were marked as valid for any country in the world but there—but then they replicated the society as closely as they could." She pulls herself out of her chair. "I should relax, right? The Germans have been paying for their history for decades; reparations practically built this country." She goes to the door, puts her hand on the knob. "And all those earnest young volunteers who come on atonement missions, the most apologetic people on the planet."

I know who she means. I've seen them outside the nursing homes and recreation centers, energetic types with names out of fairy tales. Hans. Gretchen. Hedwig. At night they're at the pubs by the beach; some have turned up in my beginners Hebrew class, part of the deal I made with my American university. In exchange for a shockingly generous stipend, I'm supposed to be doing research on a community of so-called displaced persons inside the country—foreign workers from the Philippines, refugees from Sudan, irradiated children from Chernobyl, pick your desperate subgroup, plenty to choose from right here in Tel Aviv—then go back to the States and write up a thesis and collect my degree. Problem is, I don't feel like doing any of that. Especially the part about going back.

"Hey, wait," she says, stopping at the open door. "What about you?"

"What about me?"

"Maybe you can be the one to tell my mother about Gideon." A revelation. "Yes! She loves you, nothing you could say would upset her. She's always asking about the nice American across the hall."

"Are you crazy?" I say. "I don't know how to talk about twenty-year-olds; I just finished being one myself. Or about Germany."

84

"No, no, it'll be fine." She's smiling broadly. "You'll see, you can do it."

~

It's not entirely true that I didn't know any survivors as a kid. I met one once. She came to my friend Elise's seder when I was sixteen. My father had finally left for good, and my mother wasn't in great shape. I wasn't either, but I did a better job hiding it. My mother's sister Carla was urging her to go with her and my Uncle Dave on a Caribbean cruise, it would cheer her up, she had vacation time coming from the insurance company where she and Carla both worked as claims adjusters; their specialty was vehicular wrecks. My mother wasn't so sure it was a smart idea, all that forced gaiety, but Carla was insistent. A college student, Lori, stayed over each night so I wouldn't be alone.

The cruise fell during Passover, not a big deal in my family. Elise invited me. We weren't particularly good friends but I sat next to her in Spanish and she lived around the block. Her mother had probably suggested it. They liked to have guests, her mother told me when I arrived with a box of candy. We distributed ourselves around a long table and took turns reading from the Haggadah. Her father could read in Hebrew; the rest of us stumbled through the archaic English. *Once we were slaves, now we are free. Rescued from bondage with an outstretched hand.* Elise had a big family, cousins and uncles and aunts, and they were all there. Her grandparents drove up from New York and brought a friend.

The friend was a slight, brittle woman in her seventies with a severe black bun, sapphire earrings that sat like giant blue marbles alongside her face, and a thick accent. She seemed to look down her nose at everyone at the table. She spoke to nobody after the initial hellos, and when it was her turn to read, she waved the moment away like she was dismissing a servant. I was seated opposite her, and though I tried not to look at her, it was hard not to notice the constant frown and bird-like appetite. Every time I took a bite I felt disapproval washing over me, as if I was committing some disgusting act of gluttony.

After the main course I got up to help clear. When I got to the woman's seat, I lifted her barely touched plate, balancing the knife and fork on it as I raised it over her shoulder.

"You must not kerry ze plate zet vay. It is rude."

"Excuse me?" I said. I was sure I hadn't heard correctly.

"You hev poor menors," she said, looking up at me. "You should vemove ze knive und kerry it in de otter hend. American yung pipple hev no refinement."

I didn't know what to say. Elise had told me the woman was a Holocaust survivor, that her grandmother knew a few in her building. In the kitchen I repeated to Elise what the woman had said.

"Old people can be such pains in the asses," she said, scraping plates over the trash can. She glanced around the empty kitchen and lowered her voice. "Let's do some weed before dessert, before my mother notices we're gone."

"What about your cousins?" Four preteen girls had been hanging on to Elise all night. I was surprised none of them had come into the kitchen to admire her over the garbage pail.

"We'll tell them we're getting their presents ready."

"What presents?" I whispered. Elise's mother and aunts had returned from the basement refrigerator where they'd retrieved her mother's signature holiday desserts: chocolate mousse cake, homemade sorbet, frosted macaroons from a famous bakery in downtown Hartford.

Elise rubbed her thumb and forefinger together. Money. In her family, people gave the children silver dollars on Passover. She'd give the girls paper bills if she had to. Anything for a little privacy so we could get sufficiently stoned.

I followed Elise out and moved quickly through the dining room on the way to the stairs. Immediately the four girls appeared by the banister.

"We'll be right back; we're getting something special for you, but you've got to be patient," Elise told them. I looked up. The old lady was watching, her head cocked slightly to the side, appraising, mouth in that frown. On her list of rude behaviors, leaving the dining table during the meal had to be way up there. Elise's grandparents were going to get an earful on the drive home.

I caught the woman's eye. *I'm sorry about your past,* I wanted to call out, *but that doesn't mean I should feel guilty for eating or sneaking off with my friend or getting high or living.* But of course I didn't do that. I considered waving, or even smiling, but before I could make up my mind she had turned her head and was glaring at the lushly excessive display of sweets.

~

After Sigalit leaves, I head out to the African Refugee Center in south Tel Aviv, my chosen displaced community where, to aid my alleged research, I teach English two nights a week to fourteen men from Sudan and Eritrea and Ivory Coast and other hemorrhaging places. Fifty thousand Africans are in Israel after managing to cross the border with Egypt. The Israelis don't know what to do with them. If they welcome them, they're afraid a million more will come; if they send them back, the Africans will get killed or tortured. The men in my class are in their twenties and thirties; one is married. I don't ask where their families are. The center's coordinator, a volunteer like the rest of us, told me: *Don't ask personal questions. These are private people. Anyway, you read the newspapers. So you know.*

"Hallo, Miss Zhenna," Habib says, out of breath as he enters the classroom after jogging up the narrow stairs. He's always the first to arrive and the last to leave. He's twenty-two, from Darfur, and in four months has picked up more street Hebrew than I have in almost a year and is doing pretty amazingly in English too. Before arriving in Israel he'd never seen a computer or a movie. Now he tells me he's learning English from the films he catches on TV in the three-room flat he shares with seven other Sudanese. Four to a room, they sleep on mattresses and have a working kitchen and bathroom, deluxe accommodations compared to some. Habib works at a car factory in Jaffa. He starts at 5 A.M. and finishes at 7 P.M. except on nights when he has classes and his employer lets him off early. He's lucky to have a job.

"Jenna," I say, emphasizing the J. "Try it, Habib. *Jenna.*"

"Zhenna," Habib says, watching my mouth. "Shenna," he tries again.

"Much better. How's everything?" I ask, knowing what's coming. The reason Habib is always first is because he wants to find out how to get to America and is certain I must know people who can help. He knows he can't become a citizen of Israel anytime soon because he is neither Jewish nor an officially UN-approved refugee, a process that can take years. But in America anyone can apply anytime, he says. America is for everyone.

"Everything fine, Miss Shenna. I love this country. *Kol b'seder,*" he adds in Hebrew. Everything's all right.

"Good. I'm glad to hear it," I say, unpacking my papers and getting them ready on the desk.

"But is difficult for me here. I not Jewish. I not Hebrew. I want citizen but cannot get."

I nod. "I know, Habib. You would like to get citizenship."

"I would like."

"I know," I say, hoping the footsteps on the stairs outside belong to someone in my class and not in the room opposite because Habib is smart and sweet and achingly persistent, and every one of these pre-class conversations tears me up inside because there's nothing I can do. All I can do is teach him some English so that wherever he goes next, he'll at least have that. "Well, for now you have a job and a place to live, so things are okay at the moment, right?"

"Yes, yes, very okay," and then there's a crush of bodies at the door. Everyone arrives at the same time. Habib high-fives whoever will high-five him back and goes to the table and takes a seat. The others smile at me, shyly say hello. They are exceedingly polite. At their seats they take out the name cards I insisted everyone make the first night. Emanuel. Yohannes. Mamadu. My PhD plan was to write a pithily incisive chapter about each one, laced with shimmering insights about what it means for thousands of traumatized 21st century refugees to seek shelter in a country defined by thousands of traumatized refugees of the 20th, but I haven't written a thesis-worthy sentence all year. The thought of reducing their lives to case studies for the purpose of netting me a university degree seems obscene.

Today I have brought maps of the United States, courtesy of an acquaintance who works at the U.S. embassy. The center has no materials and no money to buy any. The students are thrilled to each receive their own map, which opens to the size of an umbrella. Yellow and pink and red and blue states cover the big table like a colorful tablecloth at a July Fourth picnic.

I tape mine to the whiteboard. We go around the room taking turns reading the names of the states aloud. New Chair-See. Flow-ree-dah. Mary-Land. O-hee-oh. Nobody can say Louisiana or Massachusetts. I describe snow, but it is impossible to explain. It is not ice, not rain; it is not anything anyone in the room has ever seen. I pronounce Connecticut, my home state, and tell them about the beaches, the ships at Mystic Seaport, the stone architecture at Yale. I write vocabulary words of questionable utility on the board. Cathedral. Lighthouse. Aquarium. It was at Mystic where my father conducted his first flagrantly outrageous affair, which was with my mother's best friend, Bonnie. I was twelve; Bonnie's girls and I went to day camp together. My father liked to pick women close to the family.

Issa from Eritrea raises his hand. There's a rumor going around that Meredith, one of the other American volunteers who's killing time in Israel while figuring out what to do next, is angling for a relationship with him. All the other volunteers say it's a bad idea, she's just playing with him, Issa will get hurt, they can't possibly bridge the divide. She'll leave when her year is up and resume her cushy life in Teaneck or Skokie or wherever and he'll still be a dishwasher without a passport in Tel Aviv.

"Yes, Issa?" I ask.

"What you miss in America?"

"Miss?"

Issa nods. He is handsome and sincere and I understand why Meredith is interested. Fourteen pairs of eyes watch me. Their expressions are somber. I know what they miss. They miss their families, their homes. They miss what they will never have again.

"I don't miss the snow and ice," I say and laugh, but they don't get it. "What I mean is, I don't miss the difficulties of living in a cold climate."

Another hand. Namanya, who wants to become an English teacher in his home country if he can ever go back. "No, no. We not ask what you *don't* miss. We ask what you *do* miss."

I can't joke my way through this. The men have no taste for glibness. "My mother, I guess," I say, surprising myself, and they nod. Of course. There is no question. Of course I'd miss my mother. Everyone in the room misses their mother.

What else? they ask.

I draw a blank.

Nothing? They are incredulous. They miss everything: the fields, the sky, the fruits and trees, the quiet. Even what they never had. Emanuel, in the back, says he has not lived in his own country since he was four; he was born in Liberia but his family was kicked out and he lived the next eighteen years in five other countries. "I am remembering only one yellow wall of the house of my grandmother. I do not see it for nineteen years." He puts his hand over his eyes so we won't see that he is welling up.

Nothing else? they ask again.

"I miss the libraries," I offer. "We have big public libraries in America. You can borrow all the books you could ever want. No charge. All free, all the time."

They smile dutifully. They cannot fathom why I don't come up with something more visceral and heartfelt than a house of books. How can you live somewhere for thirty years and not miss its textures, its colors, its smells, its sounds? The men sense my discomfort. Mamadu, thirty-five and married, wants to go back to the map. He has heard of Martin Luther King and civil rights but doesn't know which state this important man came from. Can I show them?

I turn to the whiteboard. This, I warn them, will be a mouthful. While I slowly draw out the word, a chaotic chorus of *Mee-sees-aye-pi* behind me, I make a mental note to tell Sigalit that Gideon will miss her, that she shouldn't worry about that at least. But then I decide not to bring it up. What if Gideon doesn't put *Mother* high up on his list? What if he, like me, decides he doesn't miss very much of his home country at all?

~

When my advisor, Professor Audra Silk, offered me a choice of research countries, I roamed all over the map for days. Rwanda? Ukraine? India? There were displaced people everywhere. The whole world was carrying their belongings on their backs and walking in lines.

"How about a place where you have some attachment?" she said kindly. "Perhaps an emotional or personal connection?"

Attachment? Connection? I'd never thought of that. I went back to the atlas. It jumped out at me. I was Jewish, if minimally. What about Israel?

"That sounds like a good idea," my mother said when I reached her in Hartford. "I've never been there. Maybe I'll visit."

"Israel?" my father said in a rare phone call from his current home in Boca Raton with his current wife. I was pretty sure he was cheating again; he only communicated when his marriages were on the rocks. "I hear it's just like Florida. Hot and humid. Great beaches. Jewish food. Why not just come down here to bake in the sun like the rest of us?" Then he laughed.

That cinched it. I turned in my proposal and bought my ticket the next day.

~

Gideon has been accepted at Humboldt University in Berlin. It's all happening faster than Sigalit expected. If word gets out, if one of Gideon's friends tells another, who tells another, who tells his parents who then tell a grandmother at the old folks home in the neighborhood, the news, Sigalit is certain, will kill her mother.

"We have to make a plan right now," she says. We're taking a morning power walk on the promenade by the sea before Sigalit goes off to the fancy private hospital in north Tel Aviv where she works in the gastroenterology department handling the paperwork for diplomats and tourists who require professional level English. Two bicyclists in racing gear whiz by. "Next time I bring her home for dinner you come too. How about tomorrow? We'll eat, then I'll run out on an errand and you can slip it into a conversation. *So I heard about Gideon, what a smart boy.* Something like that. Okay? I'll be nowhere within shouting distance."

"Are you afraid of your mother?" I ask.

Sigalit huffs and puffs. She's almost fifty and out of shape. Plus the ambassador from France had a colonoscopy last week and sent everyone in her department trays of French pastries in thanks. She looks over at me. Sweat drips down her nose. "Of course I am. Isn't everyone?"

I tell her my mother is a pussycat.

"You're lucky. My mother's tough. The war toughened her, the DP camps toughened her. Then Israel toughened her."

"Maybe she'll see it as getting even," I try. "Sticking it

94

to Hitler. Free tuition for Gideon. Like private reparations."

She gives me a sour look. "My mother refused."

"Refused what?"

"Reparations. A German funded pension. She's entitled, you know; they all were." She stops to wipe her face with a towel while a woman on rollerblades glides past with a little dog in tow. In her spiffy lycra shorts and matching shirt she dodges around us, two slowpokes in sweats and fanny packs. "My mother is very proud," Sigalit says. "She says she'll never take The German Money. That's what she calls it. The German Money. She says her forgiveness is not for sale."

~

The day after the seder, Elise and I hung out at my empty house because it was exciting to be unsupervised. I'd promised my mother I wouldn't do anything risky when Lori, the college student, wasn't there, like have a party or let anyone use drugs, and I had no intention of breaking her trust. But just the thought of something forbidden was thrilling. Plus Elise's grandparents had slept over at her house and she needed a break from all the people.

"Where's their friend?" I asked, passing Elise the peanut butter and jelly sandwich I'd made for her. Bread was outlawed at Elise's on Passover, giving my house even more added allure. Personally, I'd been intrigued by the matzoh-only concept, but Elise wanted to break rules.

"My dad drove her to some people in Avon last night while my mom and grandma did the dishes." Elise licked the jelly oozing out near the crusts. "My grandma says she has hardly any family. Which is why she invited her to our house."

I watched Elise eat. Bread was no big deal to me; I could have bread all week, and probably would, though my mother had bought me a box of matzoh before she left, in case I wanted to be a little more Jewish on my own. We'd called it the bread of affliction at the seder to remind us of being in bondage. One of Elise's little cousins had opined that matzoh was probably pita because that's what they ate in the Middle East, and that the only thing the Exodus story said about the flight from Egypt was that the Israelites couldn't wait to let their bread rise because they were in a hurry. My father, who'd also been in a hurry, hadn't bothered to say goodbye. Six months later, when my mother would have to sell the house and she and I would move to a small apartment in downtown Hartford, my father would come to get the rest of his stuff and explain his hasty departure when my mother was out of the room by saying he'd finally found the love of his life and he'd be damned if he was going to let some youthful mistakes— presumably my mother and me—hold him back.

"Your grandparents' friend," I asked Elise, "was she, like, in a concentration camp?"

Elise shrugged, focusing on the jelly.

"Well, do you know what country she's from? She's got a majorly heavy accent."

"I can ask my grandma. Though I don't think her friend talks about it." She looked over at me. "Why do you want to know?"

"Just curious. I don't know anyone who survived the Holocaust."

Elise went back to her illegal lunch. "You're so serious, Jenna. You should lighten up sometimes."

~

A crew of students from a local college is filming the Refugee Center for a project. The coordinator has arranged for them to interview Issa and Habib after class. Would I be willing to stay to the end and lock up?

At eight-thirty, Issa, Habib and I are still waiting for the Israelis to straighten out a glitch with their equipment. I go down the steep stairs to find out if there's been any progress.

"Almost ready," Gila, the apparent director, says. "We testing the sound." She's short and squat and doesn't make eye contact. Her cameraman, a lanky guy with glasses, is on the floor, hunched over a swarm of cables. They've been at the center since six. Issa and Habib are the only people they're interviewing. They've had two hours to test the sound.

"Did you just notice the problem?" I ask. Habib gets up at four, Issa at five.

"I thought he tests at school," Gila says, gesturing at the guy on the floor.

"You were supposed to do it," he mumbles without looking up.

Gila lets loose a flood of irritable Hebrew. A third person shows up, a skinny kid holding a tangle of wires and cords who nods at me and hunches over the

97

equipment with the other guy.

"Look, Gila," I say, "the men upstairs have been waiting since eight o'clock. They have to be at work at five in the morning. Which means they were at work at five *this* morning." I'm aiming to be polite and subtle, though that isn't always the best tack to take with Israelis, who usually do better with in-your-face directness. "You can't keep them here much longer."

Gila waves, still not looking at me. "One minute more," she says.

I tromp up the noisy stairs. Issa and Habib look up hopefully. Neither has uttered a word of complaint; all the complaining is coming from me. It occurs to me that neither of them has probably had any dinner.

"They say only one more minute. I'm really sorry."

"Is not your fault," Habib says, though it is my fault. Why didn't I tell the coordinator that the visitors couldn't start filming at eight-thirty, or even eight; that these men have to go to work in nine hours?

We use the time to conjugate a few more verbs. *I wait. I waited. I will wait. I am still waiting.* Clattering on the stairs. Gila strides in, hand on hip. "We do a sound test now," she announces.

We file down the steps. By nine o'clock they're ready. Gila sits Issa and Habib at a table in the hallway. I take a seat in a torn easy chair to the side. "Okay, look at me, not the camera," Gila commands, loud, as if the men are deaf. Her own English is thickly accented and I know they'll have trouble understanding her. She seats herself opposite them, then motions to the guy with the glasses to move the camera closer.

"Tell me your name and where you from." She points at Issa. "You first, please."

"My name is Issa. I am from Eritrea." He folds his hands.

"And you?"

"I am Habib. I am from Darfur. You know about Darfur?"

The cameraman, trying for a close-up, stumbles against a chair, rights himself. Gila watches him, then turns back, distracted. "Okay, tell me how long you are in Israel and why you come here and what happen to you that you come." She points at Habib. "You first."

"I come from Sudan four month ah-go," Habib says.

"I come one year ah-go," says Issa.

"So why you came here?"

"Very bad in my country," Habib says. "Civil war. Israel is wonderful country."

"But what is happen to you in Sudan? To your family? Tell me exactly." Gila motions to the cameraman to come closer to Habib. I move up to the edge of my chair, ready like a TV lawyer to bounce up and object. Her course at the college is called The Sociology of Displacement. Nobody has prepared her for how to talk to these men. Nobody has prepared her for anything.

"Many refugees from Darfur. People dying. Not enough food. Also disease," Habib says. The camera is inches from his face.

"But what about you, what is happen to you there?" Gila prods.

"Very difficult. So I am walking to Israel. Across Egypt. Israel very good place," Habib says, trying to ignore the looming camera.

"Are your parents alive? Were they murdered? Tortured?"

"Gila!" I'm up like a shot.

"You interrupting," she says.

"That's right. You need to change the subject. NOW."

She purses her lips, motions to the cameraman to start again. "What about rape, did they rape the women in your family?"

"Gila!"

She looks at me blankly.

"New topic," I say. "Otherwise –." I point to the front door. No more subtlety.

She exhales loudly. Turns back. "You like Tel Aviv? Israelis, they are nice to you?"

I sit back down, perch on the edge of my seat.

"Everybody very nice," Issa says. "Help us very much."

"What do they help with? Jobs?"

"Yes, jobs."

"You have a job?"

"I work at a car factory in Jaffa," Habib says, smiling.

"The owner, he is Moslem? Like you?"

"Moslem, yes."

"Jews not offer a job?"

"I work at Jewish restaurant," Issa says. "Dishwasher. Very good."

Gila trains her sights on Issa. "Is good to be a dishwasher?"

"Very good."

"Do you think Israelis are racist?" Gila says.

100

I start to get up. "Racist?" Habib says.

"Treat you bad," Gila says. "Because you black." She motions to the cameraman to pan them, capture their faces.

"Nobody racist," Habib says.

"Are you crazy?" Gila says. "Is a big problem here. We have to learn tolerant."

Habib arches his body away from the hovering camera. "We very happy here. I have job. Issa have job. We learn at this center. Miss Shenna, she teaching us Anglish. I learning Hebrew, computers."

I've had enough. I stand up. Then, a miracle: the cameraman is having a technical problem. He lowers his equipment, examines something.

"Okay, it's a wrap," I say.

"I'm not finished," Gila says.

"Sorry, time's up." I tell the two crew to pack up, they can work on their equipment outside. *Chick-chock,* I say, Israeli style. Get moving.

Issa and Habib wait at the table. "You guys can go home now," I say.

"My Anglish very bad," Issa says.

"Are you kidding? You sounded great," I tell him. "Both of you sounded great."

"Really?" Habib says, grinning.

"Absolutely." I want to tell them that only one person in the room sounded bad and it wasn't me, but that wouldn't be nice so I refrain. "You spoke beautifully."

They are beaming. "Maybe one day I be on TV!" Habib says. "Movie star!" He lightly punches Issa on the shoulder. "Yah, Issa? You too."

Issa blushes. He really could be a movie star. He has the high cheekbones and almond eyes of the young Yul Brynner in *The Ten Commandments*. I hold the door open for them and wish them good night. I want to give them fifty shekels for a couple of falafels and Cokes, tell them it's from the interviewer's college, but that would be a lie and a violation of the center's rules: no money to students, it's insulting and patronizing. Before they step out into the night, they ask if I'm okay by myself, do I want them to wait, they will walk me to the main road, but I tell them I'll be fine, and that they should go home and get some sleep.

~

After my mother returned from the cruise she asked about the seder. I told her it was different from the four or five seders we'd managed to pull off when we were still a regular little nuclear family, lurching affairs for which my mother would make all the traditional foods from a cookbook and my father would dig out a few dusty Haggadahs and we'd all go through the motions without much conviction, as if we were actors in somebody else's altogether too long play.

"Different?" my mother asked, unpacking her suitcase on the bed. "How so?"

"Lots more desserts. Her dad could read Hebrew."

"Uh huh," my mother said, hanging up a pair of silk pants. She'd hardly worn any of the fancy clothes she'd brought and had mostly sat on the deck in jeans and a sweatshirt. The finality of my father's departure had hit her out there on the ocean in a way, she said, that sitting in our house in West Hartford hadn't. But Carla and Dave had been great, thank God for Carla and Dave.

"There was a Holocaust survivor there," I said. "A friend of Elise's grandmother." I made it sound casual, but the truth was I couldn't stop thinking about the woman. I wanted to know the whole story, all the lurid details, and it made me feel vaguely dirty and depraved, like wanting to see pornography.

"How did you know she was a Holocaust survivor?" my mother asked from inside her closet. "Did it come up?" she said, passing me to go into the shower.

"Elise told me," I called over the spray, then went downstairs to make dinner. After a little while my mother came down. Her hair was wet and she looked really tired for someone who'd just been on vacation.

"I think there's something wrong with me," I said.

"What makes you think that?" my mother said, picking at the splendid pasta and jarred tomato sauce dinner I had prepared.

"I can't stop thinking about this survivor. I want to know what happened to her. Everything. I'm talking about all the horrible stuff."

My mother put down her fork. She needed a glass of wine, I could tell. Or a stiff drink. "That's normal, honey," she said. "You know how when there's an accident on the highway, everyone turns to look? It's a little like that. People want to see the carnage. Just like they want the gory details of a divorce. Who cheated and where and all the juiciest parts. I don't know why. Maybe because they want to know how bad things can get. The things we're

103

all afraid will happen to us. But then it goes and happens to somebody else." She picked up her fork and pushed around a few tubes of ziti before giving up and going for her water glass.

"But that's not the worst part," I said, and lowered my voice. I was in my own kitchen with my own mother and nobody else, and still I needed to whisper. "She wasn't very nice, Mom. Actually, she was kind of mean."

My mother folded her hands, choosing her words. "That's a hard truth, honey. Suffering doesn't necessarily make you a nicer person. It also doesn't make people like you. Though usually it makes them pity you."

~

I write Professor Silk to say my displaced persons group is proving harder to write about than I'd thought.

Language barrier? she emails back immediately. It's one in the morning in New York. Professor Silk is a dedicated teacher. *Cultural diffs? Over-identification with subjects? Lack of professional distance? Second thoughts about continuing degree?*

Yes yes yes yes yes, I write back.

~

A month before my mother went on her cruise, I came home early from school with a headache and let myself in. Carla's Toyota in front of the house meant nothing; she and my mother often went shopping in the afternoon or out to lunch, coordinating their work schedules at the insurance company so they could spend time together.

My father's car in the driveway was more surprising.

They hadn't closed the bedroom door all the way. Later, I thought it had probably excited my father to do something so reckless. I lay on my own bed staring at the ceiling and listening to the moans and the creaking headboard and Carla's loose laugh, my door wide open, waiting for them to find me, but then I heard them on the stairs, the front door opening and closing, their ignitions starting, and made a decision right then never to tell my mother.

~

Gideon's grandmother didn't drop dead or rip her shirt in mourning or even whimper. She sighed and said it was Gideon's life and that he should make sure to tell everyone he met in Germany that he was a Jew, an Israeli, and stand tall.

"Incredible. Do you think I've been delusional all this time?" Sigalit says when I report. We're having a celebratory post-dinner glass of wine in her kitchen. Omer has driven her mother back to the old age home.

"People change," I offer. As if I would know. Sigalit gets up and brings a little box of chocolates to the table to add to the festive atmosphere. She fills the hot water pot for tea. I like Sigalit's apartment. It's messy and cramped and always smells of cooking and laundry and teenage boys and their dozens of friends tromping in and out. This morning I received a surprise email from my father. He'd seen something on the news about Israel and wondered how I was; a friend in Boca had mentioned it. From this I gleaned there was a new woman. The new women

105

always pressed him to contact me, which he would do once or twice before going back to his old disinterested ways; I used to write back hopefully and wait for an answer but I've learned not to do that anymore. A year after the cruise, my mother found out about the affair between my father and Carla. A neighbor had seen them trekking in and out, and had asked. In Carla's tearful confession, she said she'd wanted my mother on the trip because she felt guilty and thought it might help her break it off. And because she wanted an excuse not to spend so much time alone with Dave. Now she and Dave live in California.

I take a chocolate and say to Sigalit, "I told your mother: Look at me. I've come here, and I like it despite the impossibility of everything. People are always moving. My father's in Florida, my aunt and uncle are in L.A., my students are in south Tel Aviv. So I'm here and Gideon's over there and though it might not be what you want, it kind of evens things out. Overall it's a wash."

Sigalit lets out a whistle and takes down two mugs. "Well, I owe you. Anything you want, just say the word."

Across the hall, back in my apartment, I email my mother to say I won't be returning to the States in June after all and to ask when she's coming to visit. Then I go to the window. It's already dark. Two African men are walking quickly along Ben Yehuda Street in the direction of the bus station, carrying plastic bags of groceries. Maybe they're dishwashers like Issa. Or cleaners like Yohannes. Or have something on a factory floor like Habib. Soon after Carla and Dave moved away, my mother told me she'd long suspected her sister of playing around but had never

106

put that together with my father. Though it was right there under her nose, she said. Her whole professional life had been spent viewing wrecks, but this one she couldn't see. Though maybe it was just as well, she added. It was bad enough losing her husband. To lose her sister at the same time would have been terrible, even if she had to lose her a year later. Sometimes you can't take it all in at once.

The men walk purposefully, heads down. The evening is warm but there's a sea breeze, and their cotton shirts billow, puffing out their slender frames. Soon they're joined by dozens more—secretaries leaving the office, laborers packing it in for the day, university students with backpacks stuffed with books, everyone thinking of the meal that awaits or the family around the table or the soft spring night ahead, and I watch the two men with the plastic bags, their dark forms gliding swiftly down the twilight street, wondering if they too are thinking of home.

WONDER WOMEN

· ◊ ·

TAMI GEVA IS A BUSY WOMAN. Three boys under the age
of eight, a husband with an appointment at the university, a teenage stepdaughter two nights a week and alternate
weekends from the husband's first marriage, and a job at
an ethically questionable outfit over a shawarma place
on King George that specializes in dicey international finance, for which Tami atones by driving around Tel Aviv
collecting for the city's food bank. Today, she and two
British volunteers picked up donations from five bakeries,

four restaurants, and a symposium on the future of wind farms that had optimistically prepared lunch for seventy but fed only thirty-five. All afternoon her car smelled of lemon-infused grape leaves and saffron rice. She had to take the volunteers out for coffee and a pastry because the smell was making them all want to eat the upholstery.

"Nice ladies. They come for a month to see their grandkids," Tami says to her mother, cradling the phone on her shoulder in her kitchen on Brenner Street a stone's throw from the shuk. She's chopping vegetables for soup. The tomatoes are wrinkled. If she can pry herself off the phone, she can make it to the shuk and back for fresh ones before the boys are dropped off from aftercare. Her mother wants to know what else she's making her husband for dinner, a question Tami lets pass.

"We used to get lots of Swedes volunteering in my day," her mother says, wistful. "All kinds of Scandinavians. Of course it was a kibbutz, so everything was different." Now that all the kibbutzim have been privatized, Tami's mother has become sentimental about the fanatically communal life she couldn't wait to flee. A sound like gunshots ricochets off the walls and Tami looks out the window. A creaky truck loaded with building materials trundles down the narrow street, tailpipe stuttering. Renovations. Tami's own renovation, converting the terrace off the living room into a bedroom for Adi, Ranen's moody sixteen-year-old, so the girl won't have to bunk with the boys during visits anymore, is stalled for mystical reasons known only to the contractor. "The Scandinavian girls loved it," her mother sighs. "They came for the sun and sex and stole all the men. When we went home to the kibbutz on weekends from the army, the boys in our unit went crazy for them, such trophies, those long-legged blondinis. And exotic, like from another planet. This was before we all started to travel. Planet of the Long-legged Blondes. Like the Amazons in that movie with the pretty Israeli with the metal across her forehead."

~

A kilo of shuk tomatoes later, Tami returns to the flat to find Adi sitting on the low concrete wall out front.

"Hey," Adi mumbles, lifting herself off the barrier with effort. She picks up her silver backpack, slings it desultorily over her shoulder.

"Hey," Tami says. She wants to say *What are you doing here?* She wants to say *It's Tuesday, Adi, you're not supposed to come until Thursday,* but instead she hands Adi the tomatoes and pulls her house key from her pocket. Adi has a key but pretends she's forgotten it so that her father or Tami have to unlock the door and take her in.

"You want something to drink?" Tami asks when they're inside. Adi shrugs and Tami fills a glass with orange juice and hands it to her. You don't need to be Freud to know the girl is depressed. There are a thousand reasons, starting with the fact that Nurit, the child's mother, brought her back to Israel three months before at the height of a July heat wave after seven years in the States, for no reason other than that Nurit's new boyfriend was Israeli and Nurit decided she'd had enough of America. That Adi would have to finish high school where she'd last

111

attended school at age eight didn't figure into it. Ranen tried to reason with Nurit, couldn't she hold off returning for one more year, let Adi graduate in the States, her whole class in Tel Aviv would be preparing for the army, she wouldn't have a clue let alone any friends. To which Nurit replied that if he was so concerned, he could pick up and move to Miami, but she was done.

The juice drained, Adi leaves the glass on the counter and goes to the living room. Tami finishes the soup, then goes to the couch where Adi is stretched out, eyes closed. Tami perches at the end by Adi's unwashed feet.

"I know it's not Thursday," Adi says in English, eyes still closed. She hates talking in Hebrew, she says. Her vocabulary is terrible, she has a humiliating accent, she wants to die rather than speak in public. "But I can't stand my mother and have to get out. I want to move in here. Like live here. All the time."

Tami closes her own eyes. She can't say she's surprised. Nurit is a piece of work. Impetuous, hotheaded. Also beautiful and blunt. Adi is an average to perhaps slightly overweight teen with the occasional island of acne and a pensive, introverted nature inherited from Ranen which, in both father and daughter, crumples under Nurit's withering gaze. Tami can only imagine what passes for conversation at Nurit's dinner table.

Voices beyond the door. The boys and their aftercare driver. Tami pats Adi's knee and pulls herself off the couch, says they'll talk about it when Ranen gets home, but she knows he'll say yes. Anything to get his girl away from her overbearing mother. Knows too that Nurit will be thrilled to pass Adi's maintenance onto her unfaithful ex and his Jezebel of a second wife; she only spirited Adi out of the country to get even with Ranen for leaving her. She's already told Tami she's done with child-rearing. Enough is enough. At Adi's age, she was responsible for her five younger siblings so her parents could work at their restaurant day and night. Parents these days coddle their kids, she says. Keep it up, and they'll have a country full of weaklings and babies.

~

That Tami's mother might hint that Tami wasn't being a good wife by not making a proper dinner for her husband is forgivable considering that her mother was raised in a militantly communal collective where her own mother never cooked a day in her life. Hadassah Golan was determined to free women of the tyrannical stranglehold of the patriarchy (her words). She refused to bend to the conventions of marriage, had a flock of doting lovers, one of whom was presumably Tami's mother's father, and made her way up the ranks to become the kibbutz's all-powerful secretary, the party's equivalent of president, where she insisted that men work in the kitchen, laundry and children's houses. Bravado for which she was both heralded and hated. A revolt erupted, the mutiny coming, to Hadassah's horror, not from the men but from the women, who claimed to miss not only cooking but children, and demanded that the children's houses be shuttered and their offspring released to live with them. There was a furious intra-kibbutz battle, screaming matches every night

113

in the dining hall, the rebels fulminating that separating children from their mothers was a perversion of nature promoted by traumatized founders afraid of intimacy, the stalwarts firing back that the nuclear family was the most regressive, suffocating, stultifying environment possible in which to raise fully developed human beings. Eventually the children's houses fell, as they were falling in kibbutz after kibbutz, though the diehards managed to keep one small one open for those unwilling to endure the indignity of having to be someone's full-time parent. Naturally, Tami's mother was among those who remained in the children's house to the bitter end.

~

"It's going to be up to us to help Adi, you know," Ranen says, hanging up his newly laundered clothes after the soup and baths for the boys and a chick-chock five-minute phone call with Nurit who, no surprise, was delighted—Tami might say overjoyed—to hear the new living arrangements; Adi would move in as soon as the terrace bedroom renovation was done, Tami would start bugging the contractor tomorrow. Tami folds laundry at the foot of their bed. Ranen works a shirt onto a hanger, then stuffs it onto the overcrowded rack. For a man who professes to be against the excessive acquisition of material goods, he has a lot of shirts. "Because, as we just heard, Nurit is bowing out." He waves toward the rack, his back to Tami. *"It's your turn, Raneni,"* he trills in the annoying sing-song he uses to evoke his ex-wife. *"I paid my dues and am going off to travel the world, me and whathisname.* What's his name?"

"Ori." Tami rolls up another pair of little-boy socks and adds it to the pile. On Friday Ranen will drive their sons and a week's supply of socks and other clothes to his parents in Metulla up by the Lebanese border because the schools are closed for the autumn New Year holiday. All the grandparents in their circle have the grandchildren for the holiday, Ranen's parents say. All the grandparents in the country do, as far as they're concerned. They'd be hurt if Tami and Ranen didn't deliver.

"She doesn't need therapy. We all know why she's unhappy," Ranen says, picking up another shirt. "It's situational. Situational depression. Where you have to take action and change the circumstances, not sit around analyzing." Tami rolls up another pair of socks. She knows where this is going. "What she needs is to do something meaningful, something for others. There's nothing like altruism to lift a person's spirits. I read that psychiatrists are prescribing it for addicts to help with self-esteem. They go visit old people or work in a soup kitchen. It does something to the brain." He shoves the densely packed clothes to the end of the rack, jams the new shirt in. "Preferably in a setting where her bad Hebrew and mashed up cultural background won't be an issue. Something hands-on, you know what I mean?"

Tami puts another sock ball on the pile. They sit beside her like baby chicks.

Ranen plucks another shirt from the basket, looks over at Tami. "Hey, here's an idea. What if she comes along with you on your drives for the food bank? She's young, strong. She can carry a lot of trays of leftover schnitzel."

115

~

Tami has always understood that when you married a person with children, you married their children too. Her mother warned her about this early in her relationship with Ranen, less concerned that her daughter was sleeping with someone's husband than that he was someone's father. Did Tami really want to inherit a seven-year-old? Most likely a troubled seven-year-old since divorce, you know, left its scars. Tami was only twenty-two; it was nice that her handsome young political science professor had fallen for her, but he brought baggage. Tami told her mother that she shouldn't call a child baggage and anyway she was smitten. Plus there was the small matter of her own newly discovered pregnancy, which immediately pivoted the conversation to wedding dates.

But Tami had to admit she was relieved when, a year later, Nurit took herself and Adi off to America. No more last minute schedule changes, no more volleys of parental vitriol. Ranen objected but he had no leverage, so instead Adi came to them every summer. Off from teaching, Ranen took Adi, along with her successively added little brothers, to the beach and the parks and to visit the grandparents, his parents up at the border, Nurit's in depressing Kiryat Gat, while Tami went off to her various jobs organizing enrichment programs for Bedouin girls or free daycare for refugee kids or prison visits for mothers and their babies. Enlightened work where the need was heart-stopping and the pay laughable and which Tami eventually had to trade in for soul-killing positions in finance to cover the exorbitant child support Nurit had managed to extract. Yet even

the worst of the finance jobs have given Tami a grateful
reprieve from the brimming chaos of domestic life.

You can love your family wildly, one of her co-workers
with six kids told her, and still need a separation. A firewall
to keep you sane. Even the thinnest one will do.

~

When, at age ten, Tami's mother began pressing her
own mother to tell her which of the men dropping by
during their daily family visit was her father, Hadassah
brushed her off and said that designations of patrimony
were bourgeois holdovers and that she and her vision-
ary comrades were building a new society where people
would be free of petty possessiveness and iron chains. If
her daughter's friends were boasting that they had two
parents, that was their business. Were the two of them
missing anything by not having a male assigned to them?
Did her daughter lack for anything because there was no
specific man she could claim as her forbear but instead was
attended to by the entire kibbutz, any one of its members
happy to fix whatever needed fixing or give help whenever
needed?

What she had to understand, Hadassah told her
daughter while they sat on the concrete steps outside Hadassah's room, Hadassah taking long drags on her kibbutz-issue Noblesse cigarette and blowing smoke rings
into the oppressive afternoon heat, was that your strongest
bonds in life should be with your cohort, your peers. Not
your parents. Not your lovers. Not your children. That's
how communities stayed strong and countries survived.

Not by devoting yourself to your private little fiefdom but to the collective. Hadassah passed Tami's mother the lit cigarette, inviting her to take a puff, and said, Anyway, wasn't it better to have five men come and enjoy her kibbutz-issue birthday cake each year instead of only one? Wasn't it better to have ten, fifteen, fifty people celebrate her arrival into the world instead of a lonely little island of three?

When Tami's mother told her this story, they were at a café on the sand. Tami was nursing her second son, a blanket draped over her shoulder, two icy Cokes on a wobbly table beside them. Watching her nurse, her mother said she didn't have another baby after Tami was born because she was afraid she'd be a bad mother.

"But you were a good mother," Tami said, surprised. "You didn't hover like the others. You let me roam the neighborhood and bring home all kinds of junk and didn't care if I brushed my teeth at night or had perfectly combed hair."

Her mother reached over and adjusted the blanket to better cover Tami's breast, though the bikinis on the beach exposed far more. Tami's father had died three years before, and Tami had been urging her mother to date; she was still young, attractive, plenty of men would be interested. No, no, her mother said. She didn't need anyone else invading her space thank you very much. "I had no idea what I was doing when you were born," Tami's mother said, fussing with the blanket. "We didn't have mothers when I was growing up. We had adults with our last names whose rooms we visited two hours a day before supper and

118

who took us on holiday once a year to a kibbutz-owned flat in the city to observe how the capitalists were exploiting the workers or to a kibbutz-owned cabin on the Kinneret where we stared in awe at the families driving in with their private cars and transistor radios and pillows from home." She finished with the blanket and sat back. The sea made its rushing noises. "I might have looked like a mother, but I was like the people in those science fiction movies who look human but have no idea what that is or how to be it. That's what I felt like. Mr. Spock without the pointy ears."

~

Tami is at work writing up a trade involving oil from the South China Sea for a Russian-Israeli billionaire in Cyprus she wouldn't want to run into in a dark alley when her phone beeps.

The contractor. "Good news, Mrs. Tami," the man says. "I spoke to Mrs. Nurit. We're coming today, four o'clock. You'll be there?"

Nurit? Who'd obviously pried the man's name from Ranen because she didn't trust Tami to call. Tami checks her watch. Three-fifteen. She's supposed to pick up leftovers at the Hilton from an event the night before for the Belgian ambassador; everything is packed and ready to go and has to be collected by four, otherwise they'll throw it out. She tells the contractor she'll be there, then calls her mother who she happens to know is in central Tel Aviv visiting a museum after meeting another retired librarian for lunch. Can her mother do the hotel pickup? And, oh, by the way, Adi will be helping.

"Adi? I wouldn't have thought she'd be interested."

"She's not. Ranen's idea. Says it'll be good for her. She's moving in, also by the way."

"A teenage girl full-time," her mother murmurs. "Different from a month in the summer and a weekend now and then."

Tami drums the desk. "So will you do it, pick up the food?" She's never asked her mother to drive for the food bank, all that shuttling around, talking to people, it's not her mother's thing. She's also never asked her mother to drive her sons or keep them overnight. Children make her uncomfortable. They're like a different species, her mother says. She's not one of those grandmothers who needs the grandkids on holidays. Tami doesn't have to ask to know this is true.

"You should do the pickup," her mother says. "I'll wait for the contractor."

"But how will you get in? How will you know what to tell him? He needs constant supervision. There's still no ceiling in the new room. Last time he forgot to measure for windows. You have to check everything."

"You'll tell me on the phone. I'll get the key from Levy on the first floor."

"But the contractor's going to ask for a payment. He always does when he shows up."

"I'll tell him you had an emergency. I'll tell him I'm your mother and can guarantee you're good for the money." A pause. "Are you afraid to go out with Adi?"

"What? Of course not." The woman in the next cubicle glances over at Tami. Tami lowers her voice. "Forget me—what about you? Are you afraid to go out with Adi?"

"No, no. Why would you say that?" Another pause. "Well, maybe a little."

~

When Tami was growing up, her parents' flat was different from all her friends' flats. While her friends' parents converted theirs into bright airy places with open floor plans and whitewashed walls and spare furnishings, Tami's was a warren of tiny rooms jammed with stuff—oversized chairs and rugs and tables and lamps, decorative plates and cheesy souvenirs, not a surface left uncovered. After work, her mother liked to spend long hours by herself in these rooms reading or knitting or listening to music.

Compensation, her father explained when Tami asked. All through her mother's childhood, she never had a single thing to call her own, not a T-shirt or a pair of shorts, not a toy or a stuffed animal; even her toothbrush wasn't technically hers. Each week she took clothes from a communal bin and returned them a week later to another communal bin. The bedrooms in the children's houses were as stark as a prison's, nothing on the floors or walls, which were kept hospital-bare so they could be scrubbed daily to ward off germs.

But why all the little rooms? Tami pressed. Why not open up the flat like everyone else did, break out the space and let in light and air with sliders of glass?

Her father leaned back in the big chair, a bowl of almonds on the side table, a glass of lemonade for each of them, a man who exercised and watched his cholesterol and tried to control his tendency to overwork, the son of Polish survivors who'd washed up after the war, dragging their terrible histories with them, a man who'd be dead two years later of a heart attack, and said, did Tami have any idea what it was like to grow up and never be alone, not even in the shower? Her mother, he said, pointing with his chin to the kitchen where her mother was assembling dinner, had in many ways an idyllic childhood, the kibbutz lush with flowers and trees, whole days spent outdoors with her friends, lessons held in nature, no talk of money or careers or ambition. A utopia. What he wouldn't have given, her father sighed, to have had that freedom.

But it came with a price. Her mother was part of a group from the day she was born until she went into the army. They lived together, ate together, played together, studied together, never went anywhere without each other. It was like having sixteen twins, all of them watching you all of the time.

That's why her mother wanted all the little closed-off rooms, her father said. Why her mother was sometimes a little reclusive. She needed to be alone to hear herself think.

~

Adi is slouched outside the Hilton's double doors when Tami hurries up the walk. Tami waves and Adi gives a limp gesture in response, something between a hello and a goodbye.

"Great that you got here so punctually," Tami says, trying for upbeat while they wait at reception for the catering manager. The frown on Adi's face could sink ships.

"Where's your backpack?" Tami asks, noticing. "Did you leave it at school?"

"No. I brought it home."

"Ah." A stopover at Nurit's. She probably had to cut her last class to do it. Tami doesn't ask.

"I saw your mom," Adi says.

"My mom? Where?"

"At home of course. She was there to meet the contractor."

At home.

"She was about to buzz Mr. Levy on the first floor when I got there," Adi says. "I used my key to let her in. She's nice. We talked about books. Also movies. We have the same taste."

"Oh? I didn't know she had taste in movies."

"Oh, she does. We both like sci-fi, especially the ones about aliens. She said they're not really about aliens but about misfits. People who feel like they don't belong. That's why they're so popular. Because a lot of people feel like they don't belong."

The catering manager appears and they load up Tami's car and bring the ambassador's leftovers to a shelter for battered women and a halfway house for ex-felons and a flat housing four Somali families where it's one of the mothers' birthdays, thirty, same age as Tami, and through it all, Adi silently does as instructed, carrying foil pans of poached sole and pesto ziti and baby asparagus and cake, mutely declining offers of water, Coke, lemonade. Between drop-offs, Tami tries to engage her, asking what she thought of each place they visited—*all right, okay*—then prattles on to fill the air. The felons are in an experimental program, some battered women come from rich homes, the Somalis walked all the way across Africa to get to Israel. On and on she prattles until she can't stand the sound of her own voice. When they finish and the smells of fish and garlic and basil have finally drifted off, Tami says she'll drive Adi back to Nurit's but first has to stop at her own apartment to see how her mother and the contractor are faring.

"I don't need to go to Nurit's," Adi says. "I already brought my stuff to your place. Can I stay? My school is also closed for the holiday. I'd much rather be with my dad and you."

"She just wants to feel welcome," Ranen says to Tami that night. He has driven the boys to his parents on the border and Adi has spread out in their room, clothes draped over the beds, shoes and headphones and books strewn across the floor. She brought a suitcase and not just one silver backpack but two. "Can you blame her? She wants a family. Who doesn't want a family?"

All week Adi keeps herself occupied—doing what, Tami doesn't know—and when Tami gets home from work they go together to do the food pickups and deliveries, the girl polite but always trudging behind as if dragging herself through wet sand.

"I don't think the volunteerism is working," Tami says to Ranen in bed on Friday night. Party-goers whoop it up in the street outside their windows. The next morning they will drive to Metulla to bring their sons home. "It's been five days. I think we need to declare our attempt at emotional uplift through altruism a failure. She seems a little happier, I grant you, but not, I think, because of that."

Ranen, eyes closed, concedes. He's a passionate man but not an unreasonable man.

"More problematic," Tami says, "is what we'll do when the boys are back and she wants to stay. There's no space for her in their room anymore. She needs her own. Which might not be for a while. I heard from the contractor today. Seems he forgot to get a permit. He swore he did but, well, you know how that goes."

"Mm. We'll make do."

Tami curls up against her husband's back. Make do. A shower curtain dividing the terrace from the living room. A folding cot. A set of plastic bins on wheels. An all-night view of the starry sky.

~

When, at ninety-two, Hadassah Golan died, six hundred people came to the funeral, and that was only because there was a fluke summer storm that made traveling on the coastal road to the kibbutz iffy; otherwise there would have been a thousand. Speakers compared her to Golda Meir and Rosa Luxemburg, towering superwomen who carried the torch of equality and justice worldwide.

Among the attendees were four middle-aged women nobody could miss. Long skirts, sleeves down to their wrists despite the blistering heat. A clutch of the pious amid a sea of fervid atheists who prided themselves on having barbecues on Yom Kippur. The visitors swept toward Tami and her mother after the assembled had converged on the old dining hall for refreshments. Ranen was outside entertaining their boys, spinning them around on the rusty roundabout; Tami could see them from the dining hall windows, squealing with joy. Later, Ranen would say, only half-joking, why not ditch the city and move to the country, fresh air and freedom? The kibbutz was selling off lots. Suburban-style houses, but you could still taste the old strident socialism in the breeze.

"We're Moshe Gruenfeld's daughters," one of the women said to Tami's mother, reaching for her hands. "Moshe was Hadassah's brother. Our condolences, please."

"What brother?" Tami's mother said. "My mother had no brother."

The woman produced a plastic sleeve of snapshots, and there they were, Hadassah, seven or eight, unmistakable in a canvas hat, standing beside a pair of grim-looking adults and a gawky boy in khaki shorts hiked up to his waist. The story was straightforward and sad. Hadassah and Moshe's mother had what they called in those days a nervous breakdown and was sent to an asylum an hour away in Nahariya, never to return, following which their father disappeared, surfacing every now and then with a new woman until the kibbutz powers-that-be told him he wasn't pulling his weight and was no longer welcome.

"But the children were allowed to stay," the woman who'd been doing all the talking said. "Moshe, our father, didn't like kibbutz life so he left and went to Jerusalem. Your mother, on the other hand—." The woman waved around the dining hall.

126

"How could I not know about this?" Tami's mother said, distressed. "A brother? Cousins? A whole raft of relatives? How did I not know?"

"We also," another cousin put in. "Only on his deathbed did our father tell us. He contacted your mother over the years but she didn't want to see him. Family; it was too painful for her. Like for so many in that generation." The woman shook her head sadly. "They had to lock the door and throw away the key."

~

The boys come home and Tami and Ranen make a makeshift bedroom on the terrace for Adi with a shower curtain and a cot and plastic bins that can be stashed in a corner. The children return to school and Ranen's semester at the university begins and Tami goes to work and continues ferrying food around the city, and then one day Adi's principal calls to say that Adi has been cutting class and skipping out early, and while she's a good student, the principal is concerned and thinks her father and his current wife—the principal understands the girl's mother is traveling—should know.

Adi is sheepish when Tami asks for an explanation. Can she call someone?

Twenty minutes later, Tami's mother arrives with a box of pastries. She puts the box on the kitchen table. "I can explain. We've been spending time together instead of Adi going to school."

Tami looks from one to the other. Her mother? Adi? They hardly know each other. "The two of you?"

127

Adi says eagerly, "It's fun. We talk, exchange books, go out for coffee, watch movies." She looks at Tami's mother. "Right, Safta?"

Safta? Grandma? Another one? The girl already has two of those.

"It's true," Tami's mother says. "We started during the holiday break when there was no school, then we just carried on. I pick her up early a few times a week and let her play hooky. I know the librarian there. She said nobody would notice. You know how Israeli schools are."

Tami looks at the two of them again. The truth is, Adi doesn't really need to go to school. She's way ahead of her classmates and is studying on her own for the matriculation exams so she can go to university after the army. Though she might bypass the army and do national service instead. She's been giving it thought and doesn't think she's cut out for the military. Too rigid, plus she doesn't think she'd do well with communal living.

"I'm sorry," Tami's mother says, reaching for Tami's hand. "I should have asked your permission. I just figured you were so busy, what with your job and the little ones and the volunteer work and your husband." She looks over at Adi. "We won't do it again."

Adi grins broadly. "Absolutely. We won't."

Tami makes coffee and they eat the pastries and when her mother sees the shower curtain, she suggests Adi move in with her until the renovation is done. A curtained-off porch is no place for a teenage girl who needs privacy and a proper door so that she can be alone to hear herself think.

The boys arrive with their aftercare driver just as

128

Ranen appears, and they hug Tami's mother hello while Adi packs her things. Tami's mother plants a kiss on Tami's forehead and she and Adi leave, declining Ranen's offer of a ride; they will take the bus. The boys have already gotten busy turning the terrace into a fort, piling pillows on the cot and insisting the shower curtain remain. Ranen thumbs through the mail.

Tami takes the coffee cups to the sink. A coral dusk is beginning to spread. She tips closer to the window, looks down onto the street. Adi and her mother are pulling the big suitcase between them, each of them wearing a giant silvery backpack. The waning sun glints sharply off the shiny fabric: two astronauts preparing for space. She watches as they disappear around a corner. Behind her, squeals and laughter billow up from the terrace into the open sky.

REMITTANCES

· ◊ ·

I HEAR IT EVERYWHERE, and this morning I finally read it in the English-language daily I buy each morning at the kiosk on Tel Aviv's Ben-Yehuda Street: Jewish is in in Germany. An enterprising brewery in a small town in Bavaria is making the first officially kosher beer in the old Reich, called King Solomon ("the beer for the wise," the brewmeister says), even though all the beer in Germany is already de facto kosher. Hops, barley, yeast, malt—these are the only ingredients, the article says. So King Solomon's kashrut certification is a redundancy, a non-necessity. But the brewmeister wants it, he tells a reporter, because things Jewish are hip in Germany these days. The populace, especially the young, is drawn to them. King Solomon will make for good business.

When I tell this to Aryeh he sneers. This disgusts him, he tells me, even though his grandparents' wretched personal history also once disgusted him. This was before Israel's Official Embrace of the Holocaust. After decades of a barely disguised silent national shame—*how could they let themselves be led like sheep etcetera*—the country is finally able to look these old people in the eye. It wasn't always this way. When Aryeh was a kid, people used to tell the crones at the beach with numbers on their arms to cover themselves up.

But now this latest news from the Deutschland makes him ill. He gets up from the table and tells me to stop reading the English-language dailies and learn better Hebrew already so I don't have to read that kind of drivel.

"I think it's probably in *Ha'aretz* too," I tell him, collecting the coffee cups from the table and carrying them to the sink. "They cover the same things, you know." Which I know because my paper is just an English translation of his.

"Well, I don't understand how anyone can call that newsworthy, Robin." He takes his plate to the counter. Shells of three hard-boiled eggs jostle on the glass. He eats like a kibbutznik—boiled eggs, half a dozen skinny cucumbers, a tomato, thick bread and salt—even though he's lived his whole life in Tel Aviv. "Enough already with Germany. We've been obsessing about them for sixty years. Who gives a shit what they think of Jews now? Who gives a shit what they think of anything?"

"It has the fastest growing Jewish population in the world," I call to him on his way to the bathroom where he'll brush his teeth before heading out the door to work. He's fastidious that way. Likes to have his teeth brushed, hands washed, hair combed just so before he walks out into the muggy soup of the street. It's the *yekke* in him, his German-Jewish ancestry. Though of course I won't tell him that. "All those Jews from the FSU," I call. "The second language in Berlin is practically Russian."

"Same as here," he calls back from the bathroom, the water running. Instinctively, I glance out the kitchen window at my neighbor's balcony. The Russian cleaning woman is beating a small rug on the railing. Puffs of dust billow up like little genies. All the Israelis in these buildings employ Russian women, Ludas and Irinas and Galinas, to clean their apartments; they're shocked to hear I clean ours myself. *It's not exploitation,* they tell me in their excellent college-level English. The Russians were engineers or physicists or dentists back in Moscow, but if they don't speak the language they can't find work. *Think of it as giving an illiterate immigrant a job.*

At that, I usually smile and end the conversation. They could just as well have been talking about me.

~

I met Aryeh my third week in the country and latched onto him like glue. My image of volunteering at a leafy kibbutz redolent with citrus groves had run up against reality when a sharp-tongued bureaucrat in a windowless office next to the Tel Aviv bus station informed me that the only spaces available were in a collective in the desert where I could work eight hours a day in a plastics factory. I chose to politely decline and found myself a room in an apartment on Allenby Street with two other Americans. One was thinking of entering a women's yeshiva and finding God, who she had not been able to locate in L.A.; the other had burned out in high tech in Silicon Valley and was working under the table as a waitress in a vegan restaurant on the beach. It was in the restaurant where I'd seen the ad for the room.

"It'll just be temporary," I told the waitress, Mia. "While I get myself together."

"That's cool," she said, sipping her lemon-eucalyptus tea. She was on a break. The waves slapped the sand behind us. "So what have you been doing till now?" She was trying for casual but I knew she was appraising me. I was a total stranger and there was probably something about me.

"Dropped out of grad school. Medieval history." Which was basically accurate. I'd been required to withdraw after the so-called incident. It wouldn't have looked good for the university for me to stay during the investigation. Ivy League, big name faculty, a reputation to protect.

Mia flashed a smile. She was skeptical. But there was a tacit understanding among us English speakers; we had to help each other out.

She gave me a key and I prepaid a month's rent and moved in the same day. The other roommate, Elisheva, though that wasn't her real name, which was something embarrassing and Southern Californian like Arden or Cassandra, was almost never there, checking out the religious scene. Mia got me a job chopping vegetables in the back of the restaurant. It wasn't bad. No one bothered me, and I walked the beach when I was done.

But then one day Elisheva came home from one of her Torah-For-Beginners classes and told me someone in her group had seen me outside the apartment and recognized me. That he remembered me from New Haven and had heard I'd been involved in something violent and terrible. She could barely get out the words. By then she was wearing long skirts and praying three times a day. She didn't want my messy past seeping into her newly purified present. Mia, at the other side of the table, went pale.

It was late in the afternoon. I hardly knew them. I said nothing and went to my room, leaving them frantically whispering in the kitchen. That evening Aryeh came to the restaurant for a quinoa pilaf and salad, and when he asked me if I wanted to go out and get a coffee after my shift—I was covering for a waitress who'd called in sick; Aryeh told me later that I seemed interesting—I packed up my stuff from Mia's apartment and went home with Aryeh and never went back.

~

With Aryeh off to work I finish cleaning up, then take the bus to the Interior Ministry on Kaplan Street to carry on in my lurching pursuit of citizenship. After almost three years in the country, Aryeh has convinced me I need to do this, not because I need the work permit or the new-citizen tax breaks on a washing machine or because, like the Ethiopians or the Argentinians or the Iranians or, lately, the French, I am a Jew from a country that won't especially want me back, but because I need to make a commitment to a new life so that I can let the old one go.

The waiting area is surprisingly empty. Immediately I wonder if the workers are on strike because the waiting room is never empty. But it turns out it is simply my lucky day. I have gotten there at exactly the right time, Irit, the official assigned to my case, tells me when I shamble into her office and sit down; I was hoping for a long delay so I could have another excuse to postpone. I've just missed the morning rush, Irit tells me brightly, pulling my file from a silver mesh holder on her desk. Irit is neat, organized, efficient. She likes pretty things and has been, she's told me, to Venice and Paris, to Prague and Istanbul and Barcelona, though not to the United States. The Pacific coast, the redwood forests, the ribbon of highway, like from the song: have I been to these places? I haven't, I tell her, and she *tsks tsks*. Americans don't explore their own country, she doesn't understand this.

"*Tov*," she says, wrapping up the small talk. "So did you finish the paperwork?" She squints at her computer screen. "No. I see you have for me one more form."

It's the one asking about criminal history. Citations, arrests, convictions. Aryeh has typed up a long explanation in Hebrew and carefully stapled it and all the official documents to the sheet: the hasty trial, the successful appeal, the finding of prosecutorial misconduct, damages for

136

wrongful imprisonment. Even an apology from the State of Connecticut. I'd wanted to bring in the papers smudged and wrinkled and dog-eared so that their condition might cause my application to be ignored, so that maybe Irit wouldn't read it. Never in my life would I turn in papers like that, everything always meticulously typed and clean and respectful. Because once upon a time I was a promising student at a famous university with a great future. But this morning I wanted to bring a mess. Aryeh wouldn't let me. *You are going in there with the truth. You have nothing to hide. You should be proud.* Proud. I rustle through my bag and find the pristine manila envelope. Palms damp, I hand it to Irit.

She swivels in her chair and sits back, opens the papers onto her lap. I look out the window at the bougainvillea trailing on the façade of the building across the street. Under the giant purple blooms a pair of Filipino women are walking arm-in-arm. They are here taking care of the elderly, thousands of small Asian men and women pushing ancient Jews in wheelchairs, helping them with their walkers in the coffee shops. They are exceedingly patient, exceedingly kind. I once read in the English-language daily that thirty percent of their countrymen leave their homeland to work—they go to Dubai, England, the United Arab Emirates, Israel—and send back their earnings. Remittances. The government in Manila encourages it. It's the only way to make their economy work. It's also what allows the Filipinos who want to stay here to remain. The price of admission, they call it. It's an unspoken arrangement between the two countries: if they don't earn enough to send money home, they have to leave. On Saturdays, their day off, couples stroll the promenade by the sea and buy ice cream.

Irit has put down the papers. I glance back at her. She is resting her chin in her palm, thinking. I look at the wall behind her head and register nothing. It is unbearable to me that she has read it, that now she knows.

"*Tov*," she says finally. Finished. She takes up her mouse, clicks a few times and watches the screen. There is nothing further to discuss. She will recommend that they approve my application, she says. There is just one more hurdle. Sign-off from her superior. But approval will be Irit's recommendation. The Israeli Law of Return says that anyone with a Jewish parent or grandparent—same definition as Hitler's—is enough of a Jew and has the right to become an Israeli citizen. Certain limitations apply. Killing a fellow Jew in self-defense is not de facto one of them.

"The next meeting with my superior is at the end of the week," Irit says, poker faced, all business, but later she will no doubt go home and tell her husband about the young woman who was in her office today. Thirty years old, a murderer. But justified. He could not imagine what the creep did to her. Yale University, has he heard of it? Like Harvard except in Connecticut. Irit folds her hands on top of the file. Behind the crisp professionalism I detect a slight crack in the veneer, the faintest catch in her voice. "We'll do the best we can. I call you when it's over."

~

The Russian from my neighbor's balcony is sitting on a ledge outside our apartment building clutching an over-stuffed plastic bag that contains slippers and a housedress, things she wears for cleaning. A cracked black vinyl pocketbook is tucked in beside her.

"Everything all right?" I ask in my rounded American Hebrew. It's nearly noon and feverishly hot. I've never seen her sitting outside before.

She opens a palm and says something fast in Russian. A tiny Star of David glints on a thin gold chain around her neck. Apartment three, floor two, she manages in Hebrew. She has a customer in my building. But why is she outside? I fish for my keys. Does she not have a key? I mime, holding them up. Nobody home?

Correct, she nods. Nobody home. Brassy gold caps glint on two of her upper teeth. So maybe she wasn't a mathematician or astronaut or dentist in the Mother Country; maybe she's from Uzbekistan or Kazakhstan or one of those other long-ridiculed stans, but, still, I find her cleaning person status distressing. I don't like it, no matter what my smartly dressed Tel Aviv acquaintances say. *This is how it is. Our parents and grandparents were once immigrants too. They did their share of dirty work. Now it's someone else's turn.*

"*Cham m'od,*" I say to the woman in my simplest Hebrew, fanning myself to demonstrate, in case she hasn't learned even the basics. Hot out here. "Would you like to come to my apartment for a cold drink?" I throw back the imaginary contents of an imaginary glass and make

139

pretend drinking noises.

She tips her head, uncertain. She doesn't want to stand up her employer. But her employer is not home, and someone has made a mistake. Either the Russian has a key and forgot it, or the Israeli forgot about the Russian. I'm suspecting the latter because people don't let out keys around here just like that.

I perform a series of gestures to get across that I will write her employer a note and leave it on her door. Then she can come in out of the heat.

"*B'seder*," the woman says. All right. She will come. We take care of the note and walk the stairs in silence. In Aryeh's apartment I bring her a glass of fresh grapefruit juice mixed with seltzer. She likes this, and I pour another despite her protests. Refreshed, out of the blinding sun, she's quite attractive, about my mother's age. She even looks a little like my mother, who comes from a long line of Russian Jews.

She waves away my offer of something to eat, folds her hands and looks around. A husband? she inquires. Do I have a husband?

No, no, I tell her. Just a *chaver*. A boyfriend.

She nods. "And you?" I ask. "Husband?"

"Ach." She waves away the question. From a mélange of Hebrew and facial expressions and hand gestures I deduce that the husband was no good, that he came with her to the country but soon disappeared, leaving her with a problem daughter, a son who got into trouble, and a couple of grandchildren. She lives in Bat Yam and is tired all the time.

What did she do back in Russia? I ask, pushing a plate of grapes in her direction.

"Ah." She makes a broad smile. "*Direktor*," she beams, and takes a grape.

"Director? You ran a business?"

Vigorous head shakes. *Bizness*. Same word in Hebrew as in English. No, no, not bizness. *Direktor*. She moves her hands like a symphonic conductor.

"Musical director?" I imitate the conducting, sing a little la la la.

No, no. She floats her fingers toward her face and holds her head high. Her hands are reddish and raw from detergents and scouring powders. Then I see it: comedy and tragedy, the famous thespian masks.

"Ah, theatre director!" I say.

"*Ken, ken!*" Yes, yes! "*Shekspeer. Shekhov. Bernid Sho.*"

"You directed Shakespeare? Bernard Shaw?"

She tips her head, smiles. The actor taking a bow.

"Wow. That's some change," I offer in English. "A theatre person and now you're cleaning houses for rich Israelis in north Tel Aviv."

She smiles—I know she didn't understand—and murmurs something melancholy in Russian.

"And here?" I ask. "You are also a director here?" because there's a huge Russian community, surely they put on plays and other entertainments.

She sighs. She is too tired, she says. She is telling me in her mix of tongues that it is not possible. That no one can work all day cleaning houses and then come home at night and inspire a fleet of desperate actors. That you can't feel fresh and energized after taking three buses to the city, then three more home, then coping with your difficult offspring and needy grandchildren. I don't understand a word but I am certain this is what she's saying. Life is full of problems. Full of mistakes, losses, regrets. But—and this doesn't have to be said—it's better here than it was back there.

A knock at the door. We glance over. We both know who it is. The Russian sighs again and begins to collect her bags. The slippers, the housedress. The carriage turned into a pumpkin. Art, its pulls and potent demands, has vanished. She's the cleaning lady again.

"Oh, Robin, thank you, I got your note!" The Israeli in her stylish pantsuit and impossibly high heels and perfectly dyed blond hair is breathless. "I feel terrible keeping Tanya waiting." She pokes in her head. "Tanya," she says, loud, in Hebrew, as if the Russian were hard of hearing, "I'm so sorry, I got tied up in traffic!" She turns to me. "Stuck behind a horse-drawn wagon, if you can believe it! One of those old men from Jaffa riding to construction sites to collect the discards. Crazy Tel Aviv!" The Russian pulls herself out of the chair, exhausted though she hasn't even begun, and follows her employer out the door.

~

Aryeh's grandparents never told anyone their story. Who wanted to hear it? Enough already about the death camps, the forced marches, the mutilated women. Aryeh's Israeli parents didn't want to know, his friends' parents with their identical family histories didn't want to know.

142

Nobody wanted to know. Enough, the country of wishfully amnesiac Jews declared, and insisted the newcomers change their names. Kaminetzky became Kedem, Perski became Peres, Rubitzov became Rabin. Heroic Hebrew names to get rid of the taint. Enough of the bent-over sheep-to-slaughter. The survivors were given their dim depressing flats, their shameful reparations, their new and improved last names—Ginsberg to Gidon, Mayerson to Meir—covered up their forearms and said nothing.

~

It was the surgeon in New Haven who gave me the idea to go to Israel. He'd just come back from his first trip. *Changed my life,* he said. He was making small talk to relax me. I was on my back on the vinyl table in a blue paper gown, legs spread. Pre-op exam. The ER doctors had done the best they could under the circumstances, but there was no getting around this. He apologized for the pain.

"Ever been there?" he said from down near the stirrups. They were covered in yellow golf club socks, the kind with little fringed balls on the ends, to warm up the metal. His big-chested, no-nonsense nurse stood beside him trying not to gasp at what she was looking at.

"Mm," I murmured, eyes squeezed shut, counting breaths. Six, seven, eight, nine.

"Oh? When?"

"Trip after high school. Another. In college." My mother's idea. We took two ten-day tours with women's groups where I was the youngest participant by thirty years.

"Went with a mission of doctors. Blew me away, to tell you the truth," the surgeon said. "They treat everybody. Survivors of everything. Bombs, explosions, fires. Not just Israelis. We had patients from Iraq who snuck in through Jordan, kids with cancer from Gaza. Stuff you don't read about in the papers."

A cool washcloth settled on my forehead. I opened my eyes. The nurse. She'd migrated to my end of the table. She was a tough cookie, a matron with a New York accent who would violently disapprove of the profligate behavior and stupendous failure of judgment that got me in this situation in the first place, a woman whose kids surely knew exactly where she stood and who tolerated no back talk. She took my hand and said the exam was almost over and that the man whose head was between my legs right now was the best gynecological surgeon in the state of Connecticut. And that she hoped that whoever did this to my insides would be strung up by his balls.

From southward by the stirrups a soft reprimand. "Mary, that's not quite protocol. There's a police officer outside, Ms. Bloom is in the custody of the state."

"Sorry," the nurse said, perfunctory, unconvincing. Then she squeezed my hand and brought a fresh cloth to my burning face.

~

Aryeh calls at three to find out how it went this morning with Irit.

"So are you Israeli yet? Because if you are, you have to get a fierce haircut and start wearing overly tight jeans."

144

I laugh a little. One of the things Aryeh says he likes about me is my determination not to hide my Americanness. In three years in stylish Levantine Tel Aviv, I've kept my American grad student Birkenstock wardrobe and still eat a little salad at mid-day and a big hot American dinner every night.

"Now it goes to the supervisor," I say. "Irit will let me know."

"*Tov.*" He's relieved. He thought I might not go through with it. "Tonight we celebrate," he says, decisive. "Because you turned in the papers. We'll go to the port, have a beer, some good food, listen to some music."

"Okay." I want to say *But first we stay home and make love.* But I don't. Because that's not exactly what we do. The surgeries were successful—the externals were repaired anyway—but I'm afraid it's going to hurt, even now, after five years. So some things Aryeh and I don't do. He says he doesn't mind. It could be a lot worse. Look at what's here, he tells me when we're walking down Dizengoff and someone is pushing a twenty-year-old with no legs in a wheelchair or we pass a girl in a café whose burned face is striated purple. That's how it is. A tough country. Casualties of a war-ravaged life. For Aryeh my condition is a shrug. No penetration? We'll work around it. No childbirth? We'll work around it. We have a running joke. *Your relatives who pretend not to know you? We'll work around it. Iran developing a nuclear bomb? We'll work around it.* It's not the Israeli way to stew or mull. Better to be practical. Move on. *Gamarnu.* Finished.

"This is a good thing, Robin," Aryeh says. There's

noise in the background, people waiting for him to get off the phone. He works for a software company, a start-up like in California. Dress code jeans, hours 24/7, no one there over thirty-five. "Even if they hold up your application for a while, you'll be glad you did this."

"I will?" I say, and then remember the reporters camped out on my parents' lawn, the constantly ringing phone, the smarmy ghostwriter who wanted to write my book, my exhausted mother telling them all to go away, the calls she tells me they get even now. The contrite letter from the dean that sat on Aryeh's dining room table for six months inviting me back. *Surely you understand, initial legal proceedings, university policy, full funding, stipend assured.* " Okay, yes, maybe I will."

~

I'd met him in the dean's office at a meeting for selected graduate students about fellowships the following fall. He was in Economics. His Yale recommendation was from a former Secretary of the Treasury, a friend of the family. Prep school, Princeton, parents who were hot shot lawyers in New York. A little chit-chat. Then out for coffee. We were both Jewish, had attended a few holiday events at the university, had a few mutual acquaintances. There was something about him from the start. An edge. I liked that. I'd always liked men who were a little tough, a little mean. They weren't scared off by a challenge. The nice ones were too soft. I was always afraid of hurting their feelings.

We didn't waste a lot of time. He lived in university housing and wanted us to go there, he said, because he had a suite to himself and I'd be impressed with his house-keeping. I thought it was a joke. It wasn't. He was very orderly. His desk was neat and the bed tightly made; the rug looked newly vacuumed. *I like women to be surprised when they come here. They think men are slobs, I like to prove them wrong.* He made it sound like he was a feminist; that he would never expect a future wife to do all the cooking and cleaning. A line that was bound to please. This was, after all, New Haven; we were all equals there.

He brought a chilled bottle of wine to the bedroom. It was obvious he picked up a lot of women. Who didn't? I'd had my share of hook-ups. Maybe more than my share. After some cursory talk we lay down and he tested the waters. He was trim but strong, athletic. A kiss, some stroking, unbuttoning, then a hard grab at my wrist, pinning it down. A little rough play. He turned me over and pressed my shoulder blades into the mattress, then pushed at my buttocks, shoved his hard cock in the space between. I could feel the urgency, the need. After a minute, I eased out and climbed on top of him, felt the stiffness of him, the throbbing demand. Not yet, I murmured coyly. *You have to wait your turn.* I thought he'd like that, thought he was into prolonging things, stretching out the tension.

But something was off. A darkness washed over his face. Maybe it was my taking control. Maybe he didn't like being told to wait. *Trouble delaying gratification,* a psychiatrist testified at the trial. His house master had referred him months before, some of the other students were disturbed. *He could become enraged. We discussed strategies. He discontinued treatment.* I was on him, moving up and

147

down, and then I felt it, first a stab, then a sharp burning, the pain, something trickling out of me. Then he was on top of me, doing something down there with an instrument, his other hand over my mouth to muffle the screaming, and I saw the crazed wolf in his eyes—*shut up, bitch. Just shut the fuck up.* He was pumping up and down, all the while moving the instrument, the sheets flooding, a gleam of sick joy on his face, and I knew that I was going to pass out. That I was going to bleed, bleed to death.

He stopped, finished, and slid halfway off me onto his side, exhausted, a wet bloody blade trailing across my stomach, and I understood in my delirium that this was my only chance. That a depleted man, a man whose procreative force has just left him, is a man without defenses, a window that might last only seconds. I made myself lift my arm and pulled the knife from his clammy hand, and with a final reserve of strength before I lost everything to darkness plunged it into his chest because that's what was closest and that's what I saw. His perfectly muscled smooth chest, the chest of a swimmer or a wrestler. *I should have known,* I thought in that flickering instant. *I should have expected something like this one day.* Then he fell over me and everything went black.

~

Aryeh has arranged a little surprise party for me. Lev and Galia who live upstairs are at the restaurant, along with Doron and Ronit from Aryeh's job. Doron and Ronit have recently crossed the line and gone from being work friends to lovers. Everyone in Israel thinks it's crazy to put self-imposed romantic limitations on office relationships like we do in the States. *If you can't sleep with your co-workers, who are you going to sleep with? We're a small country. Once you rule out relatives and your friend's partners, there's no one left.*

We order wine. Everyone raises their glasses. To Robin, they toast in enthusiastic English, who finally turned in the application! Who will soon become a citizen! They say they are post-Zionist, that the world's Jews should live wherever they please and shouldn't be made to feel guilty if they want to stay in Chicago or Sydney or Toronto. These are hip, left-wing, secular Tel Avivis. They've been to university and traveled all over Europe, South Asia, the Far East. The raison d'être of Zionism is over, they say; there are enough Jews in Israel now. The problem isn't getting more Jews to settle the land; it's working things out with the Palestinians so that everyone can peacefully co-exist. Still, it makes them happy when someone from America wants to join them. It cheers them up. A person who's not being persecuted, not fleeing, not broke, wants to come live there, in tiny isolated Israel. They are touched, moved that I want to cast my lot with them and their impossible leaders and constant wars and broiling khamsins and claustrophobic boundaries. Even with my bad Hebrew.

'It's a burdensome process, no?" Lev says. He and Aryeh and Doron went to high school together. Ronit and Galia were in the same class in law at the university. Everybody knows everybody. Which was why Aryeh was interested in me. I was new. A refreshing change. My past was irrelevant. *Who here doesn't have a past?* he told me once.

149

I never shot at someone I wasn't supposed to in the army? My grandfather never killed anyone to get off a German transport?

"Not so bad," I say. "A lot of forms."

Galia rolls her eyes. "Bureaucracy. You probably had to fill out everything in triplicate, and then they sent you to ten different offices and none were open on the day you showed up, right?"

I tip my head. Aryeh says it's been surprisingly streamlined.

"Good, then," Doron says, smiling. He's very handsome. Dark hair, dark eyes, neck veins like cello strings. "Nothing to worry about. One, two, they'll approve you." He takes a sip of wine. Ronit leans her head on his shoulder. Aryeh says the relationship won't last, that Doron changes lovers as often as others change shampoo brands. "I mean, if they let in all those Russian mafioso with criminal records as long as my arm, they're certainly going to let in you, a nice Jewish girl from Connecticut who just didn't want to finish her PhD."

Ronit smiles dreamily on Doron's shoulder. It's a mild barb, not meant to insult. I'm such a good girl, the Americans are all so squeaky clean. They arrive full of idealism, eager to improve society with their three hundred years of democracy and can-do spunk and sympathy for the underdog. They come with advanced degrees and a passion for recycling and the latest ideas for improving the status of women. They bring small fortunes and sometimes big ones and the habit of wearing seat belts and waiting patiently in lines. They're good citizens who obey the rules, and worldly Israelis like Doron and Ronit and Galia and Lev find them likeable and sometimes admirable but always naïve.

Under the table, Aryeh squeezes my knee. I can tell he's trying to formulate a response—*Actually, it's not so simple. Actually, she's bringing some serious baggage*—when the waitress arrives with the free appetizers the place is famous for: little dishes of olives, Turkish salad, marinated chickpeas, roasted beets, cubes of potato in mustard sauce, the mandatory tehina and hummus. She distributes six plates, sets down a basket of steaming pita, asks if we're ready to order.

"Order?" Lev says, then makes a little whistle. "We haven't even looked." Ronit lazily moves off Doron's shoulder. Everyone opens their menus. I leave mine untouched. It's in Hebrew and today of all days I don't feel like asking for the menus they keep around for tourists, the ones in butchered English.

The waitress hovers. "It's on me," Aryeh tells the others, waving away their objections. "Because," he says, scanning the menu, "it's not easy to decide you want to become a citizen of another place. That you're going to leave the richest country in the world, the most powerful country in the world, and come here." He keeps his eyes on the menu but his hand is on my knee again, as if to hold me steady. "It takes guts to go where you can't speak the language or get a job or find your way if you get lost and where there's no one who's known you longer than ten minutes and where the population is so fucking on edge they're killing each other on the roads when they're not asphyxiating themselves with cigarettes and meantime walking around with a superiority complex as big as the Mediterranean. I wouldn't have such guts, and neither would any of you, and you all know it."

The table has gone silent. The waitress is looking at me, her mouth slightly open. Aryeh orders. Plates of fries, mixed grill, beers all around. Then he glances at me, gives my leg another squeeze. The others make awkward smiles.

~

King Solomon, I read in the next day's paper, is running into problems. It seems the kashrut certification is not guaranteed, despite the brew's ingredients. *We wish the business well,* one Yitzchak Moskowitz, Berlin's chief rabbi, has told *Ha'aretz. But the question is: can a beer that's being manufactured in a plant where in 1939 Jewish slave labor made spirits for the S.S. ever be considered kosher? Can all sins be thusly erased? Certainly we'd like to move past our dark history. But using the Jewish culture to turn a profit in Germany seems, how shall I put it, obscene. There is a limit to how much our people are willing to forget.*

~

Tanya's employer is at the mailboxes in the lobby. The cleaning woman, she tells me, has been fired.

"Don't ask," the Israeli says, pulling out envelopes. "She's been stealing. That's right. For months. My friend across the street? Merav? I feel terrible. I sent Tanya there to clean and, boy, did she ever. Cleaned her right out. Jewelry. Cash. Cameras. Even a credit card. We turned it over to the police. The woman's claiming her husband went back to Russia and is blackmailing her, demanding hush money." She shakes her head. The blond hair swings like a thick curtain.

"Hush money?" I ask. "For what?"

"Who knows?" She works a catalog out of her box. "That's the Russians for you. Half of them were into shady dealings before they came. Or they're not really Jewish but saying they are. Some of them will be paying off people for the rest of their lives so they can stay. I hate using stereotypes, but you have to admit it: most of them are liars and thieves." She turns to me and smiles. "What we really need are more Americans. You obey the law, you don't drink, you people don't even smoke. So now we'll have a Filipino come clean. Not as good but at least they're honest."

Back upstairs the phone is ringing. Irit, from the Interior Ministry.

"Robin, I'm calling unofficially. Your application is going to be approved. You won't hear for three, four weeks, but I saw my supervisor this morning and she told me. So why make you wait, okay?"

"Okay." Irit goes on with details. I half-listen. A ceremony, family and friends invited, very moving, sometimes held on Masada where the Zealots held out against the Romans. Or maybe it will be at the Ministry, for convenience. Tax benefits for five years, foreign income exclusion for ten, a preferred rate on a mortgage, I should call if I don't receive anything in the post, good luck, *baruch haba*, welcome to Israel.

153

We hang up. I start to call Aryeh with the news, though I know he'll say he's not surprised, that they weren't going to turn me away, but still, something has caught in my chest, something huge and pressing waiting to exhale. But as I punch in his number I glance at my neighbor's balcony. A young dark-haired woman is awkwardly soaping the sliding glass doors. She can't reach even halfway up the glass and looks from this distance tiny. The Filipinos are excellent caretakers but not such good cleaners. They are small and delicate, and I am suddenly afraid she won't last, that she won't have any remittances to send home. That she'll have to go back.

The doors are covered in suds. It will take hours to wash them off, dozens of trips to the sink with the bucket, gallons of water to get rid of the residue so that her employer will be satisfied. And even then the tops of the doors will not be clean. She is struggling with the rag, standing on tiptoe on the rickety stepstool, trying in vain to expand her reach in hopes of earning something, anything, and I put down the phone, unable to stop watching, desperately wishing I could go over there and help so that she can pay what she has to. Send back what they demand. Do what she must so that the people here won't make her go home, and will let her stay.

BUS

· ◊ ·

I waited for the bus at the stop I was told to use by the people I was supposed to meet at the university. We were going to talk about a paper I'd written decades before, when I lived in California; the department had heard I was visiting Israel and wanted to meet. I wasn't interested in the paper anymore but didn't want to be rude, plus I had time on my hands. But when I got to the stop, I was afraid it wasn't the right line, afraid I'd misunderstood their accented English or written the number down incorrectly or had the wrong street. This happened often. I worried about getting lost or arriving late or ending up in a strange city or neighborhood and not being able to find my way back to wherever I'd come from.

So that morning I decided I would work up my courage and ask the driver, no matter how impatient or brusque he seemed, if this was the right line. I practiced words while I waited in the shelter, trying not to attract the attention of the other women standing there with their packages and bulging plastic bags of groceries. But when I climbed up the metal stairs and heard the *whoosh* of the doors closing and felt the bus lurching down the tree-lined boulevard, I forgot all about asking the driver. All around me were stuffed animals. Plush brown teddy bears and monkeys with curly tails and baby kangaroos in their mother's pouches, turtles and lions and soft yellow ducks. They were strapped to the poles and tied to the overhead hangers and swinging from the ceiling on fishing line. A pink and blue snake was threaded through the grab bars between the first three rows of seats, linking them together like a pillowy chain, and I stopped worrying about my appointment and the university and the bus line and thought about the last time my son got an infusion. It was in Los Angeles and I was sitting beside him with the magazine open on my lap. It was the same magazine I'd picked up every week for a month. It sat in its lucite wall holder in the waiting area each time I arrived, dense and beckoning, a blue cover that featured a cartoon figure waving a butterfly net at a flock of items one normally finds in a supermarket, and it promised lively commentary and witty stories and clever musings that each week I imagined would keep me engaged, though the truth was I never read beyond the page I'd opened to. I'd sit there and look at the glossy paper on my lap, at the strings of black letters arranged in neat columns on the shiny vellum, my twenty-three-year-old son next to me in his infusion chair joking with the nurses or listening to his headphones or watching something on his computer, not looking at me or the magazine. He had told me early on that he wanted no drama. That he wanted me there during treatment but that please he couldn't handle it if I got emotional, could I just keep him company, and I'd said, certainly, of course, I would just sit with him and talk if he wished, or bring him juice or ice or food if he could tolerate it, no histrionics, nothing like that. Which is what I did. I brought him pineapple juice from the little refrigerator by the nurses' station when he asked for it, and sat quietly when he chatted up the volunteers who came around with candy bars and crackers, and stayed in my seat when, restless, he got up and circled the room, pulling his pole behind him, and smiled when he came back and sank into his chair, and continued to stare at the open magazine, two, three, five hours, waiting for whatever would happen next.

Then one time, the last time, my son said to me, You don't have to do that anymore, Mom, and I looked up. It was November and the sun was a scrim of dotted light behind textured windows to keep the brightness from hurting the patients' eyes, and I saw his porcelain face, no longer the face of the eager young man who went to work each day shaved and washed in a dress shirt and pants to a

dream job at a production company, or the college fresh-
man pleased to be growing a stubbly reddish beard that
made him look like a friendly elf out of a children's book,
or the fifteen-year-old cultivating a faint first mustache
that nobody could breathe a word about lest we break into
laughter, and saw, instead, the face of a child, egglike in
its smoothness, the loveable five-year-old who permitted a
mother's nearly uncontrollable grateful kisses. He took my
hand in his, the skin of his wrist nearly transparent now,
and said, The magazine. You don't have to do that for my
sake. All around him, nestled into the corners and curves
of the infusion chair, were little blue and tan stuffed bears,
a tawny owl with yellow marble eyes, a black and white orca
whale the length of his arm, a purple snake he sometimes
wrapped around his neck when he was cold, gifts from his
friends, a loving menagerie cushioning his bony body and
holding him in place. Later, we would take them home and
put them in a closet with the other things we didn't think
we would ever give away. He squeezed my hand and said,
You can close the magazine now, Mom. It's okay. You don't
have to pretend anymore, for me.

PART TWO

West

HUNTERS AND GATHERERS

· ◊ ·

GREG IS ON A DIET where he eats only what people ate ten thousand years ago, and Gina is down with that. Anything that gets her twenty-six-year-old son out of the basement and eating at all is fine with her. She reaches for a package of something in the supermarket meat case she presumes was living during the Pleistocene or Paleolithic—her anthropology is a little rusty—and tosses it in the cart. If Stephen were to see this, he'd bust a gut. But Stephen is in Boston and he and Gina are as good as separated, or,

rather, Stephen insists, pending separation, since committing to anything was never his strong suit, so he has no idea
what Greg is eating or not. Which is all for the best, as far as
Gina is concerned. Managing the two of them was never,
as the earnest young people canvassing her neighborhood
peddling pesticide-free lawn care and water conservation
like to say, sustainable. At least this way she didn't have to
be the one to choose between them; Stephen did it for her.

She pushes the cart down the antiseptic aisles. Next
on her list is produce. Or, rather, as the *Guide to the Early Man Diet* instructs, *gathered foods*. As in hunting and
gathering. Berries, leaves, roots, the occasional fruit of a
tree. Because back in the Neanderthal or whenever, they
didn't engage in that eco-altering, unnatural practice
called agriculture. Frozen, canned, packaged are, naturally, to be avoided. Which leaves Gina to pick through the
bins of tired-looking lettuce mix, labeled, deceptively, she's
sure, organic, collecting it in a plastic bag which she will
discard, petroleum-based conveniences being frowned
upon, after paying and dumping the contents into the canvas tote she now uses. A few grabs at sweet potatoes, carrots, an acorn squash, all allowed, all culinarily primitive,
then a wistful glance at the prohibited cantaloupes and
grapes, and Gina's on her way to the register. A whippet
thin woman in tennis whites who probably doesn't have
a mentally ill son glances into Gina's cart as they line up
at the cashier, her own tidy little basket bearing a carton
of rice milk and soy sausage and tofu in the shape of a deflated chicken breast, her eyebrows raised at the veal chops
oozing blood, the special-order buffalo hearts cheerfully

announcing themselves on the picture-postcard wrapper—*fresh bison straight from the ranch!*—a whole fish staring up at her from its styrofoam tray, and Gina offers a wan smile. It could be worse. The third category of permissible consumables in Greg's holy trinity of the caveperson's dinner, following meat and vegetables, she will not purchase. If Greg is eating flies and ants and beetles on his own, that was his business.

~

The prehistoric shopping is fine with Gina because the fact that Greg is home and alive at all is no small miracle. Two months before, after being AWOL a year, the fourth such disappearance in his young life and the longest, Greg resurfaced. The day began as any other. Stephen had been gone a month and the house felt big and empty and lonely. Diana, Greg's legitimately resentful sister and yet another tangible reminder of Gina's spectacular failure as a parent, had just emailed from New Zealand to say she wasn't returning from junior year abroad, as if the University of Hawaii, not exactly a hop, skip and a jump from L.A., wasn't far enough. She had found a job and a boyfriend and was thinking of finishing her B.A. in Auckland. It was three in the afternoon and Gina was back from work, drinking coffee in the kitchen and thinking about a Scotch straight up and how to swallow her pride and ask her smarmy lawyer boss for more hours without telling him about Stephen's decamping when she thought she saw something moving in the backyard. She looked again. Someone, or something, rustling in the bushes at the edge of the property. A figure emerged, wobbly, emaciated, ski hat pulled low, and her first thought was: *Great. An addict with AIDS is going to die right here in my backyard. What a day. She* waited to see what the figure would do before calling 9-1-1 but lost sight of him in the hedge. Then the doorbell rang.

She froze. Surely he was looking for help. Or to use the bathroom. Or to tie her up and steal her mother's silver. But calling the police over a doorbell seemed a little excessive; he'd looked so frail she could have knocked him over with a feather. She sucked in her breath and went to the front door, stood behind the screen.

"Can I help you?"

The stench hit her like a wall. Then: the sunken eyes, chalky skin, trembling lips, tufts of matted hair sticking out from under the fraying hat. He was having trouble standing. "Are you okay? Do you need me to call an ambulance?"

Cracked lips moved. A sound emerged. Sandpaper on a rutted board.

"I'm sorry, I can't understand you. Can you talk louder?"

Again the lips moved. Again, the scratchy sound. She was trying to figure out what to do when he put a shaking hand on the screen and scraped out, "Mom, it's me," before collapsing on the step.

~

Now Gina's heart does its most persistent banging as she pulls up in front of the house. Greg's car isn't there.

Another mother might have been jubilant at the prospect of her profoundly depressed son going for a spin around town or deciding it was time to spiff up his wardrobe with a jaunt to the mall but Gina knows better. Greg hasn't gone anywhere. Because when Greg is this way—this way being the downward spiral of what Gina and all the medical people the family have amassed over the years know to be severe bipolar disorder with delusions and paranoia—he doesn't leave the house. He doesn't go outside. He doesn't even go near windows. The funk is long and grueling and must take place, Gina came to understand when Greg had his first big slide five years before, in a cave-like pit. Too much light or air send him into a tailspin of cycling even lower. So he stays in the dark.

Which can mean only one thing for his beat-up Civic. She sits in her idling hatchback, staring at the gaping space in the driveway. The car hasn't been stolen. It's been temporarily gifted. Which in Greg-speak means some of his so-called companions from the terrifying life he lives when he's not in the basement recovering after another crash-and-burn have taken it, along with Greg's blessing and car keys. It will be gone for three days or two weeks or a month and then it will mysteriously reappear some bleak morning missing the hood or the hubcaps or, once, a rear wheel so that it sat, hobbled, in the driveway like a three-legged animal, a defect Greg will somehow manage from his lair to get repaired, and then, one otherwise unremarkable day in the weeks following, when the darkness has lifted, Greg, roused by the sight of his ready horse, will also disappear. His traveling fellows, a revolving-door tribe of equally compromised young people, will be summoned back, by ESP or a scent on the wind or perhaps an actual phone because maybe Greg has one, Gina doesn't know, and then he will take off with them on the beginning of the climb that is the other half of the cycle. A disappearing act that will start out tamely enough, Greg still a reasonable facsimile of any parents' wide-eyed twenty-something calling every week to tell her about the job at the vegan café in Seattle or the community college in Portland or the friendly people at the collective in Sacramento, and she—and, once upon a time, Stephen—will permit herself a shameful secret desire: *Maybe he'll be okay. Maybe this thing is passing.*

But then the spell will break and the calls will stop coming. The collective won't know where he is. The restaurant will phone, the college will email. Days will pass. And Gina will know: the fever has taken hold. He'll be in its fist, and he'll be gone. As in *gone.* Later she'll piece it together. She'll learn that he took off to jump trains across Canada or hitch to Mexico, that he lived in a squat or was bilked out of all his money or got scabies; that there were grand schemes, big plans. She'll hear about it from one or two of the earnest unwashed who bring him back catatonic or hallucinating, girls usually, who in another life would have been nurses or social workers, sweet kids under the matted dreads and reeking clothes who tell her over a bowl of hot soup or a decent sandwich how they were in Texas and he signed up for a pre-med program, a genius, everyone could tell, talking his way in and taking four classes until he flamed out, or they were in Detroit and he was going to start an alternative newspaper, scored an awesome second-hand printing press, but it never got started, something happened, he was hardly talking, huddled up, they were scared. So they, the girls, volunteered to get him home, bumming rides and sneaking onto Greyhound and dumpstering food. They're going back to their friends now, thank you for the train fare bus fare meal shower spending money, really sorry he looks so bad, what's wrong with him, hope he can get help. Gina will listen and nod and pack them nut butter sandwiches and bags of fruit and protein bars and thank them for bringing her boy back.

She pulls herself out of the hatchback, takes out the groceries and walks up the driveway, trying to ignore the looming space in her peripheral vision, and lets herself in the side door. The house is quiet. It's four in the afternoon and hot. She stops in the hallway by the basement door, listens. She's adept at identifying the faintest sounds: a shoeless footfall on linoleum, the swish of a body turning on a bed, the tentative strum of a guitar missing all but two strings. It's habit, her ears perked. She needs to hear just one thing. Just one. Her heart quickens. Then: muted joy. Tinny music. He must have some kind of electronic down there. She tiptoes into the kitchen as if the slightest noise will upset a delicate ecology, attract an unwanted predator. That's how it is now. She tiptoes around her three-bedroom ranch in Valley Village, California as if she's in the wilderness. As if she and her damaged offspring must be ever vigilant, ever on the alert for wild beasts who know how to sniff out the weakest of the herd. Who know exactly when to pounce. And are just waiting for the right time.

~

On the day Greg reappeared, Gina rode with him in the ambulance to the emergency room and made a pact with the God she didn't believe in that, if in his benefi- cence he would keep Greg alive, she would scour her soul and change whatever needed changing. So when the hos- pital discharged Greg five days later with instructions to Gina to administer a liquid diet consisting of a drool-like milkshake six times a day that of course wasn't a milkshake but a mix of chemicals and genetically altered something easy on the digestion, she didn't balk. She did exactly as the doctors told her because, they warned, her son was on the edge, and they didn't mean psychiatrically for a change. To demonstrate, one of the attendings lifted the sheet while Greg was sleeping and showed her his chest and upper arms. Fur. Pale brown patches. Had she ever seen anything like it? Lanugo. When a person was starved, the body grew fur to keep itself warm. They saw this on anorexics, eigh- teen- and twenty-year-old girls with thick feathery down on their cheekbones and backs. Gina stared at her sleeping boy, little tufts on his upper arms like glued-on mustaches from a joke shop. *Anywhere else?* she asked for some insane reason, as if she were a researcher taking notes. The doctor tipped his head, sparing her.

The liquid diet was not optional, they told her. Two weeks. Imperative. His system could not break down any- thing more complex. Gradually she would add solid foods in a precise order. If she departed from this regimen, she was risking her son's life. Did she understand? No she- nanigans, said the chief gastroenterologist, a no-nonsense

168

woman with a name tag that said Dr. Gutz. Gina thought better than to probe the woman's choice of specialty. *I've seen people die from this. I've seen mothers forcing ice cream or a homemade cookie or grandma's meatloaf or deciding what their kid needs is organic seaweed and wheat germ. They think it's love but it's manslaughter. The bowel obstructs, the large intestine paralyzes, the kidneys shut down—do you need me to paint the whole picture? I don't care if you're the best cook since Julia Child or haven't bought a processed food since junior high. You'll kill your son.*

Terrified, Gina nodded at the woman. I understand. *No funny stuff. He'll never see a cupcake or lentil burger on my watch.*

Or on anyone else's.

Or on anyone else's.

~

Food and Greg have always been a fraught coupling and Gina didn't need a degree in psychology to know why. Simply put, Stephen was a food tyrant. No candy or ice pops for Greg and Diana when they were little, no Doritos and Dr. Pepper when they were pre-teens, and then, when Greg hit ravenous adolescence—the obvious tie to his current consumption—no red meat. A lapse in moral rectitude to Stephen on a par with cannibalism. Stephen's stance was explainable if extreme, coming from an extended family of eaters who, in his words, lived and died by New York pastrami and never met a stuffed veal it didn't like. The bar mitzvahs of his Long Island youth, he told Gina, were orgiastic food fests where everyone ate as if they'd personally survived the Holocaust. His mother Evelyn's response was to subsist exclusively on Weight Watchers frozen dinners until, in a cruel twist of fate, she died of a fluke staph infection contracted while having a little eyelid lift to celebrate her excellent cholesterol numbers. Stephen's response was to become despotic and fussy. Though his attempt to avoid Jewish gastronomy by marrying Gina backfired since the cuisine she'd loved and coveted most was her husband's. Matzoh ball soup, chopped liver, brisket, chocolate babka: she'd take it over her family's pasta marinara and cannoli any day. In fact it was Jewish food that had brought them together. She was a waitress at Kantor's on Wilshire and Stephen was there indulging his newly widowed father. Max Simon had ordered the stuffed cabbage special, three giant pieces with extra rice and sauce on the side, just in case, winking at Gina like some avuncular movie mogul and insisting she sit down a minute to meet his terminally reluctant son, temporarily AWOL in the men's room.

Reluctant about what? Gina asked, smiling.

Everything, Max said. *He needs a nice buxom girl like you to loosen him up.*

Looking back, Gina thinks she should have married Max instead. At least he wouldn't have regarded a slice of New York cheesecake as a mortal sin.

~

She's got the acorn squash in the oven and the turnips draining. She treads lightly to the master bedroom, closes the door, tiptoes into the little pink and green mas-

ter bath, tile untouched since it was installed in a flush of
postwar pastel exuberance fifty years before, and lights
up a Winston menthol. She watches out the tiny window. Phil Sokoll, their next door neighbor, is taking out
his trash, carefully placing the plastic bags into the giant
bin, then inspecting and rearranging as if he's loading the
trunk of his car for a family vacation, followed by the recycling—newspapers tied with string, bottles and cans in
their special bags—which he puts into the other bin and
studies before taking out the newspapers and moving the
contents around, and she wants to pull up the screen and
stick her head out and yell to Phil that it doesn't matter;
that nobody in their right mind organizes their garbage
receptacles; that it's a futile attempt to stave off the chaos
of the universe and that life's cruelties are going to get him
no matter what. But he would look at her with that horrified smile he and Sharon plaster on whenever they see her
and ask about Greg, which nowadays they do all the time,
and assume she's just as nuts as her son. After Stephen's
car was gone for a couple of weeks, Sharon and Phil felt
obliged—their words—to ask, in case it was time to mo-
bilize the Neighborhood Watch, so she had to assure them
that no such measures were necessary and that Stephen's
car had left of its own free will, along with Stephen. He'd
gone to Boston to set up his company's east coast office
and might not be coming back. Much furrowed-brow
Sokoll facial activity followed, the Job-like misfortunes of
their besieged neighbors piling up at an extraordinary rate,
and though they were too polite to press, Gina knew they
were dying for details. She, Greg, Stephen and, God help

171

her, soon maybe Diana, were a not-to-be-missed unfolding saga. The local entertainment, their own Reality TV channel. She rose dutifully to the task.

Yeah, well, Stephen couldn't take it anymore. Nothing works for Greg. ECT, meds, more ECT, inpatient, outpatient, we've tried it all. Which has kind of left us to our own devices, you know?

Sharon nodded with concern. The three of them were at the curb retrieving their bins after a ruthless tossing about by the heartless sanitation men. Phil had made a point of asking whether Gina and Sharon thought tossing the emptied bins as far as possible from their correct domiciles was one of the job qualifications. Now he positioned the wheels of his recycling container for the trip back to the garage until Sharon elbowed him to stop.

So Stephen said we either pull out all the stops and find Greg and Greg gets institutionalized, or Stephen leaves. Simple as that. It's old terrain for us, we've been fighting about it for years. I told him to go. I couldn't really picture delivering up our twenty-six-year-old son to be lobotomized, or whatever was left for them to do. Sharon welled up. Phil looked at his shoes. Their daughter Marny had just won second place in the Valley Village Middle School Essay Contest for her piece about their cat, Hilary, named for Hilary Clinton who Marny hoped would run again and become the first woman president because girls needed good role models. Gina couldn't help it if Sharon was mortified now for having gushily reported Marny's award only moments before asking about Stephen's missing Prius.

What a terrible choice to have to make, Sharon mur-

172

mured. *Between husband and son.* Phil glanced longingly at his garage.

I don't know, Gina said, taking hold of the handle of her trash bin, her signal that the conversation would soon be ending and that Phil and Sharon would be put out of their misery. *In some ways it's easier. I don't think I could ever throw my kid in front of a train—could you? That's kind of what it felt like. Sacrifice. Or martyrdom, St. Sebastian taking the arrows. Maybe that's just my Catholic upbringing talking. But if he dies now doing whatever it is he does when he's out there, falling off a freight car or freezing in Alaska like that poor kid who starved in the rusted out bus, at least it'll have been with his own mind. Whatever else goes on in there, at least it's still his.*

~

When Gina emailed Diana about Greg's new diet, Diana immediately shot back: *What does he think? That by channeling his Inner Caveman he'll build up his animal self and shrink the brainy part? Dial himself back to before the DSM-III, back in evolution to before there was manic depression? That's crazy, Mom.*

To which Gina quickly replied, *I know, honey, sure sure, but at least he's eating and it'll help build up muscle and strength so there's no harm.* But she wasn't so sure it was crazy. There was, for instance, her own life: she was nearly broke, was on her fifth attempt at an email to her boss to ask for more hours without sounding desperate, and Stephen had just phoned to say his company was axing the east coast office because they'd made a mistake with the numbers and he was about to be unemployed but still wasn't sure if he should come home. If Greg was trying to outwit his own chemistry, tricking it into thinking it was just him against the cougars and lions, that life had been pared down to the essentials—eating, sleeping, looking out for snakes and poison berries—maybe he knew something the rest of them didn't.

~

Noise from the basement. Gina is at the kitchen sink. She's brushed her teeth and scrubbed her hands because Greg's sense of smell is acute, and she suspects that in his new bid for fundamental living he wouldn't like her smoking. He's like Stephen that way. Principled. A week ago, after the mandatory period on liquids and another month-plus of fastidiously added solids, he mumbled to Dr. Gutz at a torturous follow-up to which he wore sunglasses, a ski hat, and an ankle-length black trench coat despite the ninety-degree heat to ask if he could try the caveperson regimen.

I don't see why not. Mother, you prepared to help?

Whatever you say, Doctor.

You're not going to get all squeamish on us, are you? You one of those tofu-tempeh ladies who can't handle the sight of a fresh-cut cow tongue or jellied fish brains?

No, ma'am. Not squeamish at all.

She steels herself. Greg is mounting the stairs. A new miracle: for the last five days, he's come up at dusk to eat with her. It used to be she'd leave the food for him to retrieve in the dark when he was ready. She would like to write this down, start her own Scripture: The Book of Maternal Gratitudes. *My son is eating in the kitchen now.*

The door opens. "Hi, honey," Gina says, her back to the basement door and her son, pretending to sound normal, pretending she's spent the previous twenty minutes rinsing beet leaves and scraping carrots instead of blowing smoke rings at the neighbors. The thought of Greg running off again to go hitchhiking across South America or live alone in the Canadian woods, all bravado with Sharon and Phil aside, fills her with dread. But she has a plan.

Greg sits heavily in a kitchen chair behind her. She can tell he's watching. It's a sixth sense, eyes in the back of her head.

"I'm broiling steaks and mashing turnips," she says to the sink. Even if he doesn't speak, she will. Like the way you talk to a person in a coma. To keep the language going. He has not bathed or laundered his clothing since his discharge from the hospital eight weeks before; she can tell from her post at the sink though she could tell from half a mile away. Even the turnips don't mask it. But if she were to suggest a shower or throwing his clothes in the washer, he'd as likely flee as do as she asks. It's an old script. She casually tosses out the idea every week or so. *If you leave your things by the washer, I'll throw them in later.* If he looked out his window, he'd be able to see the clothesline in the yard where the towels and sheets sway in the hot breeze.

"Any interest in eating on the deck?" she asks, because maybe the day will come when he says, Hey, great idea! California! And because she believes he depends on her to maintain the illusion—or maybe it's hope but she isn't there yet—that normalcy could one day be his, even if he can't. *Toss in your clothes? Want to eat outside? This is your home. You are, and always will be, my son. I will never give up on you.*

Silence. She mashes. The steaks in the broiler sizzle and snap. The moment has arrived. The vegetables are ready, the meat is done. She turns off the stove.

And pivots. There he is, elbows on the formica, arms up, hands together like a little bridge. He's looking right at her. His eyes are watery and red-rimmed, his skin the color of paste. His hair has clumps of gray. He's gained some weight but still looks like a survivor of Dachau. He squints often now, his vision, she believes, impaired.

She brings him a plate: steak, carrots, turnips, a potato, wild blueberries. For herself the same, half portions. She sits beside him and tries not to see the tremor in his hand as he works the fork, the knife. She doesn't know where the shaking is from, no doctor has been able to tell her. Maybe street drugs, self-medicating. The malnutrition. Nobody knows. He gets a bite into his mouth, grunts in satisfaction, works at stabbing another.

She wills herself to ignore the stench—of his clothes, his hair, his breath, her own metallic terror—and eats. Beside her, another fork-stab, chomping noises. Good, she thinks. *Eat. Breathe. Live.*

~

Hours later, she lies in bed in the dark. She drifts, daydreams. In one version, she and Stephen are dancing. It's their wedding, they are being lifted on chairs and twirled around, Jewish style, and someone tosses them a linen napkin and they each grab an end. An old tradition. The cloth links them. But the napkin morphs and is a baby now, and soon she sees: a little boy and each of them is tugging like the women in the Solomon story, tugging and pulling and threatening to tear the baby in two.

She sits up, soaked in sweat. Then she sees: headlights in the driveway. The Civic is being returned. Her heart pounds. She creeps to the den window, which has the best view. They pile out of the car, barefoot, silent, light-footed as phantoms. They are creatures from the woods, feral, half animal, half human. One looks around, confused, as if caught in a time warp, then pauses, licks a finger and holds it to the wind, testing, and then, astonishingly, miraculously, walks to the front door.

He sees her note. He takes it down and squints under the dim porch light. Then—she would utter a rosary if she could remember it, and maybe one day soon she will—he slips the car keys into the mailbox and walks to the other end of the porch. There he finds the bicycle panniers stuffed with food and drink and cash and bus vouchers, all neatly labeled in large type. BUS TICKETS GOOD FOR ONE-WAY FARE FROM LOS ANGELES TO ANYWHERE ON THE EAST COAST! MUST USE IN NEXT 24 HOURS BEFORE THEY EXPIRE! FREE TRIPS FOR ALL! The others tiptoe up like children, see the note, grin happily. Hooray, they can go on a ride! Hooray, there's food! The tickets in fact have no expiration but she's blacked that out and anyway she's betting they wouldn't have looked because they have

177

nowhere else they need to be. Meantime they've been distracted from their mission. Where is Greg? Not among them, still asleep; if they were expecting him to come out and join them, they've forgotten. They have opened the first bag as instructed—START WITH YELLOW BAG. TREATS!—and discovered the Cliff Bars and jelly beans and jars of mango and pear juice, greedily tear off the wrappers, twist off the lids. They eat and drink and softly giggle; they know it's late, the street silent but for their whispers. They huddle around the map she's thoughtfully drawn for them. The Greyhound station is less than a mile away, how convenient! They can walk on their blackened feet and wait there until a bus comes to take them on their next adventure! They finish their snacks, carefully put the wrappers into Phil and Sharon's trash bins, closest to the Civic, pick up the panniers and distribute them among themselves, turn toward the streetlight and dance their way down the road like a parade of Pans.

She watches them go. In half an hour, when she knows they won't be coming back, she will slip outside and take the keys from the mailbox, slide into her son's car and drive it to the empty field behind the old abandoned saddlery she passes on her way to work. Nobody ever goes there, the owners are absentee, but she'll remove the plates anyway, cover the car with a tarp. She knows it's just a teaspoon in the ocean, a way to buy some time. Her meager effort to keep him safe for just a moment longer.

But this is the moment she has.

WILD ANIMALS

· ◊ ·

A BABY SQUIRMING IN HER LAP. What was she supposed
to do with it? With him. Not her baby. Of course not hers.
When are you going to settle down, Ruthie? When are you
going to find a husband? A man, any man? She was thirty
years old and they couldn't stand it, a fleet of big-eyed relatives looking at her like she was supposed to answer them
on the spot. Oh I got one for us, he's outside. I'll bring him
in. You can all inspect.

Of course not.

The baby was damp, she felt it on her jeans. Her sister's arms outstretched. Give him here. Paula in her skin-tight red jumpsuit and giant hoop earrings cooing kisses on his wet face. *Mwah mwah mwah.* Who's my little boy? Who's my little mush-mush boy?

Ruthie pivoted away, swiveled her knees in the dining room chair, blotted her pants with a napkin. Mush-mush. His name was Gus. Paula thought it was cute. Sometimes she called him Gussie. *Mwah mwah mwah.* Clatter of dishes. Ruthie's mother and aunts in the kitchen. Who made this brisket? her mother accused. It's too much, you didn't need to bring this much, what are we, the Tsar's army? Aunt Eleanor replying, a fringe of fury on the edge of her words, we're fifteen people, Bea, it's not too much for fifteen. Eleanor never good enough, never measuring up, married to Mort twenty-five years (no children, suspicious) and still Ruthie's mother refused to like her, still Ruthie's grandmother glared at her from a kitchen step stool where she presided like the Queen Mother, arms crossed, surveying the proceedings, the women at women's work--daughters, daughter-in-law, sometimes a granddaughter-- jaw tight, chin up. God help you if you dropped a ladle, a spoon, a hot potato. Dagger eyes from Rose, no sweet flower (forget the name), entitled to pass judgment on everyone because of what she endured *back there*, with the real Tsar's army. Untold atrocities you didn't dare imagine. A miracle she was able to give birth not once but four times. Bea, Thea, Claire, and the doted upon baby Mort. What did they have against Eleanor? Ruthie asked her mother repeatedly. Eleanor's perfectly nice.

Gold-digger, her mother would mutter and Ruthie laughed. Gold-digging? From us?

You don't know, her mother would seethe. Morton the precious jewel, the gem of the family. Eleanor had gotten her claws into him and turned him around and taken him away to faraway Connecticut, country of the clubby antisemites who wouldn't let you live in their neighborhoods. If not for Eleanor, he'd be right there in New York being a pharmacist or a dentist, he'd studied science at City College. Instead he was a stockbroker who commuted an hour each way by train and ate shrimp cocktail and had a business card that said Mark Epps because Morton Epstein couldn't live in Greenwich, Connecticut and it was all Eleanor's fault. No point in Ruthie saying what anyone with eyes in their heads would say. Which was that Uncle Whatever-he-was-calling-himself, with his navy and white nautical captain's cap and designer polos and pressed white pants, wanted to pass more than anyone they knew, including the starveling size-six Eleanor who at least kept her name and still tried to please, with her own mother's brisket recipe and sweet and sour cabbage she'd throw into a dumpster on the Hutchinson River Parkway on her and Mort's way home to the part of Greenwich where the antisemites let them live. It was Mort who'd gone looking for the Connecticut house, Eleanor had told Ruthie during one visit when she couldn't bear another icy stare from Rose, Mort who'd dressed himself up to look like Cary Grant on the cruise in *An Affair to Remember* to go talk to the thin-lipped lady real estate broker (Epps? What kind of a name is that?), facts Ruthie later told her mother, who didn't believe her. You're so naive, Ruthie. You believe whatever anyone tells you. About the failure to produce children, Ruthie didn't even bother to bring up. It was Mort's problem, not Eleanor's, a doctor had tested them, but tell that to Ruthie's mother? To Rose? Ha. Take your life in your hands.

Now out from the kitchen came the other aunts, timid Claire and peacemaking Thea, wearing Ruthie's mother's aprons and surveying the table that stretched to the living room where the men sat on couches sipping Scotch and rye and ignoring the babies crawling over their feet. Paula had disappeared, getting high in the laundry room in the basement. Did Ruthie want to join her? No thanks. Was she sure? Yes she was sure. Paula had told her that smoking was the only way she could get through the day. Also the only way she could have sex. Barry was clumsy, his hands sweaty paws; the weed could get her to orgasm. Did Ruthie have any idea what it was like to be so turned off by your husband's hands? Though the awful part was that she loved Barry. She just wished he was an Italian motorcyclist in a leather bomber jacket and sunglasses instead of a Jewish math teacher who couldn't wait to get home and cook everyone a big dinner. Joining Paula in the basement was Marjorie, Thea's flaky daughter, and Steve, Claire's useless son who was supposedly unemployed but made a living dealing. Marjorie's three-year-old, Sparrow (really? Ruthie had asked. Yes really, Marjorie retorted; it was 1980, did Ruthie want her to name the kid Harold? Charles?) was napping on Ruthie's parents' bed. Nobody knew where Marjorie's husband Dix was. Probably in the backyard with Barry talking about his chakras. Barry was the only person who could stand to listen to him. Which left baby Gus and Marjorie's one-year-old Eagle--the family was going full-out avian--to crawl on the living room rug by the feet of Ruthie's father and uncles and the unstoppable Mort, who never ceased talking, regaling his brothers-in-law with tales of Wall Street and motorboating on the Sound and the fascinating antics of his fascinating Episcopalian neighbors. In response to which the brothers-in-law were downing cocktails at a furious rate.

A crash in the kitchen. Shattered china, clang of metal, a scream. Ruthie dashed in. A raccoon the size of a kindergartner stood upright at the open sliding glass door. Brisket was strewn across the linoleum, shards of the white serving platter like scattered carnations.

Who left the back door open like that! shouted Ruthie's mother. Brisket gravy covered her shoes and streaked her skirt where the apron didn't reach. Look at it! If it's out in the daytime, it's rabid!

Quiet, Ma! You'll freak the thing out! It'll run in here and bite someone!

What, suddenly you're Madame Naturalist? Look! It's drooling!

Stop it, Ma! Everyone! Stay put!

They froze. Her mother inches from the sliders, Thea holding a kugel with two oven mitts, Claire gripping a bottle of vinegar, Eleanor with a mixing spoon over a bowl of coleslaw.

And, last, ramrod straight on the high stool, the statue that was Rose, in a pristine lilac dress, brooch at her neck, her face granite, marble, stone.

Vilde chaya, Rose murmured with disgust at the open door.

Wild animal.

A term normally reserved for her grandson Steve or the grandsons of her inferior neighbors or the three-year-old Sparrow when he was awake. Unless you were perfectly behaved, your appearance impeccable, your appetites invisible, you were, in Rose's linguistic taxonomy, a beast.

Well, actually, Nana, Ruthie said--she couldn't help it--that seems to be a pretty accurate description, considering where it lives, don't you think? Because how was it possible that her grandmother, exacting in all things, would misuse the Yiddish she meted out so rarely and lethally, the language a weapon, her reminder to them that there were worlds--once, despite history, vastly superior worlds--they couldn't possibly understand?

Slowly, Rose rotated her regal head, encased in tight white curls like a bust of an emperor of Imperial Rome or a bathing cap from the 1950s of the sort Esther Williams wore in her swimming pool movies, movies Rose liked to watch (the precision! the perfection!), and looked Ruthie up and down, head to toe, toe to head, from the clunky black hiking boots to the frayed denim bell bottoms to the oversized man's brown sweater to the bad haircut, Ruthie's unpromising, unpartnered, unlikely-to-ever-be-married presentation to the world when she wasn't at her crummy job typing invoices in an office tower on Sixth Avenue (for which she stepped up her fashion game to a skirt and shoes but that was it), then turned away, her message loud and clear without a single word: you're one to talk about animals. No wonder you have no husband.

Then the sharpest arrow in her quiver (what did Rose see?): You're probably one of those girls who likes girls.

Thank goodness it's gone! gushed Thea after the creature dropped onto all fours and slinked away. Claire hurried to the sliders to close them, pulling the blinds across. Then a flurry of women's bent backs as the cleanup began, brisket chunks discarded, a mop produced, a bucket of suds. Ruthie's mother, steely-eyed, so like Rose, so hopelessly like Rose, left the kitchen to change. Thea and Claire fluttered busily, gave each other urgent directives. Mop over here, Claire dear. Another spot here, Thea dear. Eleanor, presumed guilty (it was always Eleanor, had to be Eleanor), followed with towels and awaited the verdict. Rose, erect as a general, even if she was eighty, observed from her magisterial perch. No one knew Rose's true age. A guess. Ruthie had done the math, her grandmother a teenager, old enough (horrifyingly pretty enough) to be dragged off and violated (for hours? weeks? the stories were murky) during a 1918 pogrom.

Thea took the damp towels from Eleanor. Claire scooped up the mop and bucket apologetically, an invisible sandwich board affixed to her--walk on me, go ahead. Ruthie's mother returned in slippers and a clean skirt.

Had Aunt Eleanor opened the slider? Ruthie ventured. Well, good for her. It's an inferno in here. Every burner on high, the soup scalding, carrots boiled to death. If she hadn't opened it, I would have.

Yes, so warm! said Thea.

And look! Claire exclaimed over an enormous foil pan, clapping her hands like a preschooler. Lots of brisket still left! Aren't we lucky Eleanor made so much!

Ruthie's mother said nothing: Eleanor released without charges. The women ferried platters to the table. In the living room, Mort was still pontificating. Sparrow waddled out of the bedroom, a twisted cloth diaper hanging off him like a caricature of Gandhi. For God's sake, commanded Ruthie's mother, someone go get Dix to change the poor thing. Eagle crawled over and nuzzled his aromatic brother and Ruthie went outside and found Dix and Barry. They came in and Dix scooped up his odorous children and carried them off to pollute a back bedroom. Barry headed to a bathroom. From the dope-perfumed basement stairs emerged a wobbly Paula, the top three buttons of her jumpsuit undone, followed by Marjorie and Steve, all of them red-eyed and grinning. Paula flashed an overzealous smile at Ruthie, its message plain: you missed all the fun. You always do.

Hungry! Steve announced, his big white teeth shining like Red Riding Hood's wolf despite his three-pack-a-day habit. Smells great! He plucked a piece of roasted potato from a platter and popped it into his mouth. Ruthie watched him conspicuously lick his lips. Her druggie cousin, handsome, vain, without shame. When they were fourteen, he tried to grope her under the table at a family seder. She grabbed his hand off her thigh and squeezed it hard enough to leave a bruise. Paula flashed her another grin. A post-orgasmic grin. Had Paula and Steve gotten each other off in the basement? It's allowed between cousins, fourteen-year-old Steve had whispered to Ruthie at the seder. Rose and her husband were cousins, you know. All the Jews in Russia fucked their cousins because they couldn't fuck the Cossacks, so the pool was limited.

You're sick, Ruthie told him and he laughed, matzoh mush in his teeth, but then Ruthie began to wonder: where was Rose's husband anyway? He'd taken off somewhere exotic when her mother was a teenager. Denver? San Francisco? Montreal? No one knew. There'd never been a divorce. *He wanted to come back but she refused. Heart of stone,* the aunts whispered. He sent money. For Thea to go to secretarial school and for Claire to get a teaching certificate and for Mort, the princely male, to go to college; CCNY was free but there were books, fees (for the gym, the pool, he liked to swim), heaven forbid he should work and interfere with his studies. No money for Ruthie's mother, the oldest, working since she was sixteen. Rose decided Bea didn't need her father's money; she could go to night school if she wanted. Rose of course was not expected to work.

Dix returned with the boys fragrant with baby powder and weed. The men shuffled from the couches to the table. Marjorie, with a spacey smile, planted herself next to Dix, a child on each lap. Paula weaved over and sank into the chair next to Ruthie's, fumbled to close the buttons on her jumpsuit, smelling of dope and sweat and Steve's tobacco breath. On the table were platters of meat, potatoes, carrots, kugels, coleslaw, the heavy white porcelain soup tureen Ruthie's mother had inherited from her mother-in-law, part of a much-prized set brought out for special occasions (matching gravy boat, the now smashed brisket platter), the lid still on the tureen while they waited for Barry to reappear. Today's occasion was a non-occasion, no one's anniversary or graduation, certainly no Jewish holiday. The family seders had fallen away, it wasn't Hanukkah, Marjorie wanted her children to be Citizens of the World and had zero interest in religion (also Dix wasn't Jewish and why should he be made to feel bad?). Only Barry had been murmuring about reviving the tradition. For Gus's sake. So far, Paula wasn't biting.

Rose had been deposited at the end of the table next to the obsequious Claire. What did Mother need? Claire asked. Rose pointed: water. Claire poured. Anything else? A roll? A pickle spear? Rose shook her head. Absolutely not. You didn't take until everyone was seated. You had to be civilized, eat like a human being, not indulge base instincts. Was Mother comfortable? Claire asked. Rose shrugged. Claire insisted Rose take her seat, better padded than the one Rose was sitting on.

Ruthie watched the ceremony of the changing of the chairs. Her mother went to the kitchen for the ladle. It was Ruthie's father who'd told her about the pogrom; her mother, let alone her grandmother, would never breathe a word. The rampage was the handiwork of the Ukrainian army, which viewed the Jews--Communist kikes, scheming Bolsheviks plotting the ruin of Mother Russia--as less than human. Within two days, every house in Rose's village outside Kiev was torched, the synagogue turned into a urinal, the men they didn't kill held for ransom after their feet were amputated or their tongues cut out, all the women, from eight-year-old girls to seventy-five-year-old widows, raped, most in the open, in front of husbands, parents, children. A hundred thousand dead and four hundred villages burned to the ground in a week.

Claire moved the softer chair, swept it clean with her napkin. Rose, reseated, shook off Claire's fussing. After the rampage, Ruthie's father told her, the pretty girls were carried off by the soldiers.

Ruthie's mother returned with the ladle. Rose glanced up, met Ruthie's eyes.

What? Rose's expression said. Don't you look at me like that. Don't you dare look at me like that.

Barry appeared at the table.

About time! Steve boomed, rubbing his big hands together. Now we can eat! Pass the kugel, would you, doll. To Paula. Doll. Hey, Barry, sit down, take a load off.

Where's Gus? Barry said.

Gus? Dix slurred. Sparrow gnawed a wet pickle.

Gus? Mort said, his captain's cap tipped rakishly to the side like the alcoholic Yankee he aspired to be.

Gus? said Paula, blinking, holding together the top of her jumpsuit with her fist.

Gus, Paula! Barry shouted. Our son! Our baby!

The words hung there, the family paralyzed as if poisoned --by dope or drink or rabies or the petty cruelties they showered on one another, or other cruelties, not petty, others had showered on them--and then Ruthie was out of her chair, racing after Barry, running to the top of the basement stairs, into the hall, the bathroom, the pantry. Gus! Gussie! Gus!

The vertical blinds in the kitchen were swaying and Ruthie ran over and there he was, the slider pried open just enough for him to crawl through, one fat knee already on the threshold, his little palm banging on the glass to get the attention of his new friend on the other side. The raccoon, standing, a giant in the bright hot light, watching, waiting, white foam oozing from the corners of its open mouth, dark eyes shining, a claw, five fingers like the little hand on the other side, scratching at the outer glass, and Ruthie dove for the baby and hit a fortress of fabric and skin and muscle and bone. Eleanor. She was grasping Gus around the middle and pulling him away from the open portal, pulling him close. Ruthie reached over them and yanked the slider shut, the family massing behind them, her mother's oh my god oh my god, Marjorie's what's happening I don't understand, Sparrow's crying, Barry's where the hell were you, Paula! The hell!, the stench in Ruthie's nose of the men's boozy exhales and the weed on her sister's clothes and the spilled meat on the floor and Rose's icy breath, and she put her arms around Eleanor and Gussie, sheltering them, the three of them in one embrace, she and Eleanor cradling Gus like the soft tender baby animal he was.

THE INNOCENT

· ◊ ·

My FATHER CALLS TO ME from the other end of the apartment, his voice thin and urgent. Nowadays everything is thin and urgent, life paring itself down to the essentials. He's eighty-six, how many days can he count on? he says. What are the odds, Pammy? he adds, the syllables slurred, as if he's got rocks in his mouth. He's coming apart so quickly I feel like I'm watching it in fast forward: first the hearing, then the dexterity, then the balance. Age, age, he tells me. *Don't underestimate, Pammy.* Number words.

An accountant, they're in his speech, rolling around and colliding with each other, his whole life in his mouth.

"Pammy?" he calls again.

"I'm here, Dad, what is it?" He's propped up on the sofa in the den, watching the nothing that's on TV. I'm feeling rushed, waiting for the soup to finish so I can dole it out into the little containers that will hold him for the two days until I return. The woman who comes in each day to make the bed, help with his shower, the laundry, warms the food so he won't burn himself. One hot meal a day, the rest he manages on his own. Something cold or nothing. He lives on air. That and cashews. It used to be pistachios but he can't open the shells.

He points to the TV, I should turn it off, a wide-mouthed woman asking about her guest's Internet date.

Did you lie to him online?

I did. I told him I was a 36D.

I switch off the set, embarrassed. "Something I forgot to tell you," he says.

"Yes?" A new prescription, I think. Or a doctor appointment, can I tell him again the name of the service that drives him. Or maybe he's out of socks.

"I spent a year in prison," he says.

I sit down on the sofa, perch on the edge. "You were in jail?"

"Prison," he says, emphatic. "There's a difference."

He waits, wanting me to ask. "When was this?" I manage.

"1948." I begin to calculate. He beats me to it. "I was twenty-two," he says. "Before I met your mother."

192

"Twenty-two," I say, stalling. I don't know where to begin. My father is not a talkative man; my mother had done all the talking for us.

"I fell in with a bad crowd," he says. Soon he'll rattle off names like Bugsy and Louie and Spats, names that go with Bronx gangsters like in the movies, like where he grew up. Tough gizzards in fedoras chewing on cigar ends and skidding down rainy streets in big Roadsters. I can't help but turn it into caricature, fat guys with scars devouring turkey legs and terrorizing the peaceful inhabitants of the city.

"What did you do?" I ask.

My father runs his hands along the tops of his thighs. He's wearing navy blue sweatpants. He can't manage buttons and zippers. "It was a scheme. Terrible. We had no brains. No, that's not true, we had schmaltz for brains." He shakes his head. "Remember Sidney Haberman and Joe Giller?" I nod. His card playing buddies in the summers. The beach club at Long Beach. Pool and day camp for the kids, canasta and diet salads for the women during the week, pinochle and Scotch for the men on weekends.

"And Seymour Krantz," my father throws in, gazing at the ceiling. "All of them."

"Those guys were in prison?" I say. "A bunch of accountants?" It sounds like a joke. *Four accountants are sitting together in a cell. One asks two of them to move to the other side in order to make it balance.*

My father shoots me a look. "Seymour wasn't an accountant. At least not a CPA. He never passed the exam."

I open a palm. "Okay, but you know what I mean.

Those guys..." I trail off. Seymour and Charlotte Krantz had a fussy house in Wantagh decorated in pink floral. My mother of the Good Taste Brigade made fun of it. Their son Jerry had a crush on me in eighth grade. He went to college in Binghamton, became a dentist.

"It was a financial scheme," my father says. "Investments. Electronics, the Japanese weren't doing it all yet, we sold some shares." He pauses. "Imaginary shares."

"You stole people's money for bogus investments?"

My father looks at his hands. "I didn't know they were bogus." He looks up at me. "At least I think I didn't know. Maybe I really did know." He looks at the ceiling again, then back at me, eyes misty. "I don't remember anymore what I knew and didn't know."

It's not adding up. My father is the most honest person on the planet. Scrupulous, he accounted for every penny. His clients loved him but he was conservative on the deductions and never shaved a nickel off anyone's income. I was the only waitress in my college dorm to report the tips.

He leans back, closes his eyes. I reach across and pat his hand. "It was a long time ago, Dad. You paid your dues, did good in your life." I'm patronizing him but we're both tired and I'm not eager to resurrect this chapter of his history because I'm afraid it will eat up precious resources, gnaw at him when there isn't enough of him left as it is.

He opens his eyes, pulls his hand away. "No, Pammy, you don't understand. I didn't pay my dues. There's unfinished business. That's the reason I'm still alive when everyone else from those years is dead. God is making sure."

"God? Since when did God get into the act? You're

194

alive and your old friends aren't because Seymour Krantz ate his way into the grave and the others smoked like chimneys. It's your good constitution, the fact that you eat fish, also that your mother lived to ninety-three."

My father waves me away. "I can't sleep, I can't eat, I have to take care of this." His eyes are silvery blue marbles, clear and direct.

I smell something. "The soup!" I say, and rush off the couch, dash into the kitchen. The pot has boiled over, tomatoes and carrots and potatoes pooled all over the stove. I yell to my father that I'll be back in a minute, that first I have to clean up a mess.

"Me too!" he calls. "Exactly the same for me!"

~

A week later we're driving in a light rain from Providence to New York in my twelve-year-old Honda, a check in my father's shirt pocket for ten thousand dollars that I wrote out because he can't grip a pen. The name of the payee is blank. He's being cagey; other than giving me a vague neighborhood—*somewhere in the Bronx, near the Grand Concourse*—he's been pointedly mysterious about the whole thing. I've pressed. Someone they defrauded? A victim's widow or child? But he's refusing to spill. All he'll say is that it's been weighing on him for years, asserting itself with increasing urgency in the months since my mother died, as though the void she left was filling with ghosts.

I check in the rear view mirror. My father's asleep, cushioned in the back in a cocoon of quilts and pillows because it's comfortable and because it's the only place I'll let him sit if he refuses to wear a seat belt. I was not living near my parents when my mother got sick, was off for the year in Oregon in a last ditch effort to save my unraveling marriage, so now I attend to my father out of a mix of love and guilt. After a futile ten months trying to coax our limp union back to life under Portland's grim skies, Jay and I spent an equally futile if sunnier July driving every inch of the Pacific coastline looking for the spark that was supposed to reignite us, as if one was right there, glinting off the ocean if only we searched hard enough, our son hiking in Spain allegedly to celebrate his college graduation but really to get away from us. We went down through California and up to Canada and passed fishing towns and scenic rocks and showy waves tossing up their monumental spray, but we didn't find any sparks and I came back to Providence alone. My mother died three weeks later. By then I'd shipped Jay's things to his new address in Oregon, the apartment of one Elena Smart, his exceptionally friendly sabbatical colleague and, it turned out, the reason we couldn't find that vivifying spark and why he'd wanted to hightail it to Portland in the first place. It seems they'd met and fallen in love the year before at a romantically stirring conference on Contemporary Applied Ethics in Buffalo, facts he'd felt ethically obliged to disclose when he called to say his stuff had arrived. Though he wondered if I'd overlooked a shelf of his books, his most valuable ones, which for some reason hadn't gotten there, could I take another look? A month after that, our son announced he was moving with his girlfriend to Tasmania for the year, wherever that is. Right now my father is all I've got.

The rain has let up and I pull into a service area outside New London.

"Coffee?" my father says brightly, suddenly awake. He's pulling himself up from the pillows, smoothing back his hair, checking that his shirt is buttoned. No sweatpants today. Once a dapper dresser, his condition is taking a toll on his sartorial pride.

I bring the walker from the trunk, help him out, fix the pant leg that's riding up his calf. He pilots himself inside, lands heavily in a booth. Once he was a swimmer. I've seen the pictures, my handsome father poised at the end of the diving board at the pool at City College, arms extended like wings.

"So where was this prison?" I ask after I've brought over two cups of coffee and a stale apple pastry to share. If I eat, maybe he will too.

"Pennsylvania. We took a bus. Traveled at night."

Already I'm turning it into a buddy movie, three Jewish convicts who've never set foot out of the five boroughs bumping along on country roads dressed in prison stripes and watched over by guards who look like bulldogs. I'm filling in the snappy dialogue, the goofy gaffes, hapless city boys asking for rye bread and Russian Dressing, the guards looking through their hair for horns. This tendency to ill-timed comic invention, I've been told, is part of my problem. *This marriage is in grave trouble and you're making jokes,* Jay had accused halfway through the fall semester in Portland. We were in his idling Saab at a bases-loaded four-way stop and I'd offered up the observation that one could expire before any of the excessively polite locals made the first move.

"So what was it like in prison?" I ask my father.

"I don't remember."

"Nothing?"

My father kneads his fingers. "They gave us a lot to eat. It wasn't bad. We played ball outside when the weather was good."

"What else?"

He lifts his coffee cup with both hands. His knuckles are purplish and swollen. "I can't remember."

"But wasn't it a huge deal?" I whisper. "I would think some things you'd never forget."

"Oh no? You remember giving birth? How you felt that day? That week, that first month? That whole first year?"

I sit back, sip the awful coffee. A dishwater smell rises up from the styrofoam like a dare. *Drink at your own risk.* The sleepless nights, the wailing infant, the leaking breasts, the resentful husband. The beginning of the matrimonial end. Who'd want to remember that?

My father takes a bite of the vile pastry, puts down his fork with finality. He's right about the birth. All I remember are the jokes.

~

What do you get if you cross a mountain and a baby?
A cry for Alp.

The sky has cleared and the coffee's kicked in. My father dozes in the back. After my mother died, I emailed Jay to tell him the news.

198

You don't have to come to the funeral. Oregon's far away and though we were married for twenty-six years, your presence would probably not be a comfort to me.

What about for your father? he wrote back. *He treated me like a son.*

Save yourself the trouble. There's a reason they stopped trying after having a daughter.

Never one to deny himself, Jay came anyway. For our son's benefit, he claimed when he showed up at my door, Sam should see that not all relationships have to end with divorce. Not that Jay was doing a very good job maintaining his own, especially with Sam—not writing, not calling, ducking at all costs. Since I was in mourning and not in the mood to argue, I let him in. The next day at the funeral home my father asked him what the hell he was doing there.

"I came to pay my respects, Herb. You and Eve were family to me. That doesn't change just because Pamela and I have gone our separate ways."

"Separate ways my ass. The only respects you need to pay are to my daughter. I don't want you here making Eve turn over in her grave before she's even in there. Go back to your trashy little tootsie in Seattle."

"Portland."

"Get out of here before I call the cops! I didn't like you from day one!"

I stared at my father. I'd never heard him talk like that. Sam watched the volley, amazed. He hadn't been able to say anything to Jay about the defection but now my father had said it for him. Jay tugged on his lapels like an insulted lawyer in a police procedural and huffed out of the funeral home.

Why did the judge grant the divorce on the grounds of religious differences?

Because the husband thought he was God and his wife didn't.

~

My father rouses himself after we cross into New York State.

"Getting close," he says. He's squinting out his window. It's all changed, I know this without asking. Six years ago, he and my mother moved from New York to Providence to live near me in one of those places you never get out of alive. But it's not the Bronx of six years ago that's changed outside the car window, it's the Bronx of sixty years ago. That's when my father last lived there, before he and my mother joined the great exodus to Long Island.

"Can I have the address now?" I say. That was the deal. When we hit New York, I'd get to put it in the GPS.

"Dekalb Avenue," he says. "3595."

I reach over and type it in.

"That's capital D, small E, small K. Capital K is the one in Brooklyn," he says.

"I know how to spell it, Dad. I know that street."

Silence. The name hangs there. It's where he grew up, the address inscribed in neat script in his City College yearbook, on the yellowed envelope containing his high school diploma from De Witt Clinton, on his birth certificate. I can't believe he still knows anyone in the building. Or does he? Is this the famous hidden dementia everyone

200

warns you about, the kind where you can't tell it's happening because the person has been cleverly covering up?

"You sure, Dad? Dekalb Avenue?"

"Yes I'm sure. Stop asking me that way. I'm not a child, I know what I'm doing. Speaking of which, where's your boy?"

Your boy. A definite cover. That's what all the magazines say. They find workarounds. "Sam's in Tasmania."

"Tasmania," he says slowly. "Is that a place or a mental condition?"

I laugh and a little satisfied chuckle bubbles up from the back. He's still got it, the family affliction. *You think everything is so funny,* Jay had said. *Life as one big hoot. Well, I have news for you. It's not that way.*

My father continues his vigil at the window. A new one comes to me, unbidden.

What's the difference between a federal penitentiary and a house in the suburbs?

In prison they actually use the yard.

~

I didn't want to go to Portland. San Francisco, L.A., even Florida would have been better. Jay and I needed a place where we could defrost. Providence was a hard place to stay warm and cuddly in after twenty-six years. We needed sunshine and beach, not rain. A place where we could frolic naked in the waves and sip Mai-Tais and spend less time indoors brooding and reading books.

But Jay was persuasive. A prestigious college was offering an office, a stipend, a once-a-week honors "conversation" that was a cross between a cocktail hour and a toga party. My work was portable; I could write sleazy marketing copy for the gaming industry from anywhere. Mostly I could feel the stirrings of Jay's discontent. Things were not good between us. He was starting to find fault and mean it. I was trotting out the names of his premarital exes with alarming frequency, an old game that had always diffused the tension before. *You want a wife who's not messy and cooks more? You should have married that Marianne. You don't want a wife whose friends throw parties with belly dancing? You should have married that Beth.* A little well-worn shorthand to remind us that we all come with plusses and minuses, assets and liabilities. Because Marianne, he'd told me, though neat and an excellent baker, had talked too much, and Beth had refused to try marijuana and oral sex. So weren't my brash friends and culinary deficiencies a small price to pay for my otherwise stellar attributes?

But now the banter wasn't working. He informed me that he didn't appreciate my poking fun at his old girl-friends who in fact had been very fine people with many exemplary qualities. That's when I knew we were on thin ice. I bought a raincoat down to my ankles and a guide to mushroom hunting and, like the pioneer women of old who, undeterred by bandits and hail, forged their way west to brave life in a log cabin on a desolate plateau, I sucked it up and sturdily told him I was game, Lewis and Clark here we come.

~

Fortune smiles on us as I successfully bribe the driver of a two-tone vintage Cadillac with fins to let us have the parking spot he's edging into in front of 3595 Dekalb in exchange for a cool fifty. I get the walker from the trunk. My father uses the occasion of the journey to the front door to open the conversation.

"So you see this is my old neighborhood."

"Yes. Very interesting."

"So I might as well tell you."

"Okay." I'm holding his arm, watching the broken sidewalk for holes.

"It's a girl I went with before your mother. That's who I'm coming to see."

A girl? From sixty years before? Now?

He turns to me. He's teary-eyed. "Irene Popkin. We were twenty, twenty-one. First love. I promised her I'd come back for her after prison. But then I couldn't do it. I was too ashamed. Sidney, Joe, Seymour, we were all too ashamed. So we decided to cut the ties to the old neighborhood. I came home to break it off, fifteen minutes in her living room, like a coward, then I fled to the East Bronx where I didn't know anyone and met your mother. I never came back here. Until today." He pauses, looks at the building, faded brick, six stories, straggly shrubs and the first green shoots of spring poking up from the dirt. "Even my parents moved, the humiliation was too much for them."

He picks up the walker, inches forward. *Clop walk clop walk.* I give him a minute. "But why are you bringing her a check?" I ask. "Did she pay for your defense? Give you a loan?"

He fixes me with a look. "A boyfriend who goes to jail? Who swindles? It was a scandal. Her parents despised me. She told them they were wrong, that I was just impressionable, too trusting. Six months with the lawyers and back and forth negotiations, then a whole year I'm in the pen where she came a few times to visit. An entire day on the train, staying in some fleabag motel by herself against her parents' wishes. And then, when I'm free, what do I do? I abandon her. Tell her I can't marry her. What I did to her, it was worse than selling phony shares."

We're nearing the building's entry. Something's not right. "Why didn't you just arrange to meet her somewhere else and get married there, take her away from here? Didn't you love her?"

Clop walk. He stops. "I did love her. But I couldn't do it. I needed a fresh start. I had to run away, even from myself." He pulls a handkerchief from his pocket and wipes his eyes. Why the visit now, I don't need to ask; he couldn't do it while my mother was alive. It would have felt too much like cheating.

"But why money?" I ask.

He looks at me, helpless. "What else have I got to give?"

~

I knew something was off when Jay came back from the Buffalo conference. He was moody and irritable. He picked a fight with Sam, accusing him of being aimless and lazy because he didn't have plans for after college. He knocked over a crystal vase and flew into a rage and blamed me for moving it. He pointed to stains on the carpet and said our housekeeping was driving him crazy. He said a man turning fifty shouldn't have to live like a graduate student, eating take-out three nights a week.

I began trawling the Web. Changes in affect, clumsiness, insomnia. I asked him what they'd put in the drinking water in Buffalo and told him I thought he was either in the midst of a midlife crisis or had a brain tumor, both incurable. He said *Enough with the jokes! When are you going to stop?*

I thought: *It really is a brain tumor.*

I told him to go to a doctor. He rolled his eyes. He said he had no headaches, no dizziness. It was just a bad mood. But justified. Sam was indolent and would get nowhere. The house was sloppy and unkempt. We ate terribly. Nobody liked turning fifty.

Then he went into his study and closed the door and made a call to follow up on a professional contact he said he'd made at the conference. The door was closed for a very long time.

~

Irene Berliner, nee Popkin, lives on the second floor. Thankfully there is an elevator. A weary-looking aide in a stained pink uniform lets us in and informs us that Mrs. Berliner is in the living room but won't be able to hear us because her hearing aid has gone missing plus she has dementia and won't know who we are and sleeps most of the time anyway. But her son Howard is coming over. He saw the letter from my father and wants to meet him.

We sit on the couch and watch Irene sleep in a wingback chair, an afghan over her lap. My father accepts a glass of seltzer; I politely decline. Irene is delicate and withered. She was probably once very pretty in a fragile sort of way. The aide takes a chair in the corner and watches a small TV, the volume on low. Within minutes, my father is asleep. The aide goes to the kitchen, comes back with a cup of coffee, changes the channel. Outside, there's a light drizzle. If my mother were living, she'd ask my father what he hoped to accomplish by giving his long abandoned fiancée ten thousand dollars instead of leaving it in his estate for me, especially now that I'm single and need the money even more, and if I were still married to Jay he'd tell me that it's ridiculous for my father to give away this much to a near stranger; that even the most stringent ethicist wouldn't characterize it as restitution since it brings nobody to wholeness, ameliorates no measurable wrong; that even in the most obvious cases—compensation for the loss of a limb, or, say, wrongful imprisonment—everyone knows that money can't restore one's faith in one's fellow man. But neither of them is here to stop us. For the fact is, I agree with my father. Just because lovers run away from each other—out of shame or fear or the dying of passion— doesn't mean the guilty party shouldn't try to make things better for the innocent.

~

For three months after Jay returned from Buffalo, I pressed him to go to a doctor. He was jumpy and on edge, sleeping poorly, closeting himself in his study for hours, and, most worrisome for a man who managed to be reliably if mechanically amorous regardless of anyone's spirits, cool toward me. He said he didn't feel well enough.

I prodded. He relented. The internist looked concerned and made a referral. Jay got the full work-up, the deluxe neurologist's special. No expense was spared. You didn't mess around with a man's brain. For a month I didn't eat. When the results came back normal, I breathed a great sigh of relief and went out for a steak. So what if the uncovered medical costs topped five thousand and meant I could forget replacing my crummy Honda for another three years? It was worth it. He was my husband. How many times had I heard of people whose personalities had changed because of tumors? That the meanness wasn't the person but their frontal lobe being colonized? The fact that Jay continued to carp after the results came in seemed unimportant; at least he wasn't growing a melon in his head.

At the shiva for my mother, I asked my father if he thought I had an ethical obligation to send Jay the books I hadn't packed for him, the rare first editions and expensive philosophical treatises that were still on the living room shelves and which I chose to overlook for no reason other than a primitive soup of anger and hurt. My father and I were cleaning up the coffee cups and cake plates. The last of the visitors had left. My father was not a religious man but he wanted to observe the whole deal in case my mother's soul was wandering and any of that hocus-pocus turned out to be true. He looked at me, sad-eyed. They'd been married for fifty-nine years, all of them, he'd told me, happy.

Immediately I realized I shouldn't have asked him about Jay, that the timing was all wrong. I started to tell him never mind, but he held up a hand and said he had something important to impart, something I needed to hear now that I'd reached a certain age. I sat on the edge of a dining room chair and held a stack of sticky plates in my lap.

"What's the difference between a nasty divorce and a circumcision?" my father said somberly.

I shook my head. What?

"In a divorce, you get to cut off the whole prick."

~

A soft dusk. The Hutchinson River Parkway winds prettily north. My father sleeps. Irene's son Howard was a nice man who said he couldn't possibly take my father's money. My father insisted, telling him to donate it in Irene's name if he didn't want to use it for her care; he didn't expect a young man like Howard to understand, but there comes a time when you have to set the past right. The aide packed us two thick tuna sandwiches in tin foil and a couple of homemade muffins. We thanked her and Howard and took our leave. Irene never woke up. My father never spoke to her.

I sip my coffee. My father ate one of the muffins and half a sandwich the minute he got into the car, then washed it down with a Dr. Brown's Cel-Ray Tonic from a grocery store near Irene's apartment that he said reminded him of the happiest parts of his youth. While my father waited in the living room for the aide to finish wrapping the sandwiches, Howard took me aside in the kitchen and told me he'd heard the story of my father from his mother a few years back, before her cognition went, and that she said she'd felt guilty all her life because she no longer wanted to marry him by the time he returned from prison. Not because of anything my father had done but because she'd met Howard's father by then, and because a year is a long time for a twenty-year-old girl to wait. The way she told it, my father came to see her after he was released and she told him she had to break it off and that she was going to marry someone else. She'd always felt terrible about that. Though she never thought he'd committed the crimes he was charged with; he was too sweet. It was the other boys who were to blame. They were older and sneakier and had bamboozled him. Everyone knew that.

"That's funny," I said. "He thinks he left her."

Howard shrugged. "Who knows? But anyway they loved each other once and that's what counts. How it ended doesn't matter. One of them is probably right."

My phone beeps. A message from Sam. It's already tomorrow in Tasmania. I pull off at the next rest stop to read it.

Heard from Dad. His girlfriend is pregnant. Says he's not sure how he feels about that at his age. Also that he wants us to be in better touch.

I write back. *That's good. About being in touch.*

A moment later, a blinking reply. *Yeah. I wrote him back with a joke. Billy: My dad's having a new baby. Bobby: What's wrong with the old one?*

I smile, swell with pride. I tell Sam it's a winner and

pull back onto the highway. Toward the end of our time in Portland, I told Jay a joke I'd heard on the plane coming back from a work conference. A flight attendant had recited it over the intercom. Our departure had been delayed and the crew was trying to keep things upbeat; they passed out extra snacks and sodas and the flight attendant said he used to do stand-up. It was a low point then for me and Jay, and it meant a lot to me to hear people laughing on the plane. I thought then: things are bad but maybe they don't have to be that bad. Maybe we can still save ourselves. But when I got home and told Jay the joke, he lost it. When was I going to wake up? he shouted. When was I going to stop trying to turn everything into fodder and get serious about life?

This was serious, I told him. That joke was the most serious thing I'd ever said to him. He shook his head and went into his study and closed the door, and that's when I knew it was over. I thought: if only he had laughed, everything could have been different. If only he had once laughed, everything might have been saved.

Why wouldn't the cannibal eat the clown?
Because she tasted funny.

THE BOOK OF SPLENDOR

· ◊ ·

THE EDUCATION OF THE EXCEPTIONALLY PROMISING begins early and ends almost never, and this Nathan Berditchev understood long before the age of twelve when, one muggy night in the cramped Berditchev living room over glasses of tea and slices of stiff sponge cake, the rabbis of the Yeshiva of Eastern Queens informed his parents that he, Nathan, had certain gifts.

It was not seemly to make too much of it, the rabbis murmured, Nathan listening from the stairs in cowboy pajamas that in the sticky August night clung to his back. A layer of humidity had been hanging in the apartment all day, unable to move; to neither escape out the open windows nor disperse among the four rooms—a two-story, two up, two down, his mother had told her mother, the only time Nathan had heard even a twinge of a boast in his mother's voice, a sin as severe as eating traife or going to the movies on shabbas, temptations, all, of an unholy world—a stillness so thick that Nathan had felt as though he were swimming through soup as he'd gone from room to room looking for something to do, the worst heat wave in New York City, the headlines said, in fifty years. Humility was a trait to be cultivated by all, one of the rabbis said softly, the nervous tinkling of a spoon against glass, just as they mustn't allow themselves to be bitten by the serpent of pride; but this was something Mr. and Mrs. Berditchev needed to know about their son, a child gifted even more, God should forgive them, than his brother Carl, himself a brilliant boy, a light to the yeshiva, they should make no mistake, a shining example for Nathan to follow. But a Nathan he was not, and never would be.

A sharp intake of breath—his mother? father?—the spoon silent; an ambulance wailed in the distance. Another casualty of the weather, heat stroke, the phrase his mother had ominously repeated all afternoon, visions percolating in Nathan's brain of a giant paint brush lapping over innocent victims walking home from the bus. The siren stopped; Nathan hunched over and wrapped his arms around his knees. *This was the way of the world, was it not,* the other rabbi said, his voice gravelly and absolute,

212

not a question but a pronouncement, moving as though weighted through a lower stratum of air, reaching Nathan at his feet and traveling through him like a current, the sort of voice you never argued with, addressing itself almost sternly in response to what Nathan could only imagine was his mother's bowed head, hearing her children compared, the terrible truth that one, in some terrible respect, had come up short. It was not her doing, the voice said, more a reprimand than a comfort. Nor was it a reflection on the merits of her sons. *This was the will of the Creator, dispensing a little more of this here, a little less of that there, and it was not for them to presume to understand. It was only for them to accept what was, safeguard what had been given, and see to it that it wasn't squandered.*

The slightest movement at Nathan's back. He quickly turned, looked up the steps. Nothing stirred on the landing above him, not the sheer curtain that hung on the airless window nor the shaft of light from the room he shared with Carl. What if this one time Carl hadn't been so stubborn? What if this one time he'd given in to Nathan's pestering to defy their parents' orders and join him to eavesdrop on the stairs? What then?

A shuffling in the living room, footsteps on the linoleum in the hall. Nathan curled himself into a ball. "Who knows," the lighter voice said, striving for cheerful. Rabbi Lerner, the new principal for the younger boys, an American, no trace of an accent, who brought in old clippings of Hank Greenberg, three-time American League champion and a practicing Jew. "Maybe one day Nathan will be teaching all of us—Maimonides, the

213

Tosefta, even"—Lerner's voice dropped to a loud whisper, a dramatic flourish—"*The Zohar.*" The four of them appeared in Nathan's vision, his father and mother, small and defeated-looking, even smaller next to the visitors, whose backs were to him—Lerner, young and athletic like the ball players he admired, and the other man, gray-haired under his black yarmulke, powerful shoulders to match the powerful voice. Nathan's father opened the door, the thick heat standing under the light of the street lamp like a sentry, and the visitors, putting on their hats, stepped out into the night.

Slowly, his parents walked back to the living room; Nathan heard their muffled voices, life never rising up in triumph to give them joy, good news clothed always in an outer layer of bad, their heads bowed as though a great weight had been deposited in the house. When he heard the stacking of plates, the rattling of silverware, he turned and ran soundlessly up the stairs, Carl asleep with his glasses on, a book open beside him on the damp sheets, doomed now in their parents' eyes though he would never know why, and hurried into his own bed and pulled the blanket up over his face. Why him? Why couldn't it be Carl? Carl, who would grow up to teach Lerner? Who would pore over volumes of commentary, *Tosefta*, Maimonides?

And, worst of all, *The Zohar. The Book of Splendor.* Nathan had been told little of it, revelations of mystics and hermits. But he had heard. Knew that it was supposed to contain the keys to the secrets of heaven, codes to all the mysteries in the universe. It was so dangerous no one was allowed to open its pages until they reached the age of forty. Because if you did, you could go crazy. Cross over to the other side. Even die.

But what if he didn't want to know? What if he didn't want to see into the hidden meaning of all things? Why couldn't it be Carl? Carl, who was always searching, who would spend the rest of his life looking for the answers to every question anyway?

The light in the hall went off; he heard his parents on the stairs. He reached across the night table and removed Carl's glasses from his face, turned off the lamp and lay on his back. He closed his eyes, the evening sitting on his chest like a safe, and swore to himself he would never repeat a word of what he'd heard, not to anyone, not even to himself, certain that neither the rabbis nor his terrified parents would either. Then he squeezed his eyes tighter and prayed to God that someone had made a mistake.

~

September, the bus to school an hour instead of twenty minutes, the new apartment with the separate dining room and built-in china closet worth the trip. His mother's tone describing it to her mother had been one of amazement, disbelief that sometimes things improved. His father was no longer a cutter but a supervisor, *maybe one day a foreman*, his mother had whispered, straining to keep not so much pride out of her voice but all hope and expectation. Too, one had to be scrupulous about the evils that came of too much talk. *What's the most lethal weapon a person can own?* she would say. *A loose tongue,* and point to each of their mouths and then her own to show that she too wasn't above such weakness. On the bus ride home, Nathan did his homework by the flickering lights of the evening traffic; Carl squinted by the glass and read his poetry. Whitman, Schwartz, Shapiro, Ginsberg, names Carl rattled off from the books he kept hidden under his bed. Poetry was Carl's religion, Nathan told him. Every few weeks, he would swear Nathan to secrecy and make him go with him on the subway to a hole-in-the-wall bookstore on Fourteenth Street, installing Nathan on the sidewalk to keep watch before ducking into the bookstore as if he were robbing a bank, then coming out forty minutes later with his loot, half to be stuffed into Carl's book bag and half into Nathan's so as not to arouse suspicion. The books were dusty and old and had a mildew smell that clung to Nathan's bag for days.

Now they strained by the dim light while rain sheeted the glass. The first bleak portents of winter. Nathan hated winter, hated waking in the dark, coming home in the dark. They lived like bats, Carl said; the only good thing about winter was his birthday. He would turn eighteen at the end of December. For one night he'd insist on light, he told Nathan. Every lamp in the house on, even the one over the stove.

The door of the bus flew open; a gust of wet air funneled in. A lady with two shopping bags of groceries sank into the seat opposite Nathan, knocking his textbook to the floor with the hem of her coat.

"Stupid assignment," Nathan murmured, bending for it. "Inventions of America. The lousy book is so old it has only forty-eight states." Everyone knew the secular studies at school were a joke.

"Ah, the folly of dry fact masquerading as language. Unlike real language," Carl said, patting his own book, the faded green cover like old cloth. It smelled of moth balls, closets that were never opened. "One day, Nathan, you'll see how the written word can change your life. I don't mean the Talmud, I mean these words. The real truth is in these." He lifted his book reverently, like a treasure brought up from the bottom of the ocean, and recited, dramatic. The woman across the aisle turned to look. "'*Of Life immense in passion, pulse and power, cheerful, for freest action formed under the laws divine, the Modern Man I sing.*' Isn't that spectacular? *Man*, Nathan. That's what he's saying. *We* are the real story. Because we have free will. We determine our lives. Without a god. Courtesy of Mr. Walt Whitman." He smiled broadly at the woman, who *tsked* and turned away. "Such a shame," whispered Carl, looking at the woman. "A philistine."

Nathan didn't know about philistines or free will. He knew only the relentless logic of the Gemara, the endless volleys of the Mishnah. He understood the law. Rules, argument, reason. He didn't understand Carl. But then again, no one did.

~

Weeks of unending rain. Ponds formed on the walkways to the apartments and never drained away. Carl wanted to go to the bookstore again.

"We just went," Nathan said. "And how do you even have any money? You're supposed to be saving up for college." Cards for the 1960 Dodgers lineup were laid out before him on the bedspread. Their parents had closed their door hours ago. Their father was out of the house by four-thirty, doing everything he could to impress the owners so he'd have a shot at the foreman's job. This was his chance, he told Nathan's mother. *If I'm the first one in and the last one out, they'll pay attention. No sick days. No leaving early on Fridays. Don't give me that look, Miriam. I can be home before shabbas or we can eat. Which do you want?*

Carl straddled the back of the desk chair. His feet were huge in his socks. There had been a call that evening from the yeshiva; Nathan, from the stairs, heard his mother telling his father. Carl's marks were slipping, he seemed distracted, preoccupied. Had he taken on something extra-curricular? Was something wrong? He'd never had trouble in the past. "I *vant* my books!" Carl said and opened his mouth wide and pretended to eat his arm. "More books! More books!"

"You're crazy, Carl," Nathan said, returning to the lineup. He needed only two more to complete the team. Lerner had offered him ten bucks for Koufax alone. Lerner was nuts; it was just a piece of cardboard. If he could find the Koufax, he'd gladly take a ten off the principal.

"Crazy? You call me crazy?" Carl was up on the bed, on his knees across from Nathan, messing up the spread and scattering the cards. "I *vant*, I *vant!*" Duke Snider was in Carl's mouth.

"Give it back!" Nathan said, pulling at the card. Carl held on with his teeth, whipping his head around like a fierce dog. He was loving it, Carl the vampire, Carl the wild animal.

218

"Give it!" Nathan yelled. Carl raised his eyebrows and pointed at the door. They'd wake their father and have to hear a speech from their mother about respect for parents and peace in the house. "Give it back!" Nathan hissed.

"Argh!" Carl growled, jerking his head before taking the whole card into his mouth. He chewed, took it out, dangled it in front of Nathan, then dropped the soggy ball onto the bedspread. In the next instant, he pulled from behind his back a perfect Duke Snider.

Nathan grabbed it. "Stinker. Now get that spitball off of here."

"Certainly," Carl said, pretend British, delicately lifting the wad with two fingers and tossing it into the air, then catching it in his mouth and making an exaggerated swallowing sound.

"Carl, no! You'll choke!"

Carl stretched his head back, giving Nathan a full view of his Adam's apple and the stubble on his neck. "Never fear, my dear Watson. It's perfectly edible." He held up a finger. "*Smile O voluptuous cool-breath'd earth! Earth of the slumbering and liquid trees!*' See? Liquid trees? Completely natural. Per the peerless Mr. Whitman."

"Eating cardboard is gross."

"Don't *vory*," Carl said. He went to his own bed. "I'm satiated now. I don't need any more *bessball* player blood." He did the eyebrow raise again. "But I do need more books. And you *vill* be my accomplice."

Nathan lifted his covers, eased himself in and slid the cards under his pillow. He lay on his back and closed his eyes, heard Carl taking off his pants, rummaging under the bed for another book. He knew Carl had been skipping school but would never tell. Anyway Carl was always at the bus stop at the yeshiva by the time Nathan got there for the ride home. He had told Nathan he didn't want to go to CCNY or Queens next year; he didn't want to go to college at all. He wanted to be free. To ride the rails and criss-cross the country. *I hear America singing!*

"Nathan, you awake?"

Nathan rolled onto his side and looked at Carl, who was on his back, his book held high above him, like the Torah after the reading. What if Carl went away and never came back?

"Listen to this!" Carl said. "*Everything is holy! everybody's holy! everywhere is holy! everyday is in eternity! Everyman's an angel!*' Allen Ginsberg. A Yid!" He grinned at Nathan. "Did you hear? Everyone's an angel! Everybody's holy!"

~

Their father didn't get the foreman's job. The company brought in an outsider. Rumor was that the factory was being sold, the foreman the new owner's man; even his supervisor job wasn't secure. He had maybe a month, then he was out on the street.

If I'd done more, maybe they'd have kept me, he said to their mother behind their half-closed door. *Maybe I could have persuaded them.*

What—get there at four in the morning instead of six? Work eighteen hours a day instead of twelve? Don't be crazy, Avrum. They wanted an outsider all along. They were

220

playing with you. Like they always do.

There were more calls from the school. Carl was absent too much, when he was there he didn't pay attention, his thoughts elsewhere, Mr. and Mrs. Berditchev needed to have a talk with their son.

"Boys his age, their thoughts should be elsewhere," his father said. "Like on getting a job." He'd gotten his notice. *Walking papers.* Nathan saw papers with little legs. They needed to think about moving, his father said; the new apartment was too much. At supper Carl had brought up the birthday lights. What kind of foolishness was that? their father snapped. Now, when he was about to be out of work, they should burn more electricity? Carl might as well have asked to burn dollar bills. "Lots of boys take after-school jobs, Miriam. If they go to the public school." The faucet went on, Nathan's mother rinsing something. Seething. His father's voice rose. "There's nothing wrong with a little more responsibility, a little less Gemara."

The water shut off. His mother was descended from a line of scholars and rabbis that stretched back to Peter the Great. In more than two hundred years, not a single male in her family had attended a secular school. Nathan and Carl had been told this a thousand times; it was their birthright. Unlike what they got from their father's side, uneducated laborers and tradesmen. It was nonsense to talk of public school, his mother said now. Hadn't he heard the rabbis? Both boys were exceptional; they needed the proper education. She was disappointed in the yeshiva. They were probably ignoring Carl and he was bored. They weren't giving Nathan all the attention they promised either.

"Well, you can forget the yeshiva, Miriam. Two weeks I'm out on the street. Did you hear me, two weeks? Even with their scholarships, we won't be able to cover. Just covering for Nathan will be impossible. That's right, even for our mister prodigy. Where are we going to get the money? You tell me—where?"

"What are you talking? The boy has a gift, Avrum! You can't let something like that come to nothing!"

"Oh no? Then you go out and get the job! You find the money!"

His father stormed into the hall. Nathan, on the stairs, huddled into a ball. Too late. His father glared at him, went out the door.

~

November. The sun was a miser. On the days Carl disappeared he no longer met Nathan at the bus for the ride home. Instead he waited for him in front of their apartment building when Nathan walked up in the dark.

Shh, don't tell. It's all right. I'm doing something important.

What, you're looking for a job?

Shh. I can't say. Don't tell anyone.

Other days, Carl slept the whole ride to school, up all night with his poetry, not only reading but writing now, pages stashed where he wouldn't reveal. His books numbered in the hundreds. To keep their mother out of their room Carl made Nathan promise to make his bed; Carl would vacuum and dust. They were helping out, Carl told her. She'd found a job taking care of newborn twins of a rich relative of someone in the building. Each day she rose at five to take two buses to Jamaica Estates where she stayed until the husband got home at night. After a cold supper she went straight to bed. Their father pounded the pavement. Nathan saw his father pounding with a hammer. Or his fist.

One cold wet night two weeks into his mother's job, Nathan waited for her in the kitchen. He'd been intercepting calls from the school: they'd be cancelling Carl's scholarship after the first of the year, more deserving boys were waiting. He set out a plate, a fork, a knife, made his mother tea. She sat down and he brought out butter, two slices of rye bread, a hard-boiled egg. He took a chair and watched her take a bite, then told her he didn't want to go to the yeshiva anymore. That he'd wanted to go to the public school for months but had been afraid to say so.

She put down her knife. "Is this because I'm working? Your father will get a job, this won't last forever."

"That's not it. I'm thinking I might want to be a lawyer. Or learn the stock market. Or go into business. I think I have a head for that."

She folded her hands. She was trying to control herself. People in her line didn't go into the stock market, into business. "You're a very gifted boy, Nathan. You could become a scholar. More than a scholar. An *illui*. You know what an *illui* is? A Talmudic genius. My father, of blessed memory, was one. In Europe. Before this country made him grovel, made him give Hebrew lessons to ignorant American children who didn't deserve a minute of his attention. You take after my family. They were intellectuals, people of quality." She stopped as if she'd said something

223

she shouldn't have. "Enough. There's time to decide all this when you're older, I don't want to hear another word."

He inched up on his chair. "You don't understand. I don't care about what they're teaching me. The Mishnah, Gemara, it's all riddles. Puzzles. Mental exercises that don't mean anything. Nobody cares about the Talmud except a bunch of rabbis who don't know anything else. I don't believe in any of it. It has nothing to do with real life."

The sting of her palm on his cheek threw him back into his chair. She stood up and left the kitchen. He heard the door of his parents' room sharply close.

~

His father found work at a striking coat factory in Brooklyn. A two-hour commute for half the pay. A scab; Nathan saw him as a thick red mark over an old wound. Each day his father wanted to flee in shame as he walked through the picket line. One morning he saw someone he knew from his old factory. The man shouted an insult and Nathan's father wanted to turn around and go home. He told Nathan's mother some indignities weren't worth it.

And being some rich girl's cook and maid isn't an indignity? Wake up, Avrum. Principles like these we can't afford. Look at your sons. Do you see how anxious Nathan is? How thin and tired-looking is Carl? We're wearing them out with our worries.

December moved in. A frozen fist. Christmas carols blanketed the radio stations. Posters in the subway showed red-cheeked Santas and smiling families sitting beside brightly wrapped presents under a tree. That's how they

224

got people to buy, Carl whispered to Nathan, pointing to the ads in their train car, his blue knit cap pulled down low. By making you believe this was happiness. But it was a trick. Because once they got you to buy things, they could get you to do other things. If Nathan had any doubt, all he had to do was look at the signs right in front of their noses. *Act now! Call today!* There were forces out there trying to penetrate their minds. You had to build up mental shields to keep them from controlling your thoughts.

Mental shields? Nathan asked.

Defenses, Carl murmured. To keep the forces from getting through. But he and Nathan were lucky. They weren't susceptible because they were Jews. So the forces couldn't invade them. For now.

Outside the bookstore, Nathan waited at his usual spot, hands shoved into his pockets, collar up against the cold. He hadn't wanted to come. But Carl insisted; he'd gotten hold of a Koufax and had weaseled Nathan out of half of Lerner's ten. Nathan would have given Carl the whole ten if it would've made Carl stop acting so strange. Everything was secret now. He wouldn't read his poetry out loud at night because someone might hear. He vanished for whole days, coming back to the apartment long after their parents went to sleep. He told Nathan he was working on something critically important but couldn't tell him what it was.

A tap on the shoulder. A man as old as his father. "Don't be frightened. I'm from the bookstore. There's a boy inside."

Their footsteps on the linoleum were drums. The man

described: glasses, blue hat, fingers gripping a five dollar bill like a life preserver.

"Carl?"

He was huddled on the floor at the end of a long row. He looked at Nathan blankly. Was this another joke? Was Carl about to jump up and play vampire? Hah, hah, got you! No. Carl only made jokes at home, never in public. His eyes darted from Nathan to the man to the crowd collecting behind them.

The man herded the strangers away—*Someone's just a little ill, let's give the boy some room.* Nathan inched up to his brother. Carl's lips trembled. The wrinkled bill stuck out of a balled fist. "Come take my hand, Carl. Let's go home." He grasped Carl's clenched fist and Carl rose, teetering like a golem. "He's not feeling well, that's all," Nathan said to the man, his arm around Carl's waist. "I think he's coming down with something."

"Sure, sure," the man said, leading them through the store. Nathan ignored the stares. At the door the man said, "You going to be all right? You want to call your folks?"

There was something in the man's face. Had he seen Carl before? Had Carl been coming to the bookstore alone? Had he acted strange before?

"We're okay, thanks," Nathan said, and he shuffled Carl out the door and to the subway. Within seconds of the train pulling out, Carl was asleep, the five sticking out of his fist. Nathan pried it loose, stuffed it into his pocket.

Two stops from their own, Carl woke up. He pressed his face against the glass. "Where are we? What are we doing on the subway?"

"You don't know?"

Carl turned to him.

"We're going home, Carl. From the bookstore. We left early." He showed Carl the book bag on his lap. "See? It's empty. Remember?"

Carl looked at the bag, then at Nathan. He looked outside the window again, then at his hands. He lifted them and sniffed. Then he looked at Nathan again. A wave of something Nathan had never seen before crossed his face. Fear. "What are you talking about?"

"You wanted to spend your five from Lerner." Nathan dug in his pocket for the bill and made to give it to Carl but Carl recoiled as if it were a poisonous bug. "I went to the sidewalk like always. You went into the store. You were there a long time. A man came out and found me." He searched Carl's face. Nothing. "He brought me to you. You were sitting on the floor."

"Had I fallen?"

"No."

Carl stared at Nathan, then out the window again. He turned back to Nathan. "Not a word to anyone, okay?"

Nathan nodded. His eyes were welling up. "Are you sick, Carl?" he whispered, leaning into his brother's coat, mildew and must clinging to the wool.

In the dark space between them, Carl squeezed Nathan's hand. "I don't know."

~

The yeshiva cancelled classes on Christmas for the first time in its history. Rabbi Lerner had persuaded the headmaster, the man with the gravelly voice, that it was time to acknowledge that they were in America and that it wasn't right to require the secular studies teachers and janitorial crew, none of whom were Jewish, to come to work.

"All of a sudden we're like the goyim," Nathan's mother said, filling a cake pan with batter. "Soon he'll tell us to go sing carols and buy ourselves a tree. It's a disgrace." Nathan watched her from the table where he sat with his father, eating a roll. A blizzard had dumped six inches on the city. Nathan had slept late, and when he woke up, Carl wasn't in his bed. His parents thought Carl was still upstairs.

"Why are you complaining?" his father said. "Better I should have to go to Brooklyn today in this weather? Better you should be at the prima donna's house, killing yourself on the ice walking from the bus? You said she was paying you for today."

"A Jewish girl giving a Christmas bonus. I don't want to take it."

"Take it, Miriam."

"Don't push me, Avrum."

His father sipped his coffee and gazed at the newspaper. *White Christmas Blankets New York.* But it was no blanket, Nathan thought. His mother slid the pan into the oven, dusted her hands on her apron. "What's with Carl? It's ten o'clock."

"So? You're going somewhere? He's exhausted, Miriam. Let him sleep."

She poured herself coffee, pulled out a chair. "I don't like how he looks. Not that I ever see him." She turned to

228

Nathan. "Not that I ever see either of you." She pulled a tissue from the apron and wiped her eyes.

"It's all right, Ma." Nathan reached across the formica and patted her hand. "We're doing fine."

"You're not doing fine. Coming home from school every day to an empty house, a cold supper. Shabbas"— she looked at his father, who kept his eyes on the paper— "hardly shabbas. We're living like animals. Existing just to eat and sleep." She sipped her coffee. Nathan finished his roll. After a few minutes he went to the living room and lay on the couch, watched the falling snow.

The doorbell woke him. Two policemen and, between them, a silent shivering Carl. They'd found him wandering in Forest Park, no coat, his clothes and sneakers soaked. He didn't know where he lived; they got the address from the phone book.

"Downstairs," his mother commanded after they'd walked Carl up to his and Nathan's room and gotten him out of his frigid clothes and layered on extra blankets, gave him tea, waited until he fell asleep. "Did you know he wasn't here?" she said when they were in the living room.

Nathan nodded.

"Why didn't you say anything?"

Nathan watched the falling snow. "He goes on a lot of walks, I don't know where." He looked back at his parents. "I just figured he'd gone for another one."

"Is he worried from something?" his father asked. "Money? College? He hears our arguing?"

"The yeshiva's been calling," Nathan said. "They're taking away his scholarship."

"I told you, Miriam! I told you we should've let him go to the public high school when he asked!"

Carl had asked to go to public school? "Carl wanted to go to the high school?" Nathan asked.

"That's not your business," his mother said.

"Don't listen to her! Yes, he was sick of the yeshiva! We should have listened! You were so stubborn, Miriam!"

"Enough, Avrum! When did you hear about this, Nathan? Why didn't you tell us?"

"Why didn't he tell us?" his father erupted. "Because look what happens when he does! Do we listen to our sons? Do we pay attention? No! Because of you! You're blind to your own children!"

"I'm blind? What about you? Working on shabbas, what kind of example is that! And not enough money to keep the same roof over our heads, we have to move again! Whose blindness is that!"

His father stomped out. Nathan watched the snow. He and his mother sat in silence. After a few minutes his mother went upstairs to check on Carl.

~

All night Nathan heard his parents fighting. By the next morning they had a plan. They told Nathan that when the yeshiva resumed the following day, his mother would go with him and Carl and demand to speak with Rabbi Lerner and find out what was going on. Then, when the public school reopened, she would go there. Tell them Carl was a smart boy, no more scholarship money, when can he enroll. Things were going to change in the family.

Peace in the house. Financial worries were for parents, not for children. They were going to take better care of things from now on.

"What do you think Carl will say?" his mother asked, teary. Carl was still asleep. His father had gone out to buy the newspaper. "Do you think he'll be happier now?"

Nathan looked at her. How could he save her? How could he save any of them? "It's his birthday tomorrow," he said. "Let's turn on all the lights."

~

The next morning Carl whispered to Nathan at the kitchen table not to worry, that he'd had a breakthrough with his secret work, but that he would go to school because it was his birthday and his absence would be noticed. Nathan listened, feverish, didn't touch his breakfast. Fifteen minutes later, the thermometer plucked from his mouth, his mother sent him back to bed. She would stay home with him and go to the yeshiva the next day. Meantime they would have a birthday cake for Carl when he and his father returned home that evening. They would turn on all the lights.

At three o'clock Nathan woke to the sound of the front door. The snow was still falling. He went downstairs. His father stood in the living room in his coat and hat, his face ashen. His mother sobbed on the couch.

"What is it? What's wrong?" Nathan said. "Why are you home? Did you get fired? Did they shut the place down?"

His father turned to the window. The sky was slate.

"Is it Carl? Did something happen to Carl? It's Carl, isn't it. Tell me!"

"Sit down, Nathan." His father's voice was shaking. "Your brother, he was on the roof. The roof of the school. Naked, no shoes, nothing, standing in the snow, the ice, yelling." His voice broke. He took a handkerchief from his pocket, held it against his eyes. "Crazy nonsense, out of his mind. Yelling about angels telling him the secrets of heaven, they were coming back for him, he was waiting, ready. Four teachers had to hold him down. He was going to jump. They had to tie him up to carry him downstairs." He began to weep and Nathan felt himself splitting in two, floating onto the ceiling and watching the living room as though it were a play being performed by people he didn't know. A woman sobbing on the couch. A bent man, shoulders shaking, in a wet hat and coat. A boy staring out at a gunmetal sky.

~

The school sent Carl to Bellevue in an ambulance; Nathan's parents went by taxi. Nathan wasn't allowed to go despite his pleas. Mrs. Gottlieb from next door came to stay with him until his parents returned. Nathan wasn't to breathe a word.

He lay on his bed and watched the ceiling. The bell at the back door rang, a single ding. Mr. Gottlieb with Mrs. Gottlieb's dinner—*a piece of chicken, still warm*—Mr. Gottlieb standing on the mat, wiping his shoes of the dirty slush from the alley where the Dumpsters were. Nathan looked over at Carl's bed. The bedspread ached for Carl,

232

the night table whispered for Carl, the curtains fluttered for Carl. Everything longed for Carl.

He looked down. But not the books.

He scrambled to the floor and lifted Carl's dust ruffle. Hundreds of them, like vermin. He reached in and pulled them out, stood up and threw back Carl's bedspread, found them under the blankets, the pillows. Then the dresser, behind the radiator, hidden in newspapers on Carl's chair. He threw them onto the floor, pulled the linens off his own bed, pushed up the mattress. Hundreds of pages scattered on the box spring. Numbers and shapes like impenetrable formulas, sentences scribbled along the tops and sides, words curled inside circles, snaked inside hexagons. *The comet's tail saves the sufferer. Bring me to the palace of radiance. A perfect world full of splendor.*

He flung the papers onto the floor with the books, emptied shoeboxes, shook out sweaters, dug in pockets and hats. Then he went into the hall. The Gottliebs were talking in low tones in the kitchen. From the linen closet he pulled down the old white sheets they took to the bungalow colony in summer—they would not go again— and piled in the papers, the books. When he got to the green one, Carl's favorite, he flipped it open.

You road I enter upon, you are not all that is here. I believe that much unseen is also here.

Carl had thought it was only words. They both had. But they'd been tricked. Words could betray you. They promised you truth and they told you things you should never know and then they took your life.

Because everyone knew there were things no one should ever know.

He filled the sheets, tied them tight, put on his sneakers. He waited at the top of the stairs. Mr. Gottlieb went out the back door. Mrs. Gottlieb rinsed her dish. He saw the kitchen light go out, heard her pad into the living room, click on the TV.

He hurried down the steps, a sheet over his shoulder, its contents digging into his back. When the noise from the television billowed up with laughter, he unlatched the kitchen door, ran out into the icy black night through the alley to the open Dumpster and hurled his terrible burden into the stinking bin. Then the next one and the one after that, two, three, four trips, heaving his burden into the trash again and again until it was all gone and he raised his trembling face to the moonless sky and cursed the God who answers his prayers.

THE NATURAL WORLD

· ◊ ·

WE BEGIN TO SEE THEM ABOUT MINNESOTA. Lone deer, sometimes three a day, pushed to the side of the highway, their long legs curled beneath them.

"There are so many," Danny says, staring out his window. He's right behind us in the van, the middle bench his personal domain. After six days, half his markers have disappeared into the upholstery, and the holder under his window overflows with candy wrappers and stale sandwich halves. "What's the matter? Do they get lost or something?"

"They come out of those woods," I say from the passenger seat, pointing to the thick trees. "They're trying to get over to the other side."

"It's cruel to put a road in their way," Jake says from the back. He's stretched out, a pillow under his head, all his stuff—iPod, iPad, sugary snacks that would land us in jail in some parenting circles—within easy reach in an overpriced nylon bag with a dozen pockets that hangs off the hook for the dry cleaning. Arthur and I spent days choosing all sorts of car things for the drive west across the country. Maps, drawing pads, magnetic checkers, plus flares and orange hazard cones and a first aid kit good for every climate from Vietnam to the North Pole. Jake's like a royal personage back there, reclining and consuming Oreos and Cokes at will. It's our own fault; the last thing we wanted on this trip was resistance. It's not the travel our sons object to; it's what comes after. Five months in a hamlet on the Idaho-Washington border where we won't know a soul and our nearest neighbors will be eleven miles away. They're not the only ones worrying. "It's not right," Jake goes on. "We're destroying their territory, their whole way of being."

I want to ask since when does he care so much about the wildlife when at home he and his twelve-year-old friends still make sport out of terrorizing squirrels, but Arthur pipes up from behind the wheel and says, "You're right. But here's a question: let's say you're the government. It's 1960, 1965, and suddenly there's a huge demand for highways, people discovering the joys of automobile travel. Now suppose this is all unspoiled"—he waves toward

236

the windshield—"except for an old two-lane road that's jammed every summer, bumper to bumper. What should the government do? Take into account the welfare of the people? Or the welfare of the animals?" He looks into the rear view mirror. "What do you think?"

No answer. Jake's lost interest. Arthur's gone on too long, taking Jake's black-and-white indignation and complicating it with shades of gray. He can't help it. *It's our job*, he tells me whenever I ask him why he always feels obligated to point out to our sons the complexity of everything. *Because they need to hear that there are always two sides. That things are never that simple.*

Arthur checks the mirror again. Jake is fiddling with his headphones. Arthur gives it one more shot. "What do you think, Danny? What should the government do?"

Danny's watching out the window, his big sad eyes sadder and bigger. "I don't know. I just feel bad for the deer."

~

We hadn't expected a sabbatical. But Arthur was feeling the itch. When his department head offered a semester off for scheduling reasons, he jumped on it. It's a big country, let's go somewhere, the company I worked for was folding anyway. He told Jake and Danny it was important to expand their horizons, that there was more to life than staying in your own little corner.

He scoped for possibilities. Oregon, Colorado, Utah, the further from New York the better. And west, he wanted to go west. Idaho fished up, a paleontologist's dream, especially a paleontologist who'd been staring at tiny marine fossils for twenty years, and where, in addition to a generous stipend, we'd get a university-owned log cabin house a hundred miles east of the city of Moscow, population twenty thousand, on a site littered with newly unearthed Brontosaurus-sized bones just begging for analysis. Rather than attempt a new school—a three-room schoolhouse forty minutes away in good weather—Jake and Danny would keep up with their classwork from home. Once a week we'd drive to Moscow to a restaurant or a supermarket or a trip to the library.

"Sounds exciting," our friend Leo said at dinner. Melanie fussed in the kitchen; we heard her opening drawers, filling water glasses. They were newlyweds, less than a year. Melanie was determined to make this one work.

"Didn't you go out west once when you were teaching?" I said to Leo, limpingly hopeful. This was Arthur's baby, not mine.

Leo glanced quickly toward the kitchen. "I did, yes. Went to Taos. New Mexico." He lowered his voice. "With my first wife."

"Oh, Taos," Arthur said expansively. "Supposed to be beautiful out there."

"Right. Nice place," Leo said, watching the kitchen.

"Funky. And cultural, too," Arthur said, pulling a little memo pad out of his back pocket—he was still in the trip-planning stage—and jotting something down. "Were you studying the indigenous peoples?" Leo had been in anthropology before moving over to development. Double the salary, he told Arthur, but Arthur wasn't interested. All that glad-handing and boosterism: no thanks.

"Not there," Leo mumbled. "I did that in Peru. With my second wife."

"So was that a year or six months in Taos?" Arthur said, still scribbling.

Leo waved, helpless.

"I'm just curious," I said. "How long after your return did you and your wife split? Wives, actually." I could feel Arthur looking over at me. *Why would you ask that?*

Leo reddened. "Oh, not immediately. Three, four months. Maybe six."

Melanie appeared in the doorway. A huge eye roast sat on a silver platter, pink and juicy, like a prize. She'd called in advance to make sure we ate red meat. *A taste for beef!* she whispered on the phone. *Such a sin!* "Talking about Leo's sabbaticals?" she said breezily, setting the platter on the table. A flutter of juice spilled over onto the white cloth, oozing in greasy pink circles. "Lethal for a marriage, positively lethal."

~

The Corn Palace in Mitchell, South Dakota is no longer entirely faced with corn, the plant more a decoration, the guidebook says, than insulation. Still, here we are and everyone's hungry, so we stop, eat oily grilled cheese at a tourist trap across the street, then wander over for a peek.

It's an explosion of corn. Orange, white, purple. Inside, one entire wall is covered, row upon row of different colors, in stripes, like a giant vegetable parody of the flag.

We gape as a group for a few minutes, then separate and browse. I drift over to the for-sale area, a scattering of folding tables. Paintings of cowboys on bucking horses, brass belt buckles, wooden toys. Half a dozen others mill around, listlessly picking up items and putting them back. Business isn't brisk.

In a distant corner I spot Danny and Jake. They've found the gun display. So far the only thing they like about the trip is the abundance of firearm paraphernalia available at every gas station and convenience store—caps, smoke bombs, plastic rifles. I'm fingering a replica of a pioneer woman's bonnet when Arthur returns from the men's room smelling of antiseptic soap.

He pinches my behind. Nothing can see besides the corn. "You'd make a cute frontier woman," he says, winking, then leaning his head against mine. We haven't had sex since getting in the car.

I hold up the limp cotton bonnet, ties dangling. "Yes, my grandmother Sadie from the Bronx prepared me well for life on the prairie."

Arthur puffs himself up and hooks his thumbs into his T-shirt where suspenders would be. "And my zayde, Morris the tailor, did the same for me. Taught me how to ranch and ride and sew up my Stetson if the band should, God forbid, get torn." He smiles. It's funny and not funny. What are we doing heading to Moscow, Idaho, a couple of myopic New York Jews on revved-up eastern standard time? We aren't the venturesome types. Arthur's only other sabbatical was in New Jersey. He gives me a pat and we go off to see the boys. They're hovering over the cases of bows and arrows. The term archery as I know it—as in *Camp Shalom offers drama, dance, radio and archery!*— seems ludicrous here.

"Great stuff," Arthur says to Danny, who's more willing than Jake at this moment to acknowledge that he has parents and that we are them. They're looking at arrowheads. I know this from the sign: *Genuine Arrowheads.* "You know, the Indians didn't have firearms until Champlain introduced them in 1610. He wanted to build an alliance with the Algonquin against the Iroquois, who were getting in the way of the French fur trade." Jake stands to the side as if he were some kid who happened to wander over and is listening to someone else's father spout off awhile but can drift away as he pleases. In the guise of a person not related to us, he actually seems to be paying attention. "It was a huge change when you think about it," Arthur says. "A history of traditional warfare among tribes that went back thousands of years, and then, *poof,* it's forever altered by a single act of colonialism and greed."

Danny nods slowly, stares into the case.

"Do you know what I mean by colonialism?" Arthur says. Danny shrugs.

"It's when someone who doesn't live in a place comes in and starts taking the local resources for themselves. Like the animal pelts for furs in Champlain's time. Or oil or cheap labor in ours."

"Like going on sabbatical," Danny says.

Arthur looks at him, brow furrowed. "How do you mean?"

"Because we're coming to a place from the outside."

Arthur smiles a smile of teacherly understanding. Magnanimous, generous, and it's going to get him into trouble. He has high hopes for our sons for the coming months; they can learn to fish and chop wood and identify wildlife and edible plants, get to feel at home in the natural world. Something he says he never got as a boy. "Actually, it's the opposite with a sabbatical," he says. "We're going to Idaho to appreciate it, not to use anything of theirs or take anything away."

Jake makes a tapping noise on the glass with his fingernail. We all turn. "That's not true," he says. "We're using the *idea* of Idaho. To make us feel cool and adventurous. Which is kind of sucking off them, you could say." Arthur stares at him, stunned. I can't tell if it's the use of the word sucking that's got him speechless or Jake's suddenly sophisticated logic. "Mental colonialism," Jake says. "To make us feel good about ourselves. And to do something to spiff up our life because you—though not Danny or me or Mom—thought our life was too boring." He waits a moment, then, like a stranger who suddenly remembers he has to catch a bus, purposefully strides off.

~

"I feel terrible about last night," Melanie said the day after the roast beef dinner, inching up on the couch and crushing an edge of the Sunday *Times*. She and Leo had rushed over the minute she knew we were awake. "I had no idea you were thinking of a sabbatical. I was in the kitchen, I missed half the conversation."

"Don't worry about it," I said. Arthur wasn't home.

242

He was at the Y playing basketball with Jake while Danny was in the pool. It was the second Sunday in a row. Father-son bonding, Arthur was determined to see improvement. First the gym, then pizza. The week before, Jake had tried to lose Arthur in the locker room and Danny had refused to eat, but other than that, Arthur said the project was going great.

"Anyway, it wasn't the sabbaticals that broke up your other marriages, right?" Melanie said to Leo. Leo nodded obediently. "See?" Melanie said to me. "They were rocky from the start. What good marriage goes down the tubes in six months? Even a year." She looked at Leo again. "It wasn't their sabbatical that broke up Jeff and Gail Sobel, right? Or those people who lived around the block from you, Bill and Aileen, they had two teenage kids, she taught history?" She turned to me. "Aileen said it had been bad for ages, the year away was just the straw breaking the camel's back."

"And think of all the marriages where nothing happened," Leo said, a little wooden. They'd obviously rehearsed. "All those couples where the time away didn't change a thing."

"That's right," said Melanie, nodding enthusiastically.

"Like who?" I said. It was ridiculous, I didn't even know these people.

"Who?" Melanie said. She turned to Leo. "What about that couple that went to Michigan?"

He shook his head.

"Okay, Bob Fenner from Sociology. They went to France." He waved her off.

"Wait, I know," Melanie said. "Gene and Marcy from the gourmet club. They had a great sabbatical. They talk about it all the time, somewhere in California, the best year of their lives."

"No, no," Leo said. "They *met* on sabbatical. They were each married to someone else. They broke up two marriages and created a third. I don't think anyone would call that a positive net gain."

~

In a Motel 6 in Rapid City I check the Yellow Pages for synagogues. Under Churches I find Black Hills Hebrew Congregation, with a post office box and phone number.

"What are you going to do? Decide we suddenly need to go to services en route?" Arthur says, a towel around his waist, his skin damp from the pool. The kids are robotically channel-surfing in their wet bathing suits on the other bed. When I glance up, Bugs Bunny is leaning against a doorway, gnawing a carrot and waiting for a bucket of cement to fall on Porky Pig. Jake laughs. Danny is braced against the headboard, hugging a pillow. His face is stone. He's hardly said a word all day. Whatever is in his head is on a long slow simmer, and he won't let it out. "Our whole married life this Jewish thing has been just an annoying obligation for you, and now, in South Dakota, you're searching the phone book for rabbis?"

"I'm not looking for rabbis," I retort, flipping to the White Pages. It's true that I resisted joining a temple until the last possible minute and only to sign up Jake for bar mitzvah lessons for an event none of us cares about and is being staged entirely for the grandparents. Still.

"No? Then what are you looking for?"

"Names. Seeing if there are any Cohens, Goldbergs."

Arthur laughs, then goes into the bathroom. I hear the shower. Bugs is madly running around in circles, making a perfect manhole for the pig to fall into. Jake's hysterical. Danny looks like he's going to cry. I know I should ask what's wrong but I'm too tired to find out.

I opt for the cowardly approach. "Don't like the cartoon, honey?"

Danny shrugs.

"Do you want to pick the next show? Jake doesn't own the remote, you know."

Another shrug.

It's not like I don't know the drill. Danny has to be prodded, pried, and then it comes pouring out. Unlike Jake, who simply emotes, then lets it go and now sits here laughing his head off after palling around with Arthur in the pool like his best friend.

But after seven hours in the car I don't have the energy for Danny, who needs to be cajoled, worked. I tell myself he has to learn. That in real life people aren't going to massage out his emotions for him. I go back to flipping the onionskin pages. Goldman. Goldstein. Arthur comes out of the bathroom smelling of shampoo and wearing a crisp clean summer shirt, and sits next to me, sneaking an arm around my shoulders. Bugs is burping his way through *The Blue Danube Waltz*. Jake is convulsed with laughter. Danny holds the pillow tight against his chest, goose bumps covering his skinny arms.

"So, how many have you got so far?" Arthur says, nibbling at my neck.

"None." I flip to the K's, trolling for Kaplan, Katz. I know this is ridiculous. I barely acknowledge the whole ethnic thing at home, but suddenly it's supremely important to assure myself there are Jews in Rapid City, a name that sounds like it was made up for a TV show.

"Good," Arthur whispers into my ear, then sticks his tongue inside. There's a tingle deep in my spine. Could we send the kids to the fogged up mini-arcade next to the pool to play games for half an hour? If Jake takes Danny downstairs and Danny falls apart, am I a terrible mother? If I ease Arthur away from me to go tend to my sad-eyed son, am I a terrible wife? Bugs is now tormenting Porky, who's a Freud caricature, confusing the pig by switching positions so that Porky's on the couch confessing and Bugs is in the chair taking notes. "We're cut loose from our moorings," Arthur whispers, his breath hot in my ear. "Nobody we know. Nothing familiar." He nibbles my ear lobe. "Free to be just you and me."

~

For a year after Danny was born, Arthur and I didn't make love. The cessation wasn't immediate, but after awhile it was obvious I felt nothing and was doing Arthur a favor. I'd lie there, trying to seem attentive, and he would be up there doing all the work. Eventually it turned confrontational, Arthur saying he hadn't married a rag doll and that lovemaking like that was like making love alone.

When Danny turned one and nothing had changed,

we went to a sex therapist. Or, more accurately, Arthur
dragged me to a sex therapist. I figured the feelings would
come back on their own, but Arthur was edgy, tense. He
was on sabbatical in New Jersey then, an hour and a half
commute he did four times a week. The therapist said
all the right things. *It happens. Motherhood. Hormonal
changes. Our bodies are not machines.* But then she went
ahead and did the machine thing anyway. Exercises.
Homework. Controlled in-house pornography. It was like
needing to re-ignite the pilot light, she said. Get the thing
to catch fire again, then it would stay lit. Like a gas oven.
Or your boiler.

For ten months we got on the subway every Thursday
evening and talked in her airless Fort Greene office about
excruciatingly personal matters: positions, my anatomy,
allegedly dormant fantasies that refused to get up off the
floor and spark anything. I felt like a lab rat, every glimmer
of private desire duly reported and picked apart as if I
weren't in the room. I began to imagine a separation. I
loved Arthur and I knew he loved me, but we were both
so unhappy that after awhile I just wanted to make the
unhappiness go away. I would think of Arthur getting an
apartment in Newark and visiting the boys on weekends;
because of the sabbatical we'd have months before we had
to go public. But I didn't say anything to Arthur about
splitting up. He said that as long as we were getting help,
nothing bad had to happen; what mattered was that we
were trying. Occasionally, to test myself, I would picture
him with another woman, holding hands or laughing or
even kissing, but I made myself shove the images away

because a heavy ache would begin to seep into my chest, like my heart squeezing itself.

Meanwhile the days rolled on, weeks and months, and we'd go out with our friends, even in our sadness, and have barbecues with our neighbors and drinks with Arthur's department buddies. A whole network of people who knew us, who saw us as a family, a couple, a team. And because of them, I'd remember what we had together and be pulled back from the brink.

~

On the highway we see signs for Whitefish, Montana, and billboards advertising local restaurants and shops. The boys don't want to hear why the Whitefish Bagel Company sounds funny; don't care to have described for them all the legendary breakfast fishes of my childhood, my newfound interest in our personal anthropology irritating. It doesn't help that it's ninety degrees in the car because the air-conditioning has stopped working.

"There's another one," Danny says. "Look, Mom. Quick."

"What?" It's two o'clock and I am forcing myself to stay awake. The hot air gusting in from the open windows isn't making it easy.

"On the median. Hurry, you're going to miss it."

It looks like a huge rat with a gigantic tail. Arthur slows down so we can see.

"It's a beaver," Danny says.

"What's a beaver doing out here?" I say.

"Probably got lost getting to his river," Jake says

248

from the back where he's in his usual baronial pose. "The highway goes right over his dam, I bet. Probably cuts his path right in half."

The tail is the worst part, unnaturally flattened. Clumps of fur are scattered on the parched grass. Danny's craning his neck as we pass. When he finally turns around his eyes are wet.

"Rough, huh?" I say, reaching for his hand. He looks pasty and hasn't had an appetite in days except for Dr. Pepper and Skittles. His breath has a treacly, decayed smell. "It's hard to see a dead animal like that."

"Why'd you have to bring us out here?" he blurts out, pulling his hand away. "Why'd you have to take us to where everything gets killed?"

I reach out again but he stiffens and curls himself against his window. "Danny," I say softly. "Sweetheart."

"Go away, Mom!" he says, refusing to look at me. "You made us come out here where it's dangerous and bad and everything dies!"

I glance over at Arthur. He gestures for me to turn around and let Danny calm down. I don't know how Arthur is keeping his cool. The hours spent researching and calling and making arrangements—the water parks, the rafting and hiking and paddleboats, visits to the automotive plant and the cheese factory: he's tried so hard to make it fun. Behind us, Danny is consoling himself with candy; I hear the crackling of the wrapper, smell the chemical fruitiness. Next he'll pop another soda. All that junk and, worse, his need for it. Another arena where I can feel guilty.

~

"Kids are resilient," Melanie says on the phone. We've checked into a Holiday Inn in Kalispell. Arthur and the boys are in the pool, working off the ride. This is my tenth call home in ten days. Two were to my next door neighbor on the pretext of reminding her to take the dill overflowing on our balcony, two to our tenant, Mr. Malouf, for no reason, one to a former co-worker to see how things are going at my old company, which hasn't yet folded and might not after all, and the rest have been to Melanie and a couple of other friends just so I can hear their voices. Arthur's trying to get me to taper off. Have a little faith, honey, he says. Don't be like Lot's wife, always looking back.

"Resilience is overrated," I say. The bed is hard and the sheet feels like sandpaper. "Danny's a mess. He's withdrawn and angry. He's always been sensitive, and now this move, I don't know."

"That doesn't mean he won't get over it," Melanie says.

"Oh? And Leo's kids are doing so great?" I snap.

Melanie goes silent. I'm not being nice. Leo's sons are exhibiting every problem in the book—run-ins with the police, suspensions from school, threatening to drop out—because of all the parental upheavals. "You're right, they suffer," she finally says. "But they do get past it. Most of them. Eventually."

"I'm sorry," I say. "That was mean. I'm just worried."

"Look, I'm not saying life is a picnic for kids," she says. The clock radio reads five o-six, the big eyeball zero looking at me, asking: what are you doing here? "But you can't protect them from every hard thing. Should you

250

deny Arthur a chance to spend half a year in a novel place because Danny doesn't like change? What if Arthur had gotten a new job? What if he hadn't gotten tenure and you had to keep moving until he did? What then?"

I pick at a loose thread on the bedspread.

"You've got to talk to Danny about this, you know."

"But what can we say? That Daddy wanted to go away and it's too bad that you didn't? It's not like this was a necessity. The work is actually sort of low level for Arthur. He's doing it because he wanted something to do, not because he had to."

"So?"

"So Danny's going to see that Arthur's needs come first."

"So?"

It's a revelation. Have we been raising our sons to think it's only about them? Still, the truth feels like a betrayal. *Yes, we love you. But not that much.* I glance at the big picture window. The sky is streaked orange, and then it hits me: this is it, the West. We're here. It's not just Danny who's afraid. "Tell me what happened with Leo's other wives," I press. "The truth."

A pause. Melanie says, "Look, things were okay when they were in their usual routines around all their usual people. But once they left home, it was different. Kind of like a table that manages to stay up on three legs until you try to move it and find out it's been propped up artificially by everything around it. When they were on their own, things were, well, not good."

"But no one's supposed to live like that!" I protest. "All alone as if you're on a desert island or dropped down from

Jupiter. You can't expect to be nonstop blissfully happy. That's the movies, a fantasy, not real life!"

Footsteps in the corridor. They'll be shivering and hungry, and all of a sudden I've had enough of motels and chlorinated towels and bolted TVs, of searching for places to eat and climbing back into the claustrophobic van. We still have ten more days, a working ranch and two more national parks and a trip to a reservation, and all I want is to unpack and make a home and find people to talk to.

"I've got to go," I say. "Give Leo a hug for me. I'm sorry for sniping about his kids."

"Don't worry," Melanie says. "You'll be fine. All four of you will."

I stare out at the huge sky, blazing crimson, alien as Mars.

~

A month before Danny's second birthday, the old feelings began to come back. It was as if a deep anesthesia had worn off, a deadness finally tiring of itself and one night just slinking away. The therapist was triumphant. *Just as I said! Patience and hard work!* Arthur was ecstatic. It didn't matter if the temperature wasn't as high as before; at least there was heat. With the pilot back on, we could safely assume the mercury would rise on its own. Moments after my first bodily shudder in two years, Arthur pulled me to him and wept. *You're back!* he cried. *I love you so much and now you're back, you're finally back!*

I stared at the ceiling. I was back. But I'd had no say over the leaving. The exhaustion, the insatiable need of two little ones, my boundless love for them, the fact that I had only so much to go around: who knew why desire had vanished? *You're going to have to limit how much you give your sons,* the therapist told me at our final session. Even Arthur looked stricken. Our children were four and two years old, and neither Arthur nor I had ever loved anyone as much as we loved those little boys. *How do you do that?* I wanted to say to her. *Tell me: just how do you do that?*

So, yes, I was back. But I had been gone. It had happened. It could happen again. And what if there weren't enough people next time to hold us together, keep us from falling off the edge?

~

Outside Columbia Falls, police cars with flashing lights huddle in the breakdown lane. The rubbernecking is causing a traffic jam. We slow to a crawl and look.

I think it's a bear. Jake says it's an elk. Danny says a horse. Whatever it is seems too big to be felled by a car. A policeman waves us on. I turn to get one last glimpse. There's something other-worldly about a creature that size sprawled on the concrete, as if a serious taboo has been violated, nature itself injured in some fundamental way.

"Maybe it's a bison," Jake says.

"I'm afraid of bison," Danny says. "I don't want to go to that place tomorrow."

Arthur and I exchange looks. He means the National Range. We showed him the pictures last night: hundreds of them, better than at Yellowstone. Jake looked at the brochures for a long time but Danny gave a quick glance and went back to the TV.

253

"Let's wait till we get there to reserve judgment, okay?" Arthur says, smiling into the rear view, trying, always trying. "You might feel differently when you see it."

"You don't get out of the car," I say, turning to Danny. "You just drive through. That's all. A beautiful scenic ride."

"I don't want to see them," Danny says. His voice is trembling. "If you go near them, they'll kill you."

"What are you talking about, sweetheart?" I say. "They're not going to kill anyone."

Tears are rolling down his small face. "That's not what Dad showed us last night. It was in the flyer: don't go near the animals, they run faster than a horse, they weigh a million tons. Remember that drawing of one attacking a man with a camera?"

"Honey, that was an illustration of their safety precautions. Some people think it would be cute to put their three-year-old on a bison and snap a photo."

"I don't care," Danny says, sucking in air, working himself up. "I don't want to get near them, and I don't want our car to get near them." He kicks the back of Arthur's seat. "We have to turn around, Dad! We can't go! Please!"

We're thirty miles from the nearest exit. I could suggest that Arthur pull over but it's not clear what Danny would do—open the door and flee, maybe even dart out onto the highway. "You have to stop this," I say, reaching to grab Danny's foot. "Dad can't drive with you kicking him like that. You may be upset, and also worried about what it'll be like in Idaho, but you can't deal with it by getting hysterical over a visit to a park."

254

"I'm not crying because of Idaho! I'm scared of the buffalo! I don't want us to go near them!"

"Well, don't *make* him go, Mom," Jake says.

"Why don't you stay out of this, Jake?" Arthur says between his teeth.

"Hey, this is my business too," Jake says. Danny has curled up against his window, softly sobbing. "It's probably all fake at that park anyway. Probably not real buffalo, even."

Jake has finally hit it: Arthur's hot button. Nothing is artificial on this trip, he has told them. The ranches are real working ranches. The mining towns are real mining towns. The pow-wows are attended by Native Americans performing their ancestral dances. Even the rodeo on the weekend will be a real rodeo, not some Hollywood extravaganza with stunt artists working off a script from a stage set in L.A.

Jake can't leave it alone. "They probably put the bison out for the tourists," he says. "No wonder Danny doesn't want to go. I don't want to go either. It probably messes up their habitat, all these people staring at them. Probably interferes with their real way of life."

"It *is* their habitat!" Arthur explodes. "It *is* their way of life! If they didn't have the National Range, they'd be extinct! Dead! Kaput! That's what brought them back! If it weren't for the Range, there wouldn't *be* any bison at all, let alone any bison way of life!"

Silence. Jake crosses his arms, stares out his window. Arthur is grinding his teeth, a habit I haven't seen him do in years. Danny whimpers. Ahead of us, on the sloping shoulder, is a small lifeless form. A raccoon or skunk, or maybe a fox. It's long and thin and dark, curved like a question mark.

~

When I was packing up the condo to make space for the Maloufs, I found the classifieds of an old *New York Daily News* in the bottom of Arthur's desk in the den. He hadn't used the desk in years, it was small and impractical, but it had belonged to his parents and he didn't have the heart to give it away. The newspaper was from the year he'd taught in New Jersey, on sabbatical. A dozen apartment ads had been circled, and there were notes in Arthur's handwriting in the margins. *Lg studio Bushwick. One bdrm Brooklyn Hgts willing to negotiate.* Next to one he'd written: *no lease, month to month, half hour from home avail Jan 1. Best option?*

I took the newspaper and put it in my sweater drawer, then cleaned out the rest of the desk. Old syllabi, outdated faculty handbooks. I doubted Arthur had any idea what was in there. When it came time to clean out my dresser, I piled everything on the bed. Arthur was in the bathroom in the hall, clearing out the medicine cabinet. He was whistling something peppy he'd heard on the radio. I hadn't seen him so happy in months. He couldn't wait to get on the road. To drive, he said, with the three people he loved most in the world across this vast beautiful country. I picked up the newspaper. It was dated November. Arthur had started teaching in September. We'd been in therapy for four months by then. I stared at Arthur's neat script, at the watery blue circles, then brought the paper over to the big trash bag in the doorway and shoved it in with the broken toys and moldy sneakers and everything else that was wrecked and ruined that we would never need to see again, then tied the bag closed and dragged it to the front door for Arthur to haul to the curb to be taken away in the morning.

~

A rosy dusk. I am driving. Arthur sits with Danny in the middle seat of the van playing checkers, and Jake has taken the opportunity to extricate himself from his backseat lair for the first time since New York and sit up front with me where he gets to rule over the maps and the air-conditioning, which, miraculously, is now working. Over dinner we talked again about the bison range, and Danny has agreed to sit in the Visitors Center with Jake and watch the educational videos.

"So tomorrow," Jake says, looking at the map, "you and Dad'll drive around the place for an hour or so, then we head out?"

"Depends," I say, watching the road.

Jake looks up. "Depends on what?"

"Depends on what we see. It can take two or three hours if a lot of the herd is out."

Jake pauses—he's deeply regretting siding with Danny and having to babysit him—then goes back to the map. Behind us, Danny allows himself to sound a little happy. He's beating Arthur in checkers, and Arthur's not even letting him. I hear the clack-clack of the magnetic pieces.

A triple jump, Danny cleaning up. The game was Arthur's idea. You had to keep trying, he told me in the restaurant parking lot, the boys ahead of us finishing their ice cream. Because in the end all we had was each other.

No one sees the deer. Later, Arthur will say he heard the faint knocking of a hoof before the sound of the window shattering, will say he remembers movement in his peripheral vision as the car swerved, the animal, almost flying, leaping over the back of the van before disappearing into the woods.

All I hear is Danny yelling that the back window is smashed. There's a sudden gust of hot air and Arthur says, forced calm, "Honey, you need to pull over. Nice and easy, just put on your signal and pull over."

I maneuver into the breakdown lane, then turn around. The van is filled with shards, tiny diamonds glinting on the floor, the coolers, the food bags. Silvery droplets shimmering in the last of the light. "What happened?" I say, frozen.

"Deer hit the car, honey. You need to turn off the ignition. Just turn the key, that's right."

There's a person by the passenger door.

"You folks okay?" I glance in the side mirror. An RV that's been behind us for several miles is parked in the breakdown lane. A woman stands beside it, looking into the trees.

Jake opens his door, gets out. Glass crunches under his feet.

"What happened?" I ask the man through the open door.

"Deer flew right out of the woods, tried to clear your

258

car," he says. He sticks his head inside. "I see he got your window."

We all look. The space is a gaping mouth. Jake's pillow looks like it's been stabbed.

"Jesus," Arthur says. If Jake were lying there, his face would be a pin cushion. Arthur opens the sliding door, climbs down, helps Danny out, then comes to my side. The man follows. There are blood spots on my leg, little rivulets above the knee. I'm the only one in shorts.

"I've got some first aid in the RV," the man says as I step down.

"Thanks, we've got a pretty good kit with us," Arthur says, trying to sound steady as we move around to the other side of the van. Danny and Jake sit on the grass. The man's wife is walking over with an armful of Cokes and hands two to the boys, puts two more on the ground.

"Awfully scary, being hit," she says. They're an older couple, maybe retired.

"Those deer look small but they're powerful," the man says. "Those hooves? One kick and they can take out a door." He walks to the back of the van with Arthur. His wife stands near me and the boys, who are quietly sipping their sodas. "Yep," the man calls from the back. "You've got yourselves a dent, all right."

"You boys see the deer?" the woman asks.

Danny shakes his head. "No," Jake says. "I was up front. With my mom. That's my seat back there," he says, pointing with his chin to where Arthur and the man are standing. "Usually I'm lying down, listening to my headphones and stuff."

"Well, that's a lucky break, isn't it," the woman says to Jake. "Someone was watching out for you today, I'd say."

"There's a row of car places in Missoula," the man says, coming back with Arthur to our side of the van. "Right off the highway. Can't miss it. I'll bet there's even a dealer there, fix up your window in a jiffy."

"We've got a broom in the RV," the woman offers. "Sweep up the glass."

"That's okay," I say. I don't want them getting slivers in their broom. Besides, it'll take hours. There's not a surface that isn't covered. "We'll vacuum it when we pull off. Or maybe they'll clean it up for us in Missoula."

"Sure you can ride all right now?" the woman asks.

"We've got some towels we can sit on," Arthur says. "But thanks for your concern."

The woman nods. The man says, "Well, then, we'll be on our way."

"Wait! What happened to the deer?" Danny, urgent. He's asking the couple, pleading, really.

"Oh, it ran off into the woods, honey," the woman says.

"Do you think it was hurt?"

"Well, if it was, it must not've been that bad. Didn't see any blood on the window frame or the car. Only blood here looks like your mother's."

"Mom?" Danny's eyes go wide. "Mom's bleeding?"

"Just a few cuts," I say, looking down at my knee. "It's not anything we can't handle."

"Oh, right!" Arthur says, suddenly flustered, reaching under the passenger seat for the first aid kit. He's got a lot to do and he can't afford to waste any time. It's getting dark and there's glass in my leg to get out and a car to make drivable and two children sipping Cokes by the side of the highway wondering what the next big thing will be. Still, there's a palpable sense of relief. Something has happened. Whatever we've been waiting for has happened, and I feel a weight lifting off me, something that had been sitting on my chest for weeks, maybe years. Even Danny's not crying anymore, and we can tell he's done with that, at least for now, and that we can go on.

Arthur pulls out the plastic case and shakes the glass onto the gravel, then spreads a clean towel on the grass next to the boys for me to sit on. "Well, we won't intrude," the woman says.

"Thanks for the Cokes," Jake says, holding up his can.

"You bet," the man says, "take care now," and they walk away.

The moon is a pale disk in the purple-slashed sky. Ahead of us is the open road, sixty miles to Missoula. Beside me, on the weedy ground, Danny puts his head in my lap and Jake sidles over, and I close my eyes and listen to the trees behind us and the sound of Jake sipping, and let Arthur tend to the wounds, carefully picking out the shards with his tweezers, gently cleaning each cut and bandaging it well enough so that we can get back in the car and, together, continue on our way.

ROOTS

· ◊ ·

HIRSCHMAN, UNWILLING TO BEND, was refusing to participate. A lifelong agnostic, and proud of it, he'd managed for eighty-two years to not observe a single of his people's canonical festivals except in its breach, and he had no intention of starting now. It was his father's way before him, and his father's father's, and now it was his. He ate bread on Passover, went to the track on Yom Kippur, and, since childhood, had miraculously avoided the trappings of this one, the relentlessly marketed Jewish Christmas when boys and girls with names like Cohen and Levy were commanded to ignore the country's love affair with eggnog and fruitcake in favor of oily potato dishes invented by starving peasants in Galicia. Not that the so-called historic origins of the holiday were any better, Hirschman liked to remind himself, the ancient Maccabee brothers a posse of religious fanatics who killed any fellow Jew who didn't agree with them and their visions of a theocracy that, to Hirschman's lights, wasn't all that different from the Taliban's or an ayatollah's Iran.

But now Hirschman's octogenarian resolve was being shaken at its root like a flimsy pine grasped around the trunk by a gorilla, threatened to be loosened of its footings by the least likely person on the planet: his daughter.

The daughter! Need Hirschman even think about all that he and his long dead wife had endured because of Wendy? A list a mile long and everything a man of his years had once read about on screaming covers of *Time*. Drugs, abortions, political arrests, the FBI knocking on their door, serial boyfriends, some, apparently, if briefly, quasi-spousal. A list so predictable that, decades back, Hirschman stopped looking to the telephone for news of Wendy's life and simply bought the magazines. And now this daughter was turning fifty—fifty! almost as old as Hirschman!—and trying for respectable, with a regular job and ladies suits and a six-months-old marriage to an actual husband, a long-faced man named Ronald who drove a Ford. A daughter who was now entreating Hirschman to come over and light Hanukkah candles with Ronald's even longer-faced thirteen-year-old son where Hirschman

264

could—in Wendy's painfully submissive pleading—rediscover his "roots."

"Roots?" Hirschman declaimed on the extension in the bedroom where he'd been soaking his feet in Epsom Salts. Of all his bodily parts, Hirschman's feet were, hands down, his least attractive. Marilyn used to say they were Satanic, with sharp yellow nails that curled under and toes bonily misshapen like the beckoning fingers of a fairy tale witch. Hirschman had come to view his feet as a separate part of his being, the workhorses of his body, the sad ugly oxen pulling the plow.

"What roots?" he said, splashing lightly in the chipped plastic dish bin he'd rescued from a neighbor's trash. Hirschman was not merely an agnostic but a frugal agnostic, platforms that seemed to him not unrelated, for what was dogma if not the lavishing of excessive belief on the wholly unnecessary, not to mention unprovable? "They were thieves, my ancestors. Crooks. They stole from their business partners and screwed their customers. They came here from Russia like the British went to Australia, as ex-cons, fleeing. What do you think, everyone had a father like Bashevis Singer's with his saintly rabbinical court? Tevya from *Fiddler on the Roof*?"

A long sigh. Wendy's forbearance. Her father was old and ornery, the sigh said to the reliably choleric Ronald, who was probably hovering in the middle distance drinking a glass of low-fat milk. Or jingling his car keys. Hirschman had seen the man maybe half a dozen times despite the geographical proximity, fifteen Queens blocks between them, and always he was playing with those keys.

Hirschman didn't know what his son-in-law did for a living and was afraid to ask.

"Look," Hirschman said, feeling sorry for his daughter, the wall-eyed Ronald no doubt lurking darkly, the reputedly brainy son hanging his oversized head, weighted down with too many compound thoughts. "You don't want to connect with these roots, believe me. Liars and cheats, and on your mother's side, no better." Though Hirschman had no idea who stretched up Marilyn's family tree. Maybe they were saints. More likely they were deli wholesalers, skimming the profits like his wife used to skim the fat off the chicken soup. With a little too much zeal.

"Anyway, what's this talk about roots?" he said and immediately regretted it. He could see the magazine covers already. *The Return to Religion: The New Tribalism*. He liked it better when Wendy was insolent and yelled *Death to the pigs*! at a couple of off-duty cops having a cup of coffee at a local diner before Marilyn pulled her away.

"Is it because he isn't your grandson?" Wendy ventured. "Your own flesh and blood?"

"Who?" Hirschman said, lifting his pruney feet, now pale and tender, and letting them down onto the stiff towel. They rested there like two tired mules.

"Who?" Wendy said. "Jason, of course."

Jason. Who must be the key jingler's boy. Hirschman didn't remember the child's name. He could say he had a bad memory but it wasn't true. He was just a bad man. He loved Wendy, but with all the human appendages she'd accumulated over the years and then lopped off like so much spring pruning, it had been hard to keep track.

"Ah, the boy," Hirschman said. "Of course not. I'd be equally disinterested if he were the fruit of your own loins."

"Oh God, Dad, do you have to put it that way? *Fruit of the loins?*"

"What? Fruit? Loins? What should I say? Issue?"

"Oh, never mind. I just thought—." His feet were dry. He slipped them into his lined slippers, his one indulgence: sheepskin outside, soft fur inside. Two warm caves. They made his bestial extensions feel at home. The same extensions that had gone through life frightening locker room attendants and lifeguards and—dare he think of it?—women after Marilyn. There had been only a few and never with the lights on. "You know, a family thing," Wendy was saying. "A few songs. Not that I know any but Ronald does. So I just thought, well—."

And then he heard it. It was in those pauses. The hopeless giving-up. Pre-emptive despair. She was trying to make a go of it. Trading in the last boyfriend, the final contestant in a decades-long parade of unwashed ponytails with no jobs who, now deep into middle age, were still pretending unemployment was a matter of principle and mouthing bromides even Emma Goldman had stopped believing in. This was Wendy's chance, a last lunge to capture a normal life with the dull office clothes, the steady job, the regular if rigid husband, the stab at motherhood which, thank God, was only part-time, she'd whispered to Hirschman outside City Hall before the marriage ceremony. A boy, thirteen years old, what was she supposed to do with him? Fortunately the child's mother was a jackhammer who had no intention of divvying up custody. Ronald had only old-fashioned father's visitation rights on weekends and one night in the middle of the week.

And now here was his daughter asking for something. She hadn't asked him for anything in thirty-five years except to get out of the way. Or to post bail.

The boy was at the house with his homemade menorah from Hebrew School concocted out of a strip of metal and a row of glued-on washers from a discount plumbing supply. "So I just thought," Wendy again sighed, discouraged. "Maybe if you could come over for a little while--."

Hirschman moved his toes in the soft cushioning. His shoes, those cruel prisons, sat in wait by the closet door.

"Okay, okay, I'll come over." Because who cared if Hirschman believed or not? If the candles slid into their plumbers' leftovers in silence or in song, with a blessing or a sneer? After eighty-two years he had made his point.

~

The boy was as Hirschman remembered. Bookish, slightly surly, sour-looking. He mumbled a subterranean greeting from a remote region of his larynx and vanished.

"Hello, Stanley," Ronald murmured. There was never a question of calling Hirschman Dad because who was anyone kidding? Hirschman would no sooner be Ronald's father than Ronald's dead father would be Hirschman's buddy, the older man, whose name Hirschman had forgotten, once some sort of higher-up in the city's Department of Education. Self-satisfied and smug—Hirschman had asked around—the type who'd look down on the less educated Hirschman, a veteran of sixty years in the oily trenches of the garment business. Anyway, Hirschman was too old to take on anybody else as progeny. If Ronald ever started calling him Pop, he'd correct him in a withering instant.

"Take your coat, Dad?" Wendy said, fluttering to the door. Who was this nervous woman with painted fingernails and gray wool slacks and a death-pallor beige cardigan and anxious trill in her voice, prim little pearl things in her ears like a schoolmarm's sweater buttons? He liked her better when she was foul-mouthed and getting arrested.

He shed his outerwear, stamped his shoes to release the city's slush onto the mat, and shuffled inside. The aroma of frying oil rushed at him, a reminder of Bronx kitchens seventy-five years past, toothless old ladies smiling and offering him glasses of spinach soup.

"Where's Jason?" Wendy asked her husband.

"I don't know. He's driving me nuts," Ronald said and strode off in search.

"Problem with the boy?" Hirschman asked his daughter, who had somehow sprouted an apron.

"Nothing out of the ordinary," she sighed, pulling out a kitchen chair for him. "Half an hour ago he couldn't wait for you to get here. Now he's disappeared." She glanced around, looking, Hirschman was certain, for a cigarette. She'd given up the habit upon meeting the clean-living Ronald. Hirschman wished he had one to sneak to her. "I'm probably not handling him all that well. I don't know how to be strict. Or consistent. Ronald says he needs consistency."

Unkind thoughts leapt to Hirschman's mind, preparing to light onto his tongue and release their trenchant substance into the overheated room. Hirschman heroically held them at bay.

"Teenagers," Wendy said, sinking into a chair opposite. "They're difficult, you know?" and Hirschman nodded. No irony? Didn't she remember? What kind of adolescent did she think she'd been? Nancy Drew? Patty Hearst before the machine guns?

He was rescued from offering useless opiates—*He'll grow out of it. Worry when he's thirty-five*—when the boy shambled in, followed by his irritable father.

"So, shall we light?" Wendy said too brightly, bounding up, and then Hirschman knew: a problem in the marriage. Wendy had told him she'd known Ronald only two months—a matchmaking service on the computer—before they'd decided to wed. She'd have skipped the legalities but Ronald said it was necessary because of the boy. There'd been enough trouble weighing on the child because of his mother, who'd been nasty, turning him against his father, and Ronald couldn't afford another ounce of ammunition in her arsenal.

The boy shrugged, eyeing Hirschman suspiciously. Wendy set up the candles, alternating blue and red and white in a patriotic display. Her husband struck a match, lit the chief candle that lit all the others, then handed it to his son, who dutifully complied. Ronald, solo, droned the blessings. Again Hirschman controlled himself. The last time he'd heard such a recitation was in the hospital a few weeks before Marilyn died. Some busybody from

Chabad insisted on dropping in on all the patients with Jewish last names to deliver tin foil menorahs and candles. Marilyn's roommate, a Mrs. Schwartz dying of lung cancer, had joyfully welcomed the visit. From behind the partition, Hirschman and Marilyn had to listen to the Hasid's chanting, but when the man slid the curtain aside and stepped into Marilyn's half of the room, Hirschman yelled at him to go away and take his implements of fundamentalism with him.

Now Hirschman felt a heat rising in the back of his neck as his son-in-law concluded the rituals. Ronald was precise, exacting, no words left out, he explained. When you do things, you have to do them right. Which called to mind what Wendy had told Hirschman about the Ford. Ronald was devoted to his automobile. Each weekend, he lovingly washed it and waxed it and wouldn't let Wendy drive it. It needed to be kept pristine. The boy glanced around the dining room in expectation. Hirschman followed his gaze. Wrapped packages on a side table, the telltale blue and white paper: Hallmark reaping an equal opportunity profit.

"All right! Everyone ready for latkes?"

Wendy was trying too hard. Which meant Ronald had something going on, something on the side. Hirschman had a nose for such things. Soon Ronald would be fishing for excuses. He'd say Wendy was a bad stepmother. Or, worse, a bad Jew.

"Delicious," Hirschman pronounced, heaping on the sour cream. "You take only applesauce?" he asked his son-in-law.

"Cholesterol, Stanley. Most of us are careful. At our

age." He looked at his son's plate. A snowy pyramid. "Sour cream is for the young. And foolish."

"So I guess I'm young." Hirschman sipped his ginger ale. "Shall I tell you about our forebears?" he asked the boy.

Jason looked up from his plate. "Your what?"

"Forebears. Would you like to know about my ancestors? My roots?"

The boy shrugged and resumed shoveling in his food.

"This is what holidays are for," Hirschman said. "To connect with tradition."

The air was heavy, cooking oil mixed with dread and the scent of looming divorce. Hirschman wiped his mouth with a napkin. "Here's one. A relative in Poland named Yankel. The original Ponzi schemer. He sold shares in a lumber business. So-called shares. You gave him your zlotkes, or whatever the currency was, for a weight of wood, and for half again more money he gave you the right to collect an equal amount of wood when your first supply ran out. This included milling, planing, curing, delivery, the works. A great deal. He criss-crossed the countryside, cleaning up.

"But eventually people starting calling in their chits. They wanted their second delivery. No dice. He didn't have the lumber and he didn't have the money to buy it. He'd spent everything on keeping up with the original orders and skimming to make himself rich. He hightailed it to a boat to America and vanished. A millionaire. Which was no small change in 1902." Hirschman tapped the table, triumphant. "This is one of my more stellar relations."

The child was open-mouthed. Finally he said, "How

272

did you ever hear this story, then? If he vanished?"

Hirschman pointed to the boy. "Smart thinking. He couldn't resist boasting. It was his downfall. He died under suspicious circumstances."

"I never heard that story, Dad," Wendy said.

"There's a lot about our family you don't know."

"Did you have more relatives like him?" Jason asked.

"Sure. My grandfather, for instance. Now, he was really something."

Ronald stood up, began to collect the plates.

"What're you doing?" Hirschman asked.

"Clearing the table."

"I'm telling a story here."

"That's okay. I'm just cleaning up."

"Sit down," Hirschman said. "I'm not finished."

Jason glanced at his father. Wendy looked at her husband. Ronald sat down.

"My grandfather," Hirschman said, turning back to the boy, "worked in a tavern. In Ukraine. Part of Russia then. But he had sticky fingers. He couldn't help lifting some of the cash. A lot of the cash. When the tavern owner found out, he had to make a quick getaway. He sent his wife and three small children to Canada and went into hiding. When he arrived in Montreal eight years later, my father had no idea who he was. Neither did anybody else. Because he'd changed his name, did a little facial rearranging, not exactly expert plastic surgery in those days but enough to do the trick. And, to complete the picture, showed up with an entirely new family. New wife, new children. First case of identity theft ever documented."

Wendy burst out laughing. "Where do you get these from?" she said.

"What? It's true." The boy was watching them. "My father told me." He held up a hand. "Scout's honor. His father maintained two separate families till the day he died. They lived on the same street. Everyone pretended there had been two brothers and that one had died young and that the surviving brother was helping the widow and children. For years my father thought the others were his cousins."

"Who did your grandfather live with?"

"Technically his first family—my father and his mother and brothers. But he spent a lot of nights down the street."

"Cool," Jason said.

Ronald drummed his fingers.

"Can we have the presents now?" Jason said.

"Sure," Wendy said and began moving the gifts to the couch. The boy followed. Ronald got up to clear the plates. Hirschman brought his into the kitchen.

"What was that all about, Stanley?" Ronald said. "That was the most ridiculous bullshit I've ever heard. And I don't especially appreciate my kid hearing about these kinds of things."

"Lighten up, Ron. Anyway, there's a moral to these stories."

Ronald piled the plates in the sink. "Oh? What's that? Crime pays? Bigamy is fun?"

"No. You can run but you can't hide. That's the moral. If you're screwing around and want out of the marriage, fine. But don't make my daughter feel like a lousy stepmother or a bad Jew."

Ronald wheeled around. "What the hell are you talking about?"

"It's written all over you. You're a bum in a fancy suit. She should have stayed with her long-haired anarchist. He had a big mouth but he kept his pants zipped."

~

What Wendy wanted to know was how he'd picked it up so fast. Practically before he'd gotten inside the house.

"Instinct. And experience."

"You cheated on Mom?" She leaned across the formica and lowered her voice so the other diner patrons wouldn't hear, even though Marilyn had been dead twenty-five years.

"No. But half my friends cheated on their wives. This was the dress business, remember. Models, buyers, they expected it. I was the exception."

"But he seemed to be so not the type. So..." She trailed off.

"Straight-laced? Fussy? It's always the ones you least suspect."

"I'm scared, Dad. I'm fifty and I'm alone."

"So? I'm eighty-two and I'm alone."

"But you had Mom."

"And you had Ronald. And Pierre and Max and all the others. *Tempus fugit* but that doesn't mean it *fugits* and leaves you with nothing."

The waitress brought their hamburgers. "So where will you go?" Hirschman asked, assembling his meal. Tomato, onion, cole slaw, pickle, all of it went inside the bun. Wendy had told him she didn't want to stay in the house another minute. Too many bad feelings and all of Ronald's belongings. Plus those drab awful clothes he'd wanted her to wear. Replicas of his first wife's wardrobe, she now realized, but two sizes smaller. He'd wanted to remake his ex and then reject her so he'd come out on the winning end this time. "You can stay with me," Hirschman said.

"That's okay, Dad. I'll find another place. We finally like each other. Why spoil a good thing?"

~

Meantime something rankled. How could Ronald get away with it? He'd hurt Wendy. This offended Hirschman's principles. His father, his grandfather, all his bold forebears: they wouldn't have hesitated.

He made a plan.

He drove to the house and parked across the street, opened his trunk, took out the big four-pronged lug wrench. His son-in-law's car, the beloved Ford, sleek and beetle black in the driveway, gleamed in the afternoon light. Unwilling to risk scratches, Ronald took the bus to work, even though, Wendy said, the office—on the other side of Queens, insurance underwriting; why was Hirschman not surprised?—had free parking. The street was quiet, even the dogs watching from the windows were quiet. Hirschman approached the vehicle. It looked like a police cruiser, a limousine, a hearse. It shone like a jewel and this amazed Hirschman: here lived a man who washed and waxed and polished an automobile each week, caressing it like a woman.

He moved to the rear of the car and brought the wrench down onto the back bumper. Nothing. He applied the tool to the fender. A slight but satisfying indentation.

"What're you doing?"

In the doorway, the boy. He stood outside in his school clothes.

"You'll catch cold," Hirschman said. "Go get a jacket."

"What are you doing with my father's car?"

Hirschman looked at the lug wrench. "I'm returning this. I thought the trunk would be open. Your father said he'd leave the trunk open."

"No. He'd never leave the trunk open."

Hirschman shrugged. "Well, I thought that's what he said."

The boy hugged himself, cold. "I'd open it for you, but I'm not allowed. I can't touch the car. My father won't let me."

"I'll take this home then," Hirschman said, lifting the tool. "I'll bring it back another time."

The boy was considering. "Well, maybe I should open it. Just this once. Then you don't have to make the trip again."

"No, don't do that," Hirschman said, because Ronald would see the dent and blame the child. Better Ronald should wonder if it was some cosmic punishment. Or hear from the child that Hirschman had come by and put two and two together.

"How's Wendy?" Jason said while Hirschman put the lug wrench into his own trunk.

"She's okay. What are you doing here by yourself?"

"I come to my dad's on Wednesdays. But he doesn't get home from work until seven." Jason looked at the house. "Want to come in?" Then he added, "I won't tell my father."

~

Jason made him tea and showed him his room. On his desk were papers he'd printed off the Internet about Leopold and Loeb.

"You know who they were?" Jason asked.

"Of course. Everyone knows who they were. Two rich kids from Chicago who wanted to commit the perfect crime. Killed another kid on purpose. Clarence Darrow was their lawyer. Argued against the death penalty, very famous oration. Before my time."

"1924. They were geniuses but they failed." The boy moved the papers around. "My dad is upset that I'm reading about them. But their case was amazing. I try to tell him that not all famous Jews were baseball players or Supreme Court judges. Some of them were criminals. Notorious ones."

"Absolutely," Hirschman said. "And good ones. Smart ones. Right up to Madoff."

"I hadn't thought about that. There's a whole tradition of Jewish crooks."

Hirschman pointed at the boy. "You bet there is. And they're your roots too. My family, all those thieves and con men."

"But Wendy isn't biologically connected to me," Jason

278

said, and seemed more than a little sad when he said it.

"Doesn't matter. It can be your pedigree also."

"How? We aren't related."

"So steal it," Hirschman said. "Who's to know? You want to give yourself a lineage? Then give yourself a lineage."

The boy let him out the front door. As Hirschman neared the behemoth shining in the wintry light, he took his own car key from his pocket and, when Jason couldn't see, held it against the paint, holding it fast as he walked from the rear door to the front bumper, making an unbroken line like the mark of Cain: a straight line across the killer's forehead so that the whole world would see and know what he had done.

~

"I heard you visited Jason," Wendy said on the phone the next day.

"Is that a crime?"

"No. Though vandalizing Ronald's car might be."

"I wouldn't know."

~

Two weeks later, Jason called. He'd been researching Jewish gangsters and had some questions. Could he come over to Hirschman's place and pick his brain?

"Does your father know you're calling me?"

"No."

"How would he react if you told him?"

"Bad. He doesn't like you."

"Good. Come on over."

The kid had done his homework. The list was impressive. Meyer Lansky, Bugsy Siegel, Longy Zwillman, Mickey Cohen, Dutch Schultz. Tough guys involved with the numbers rackets, prostitution, loan sharking, gambling; some got into bootlegging, others had funneled money to the Irgun. Jason's parents, both Ronald and the boy's jackhammer mother, were worried about his interest in Jewish lowlifes, he told Hirschman. It was one of the few things they could agree on. They were mounting a campaign to make him stop.

"Stop what?" Hirschman said. "Thinking? Reading?" He had put out cookies and a short glass of schnapps for the boy. "How can they do that?"

"They're threatening to send me to therapy. They're saying I'm adjusting poorly to the breakup of Wendy and my dad. Acting out."

Hirschman waved this away like a cloud of gnats. "Ach, that's nothing. Intimidation. Oldest tactic in the book. Radicals never let that stop them, union organizers never let that stop them."

The boy was unconvinced. "I need a counter-strategy."

Hirschman watched him devour the cookies. He hadn't touched the schnapps. "Tell them you'll be glad to go because then you'll have the chance to tell the shrink all about them. About the fights and the name-calling, anything you heard. And anything you care to make up. A whole delightfully sordid history."

The boy smiled, wads of mashed cookie dough between his teeth.

"You want something else to drink?" Hirschman said

and got up to get him a glass of tomato juice. He was wearing his cushy slippers.

"What's that?" Jason was pointing to the dish bin on the floor.

"Your father tends to his car. I tend to my oxen. This is what men do."

~

Wendy had found a nice apartment six blocks from Hirschman's and was dating a man she met at a demonstration.

"What kind of demonstration?" Hirschman asked over his pastrami sandwich.

"In the city. In front of the old Helmsley Palace. Against the exploitation of the housekeeping staff. No one else will do the work they do, but the hotel management treats them like dirt."

A week later, while soaking his feet, he saw the back of Wendy's head on TV. The demonstration was on the news, a melee had broken out. One of the protesters heckled the mayor of New York as he tried to get into the hotel to meet with a delegation from management; later, from his hospital bed, the mayor with two broken ribs said he'd gone to persuade them to meet the workers' demands or risk being shut down. But all the demonstrators heard was *meeting with management*, and things got out of control.

Five hours later, Hirschman, in his tight shoes, was in a taxi with Wendy leaving the police station with a receipt for bail in his hand. There was no mention of a new boyfriend.

"I'm getting too old for this," Wendy said, staring out the window. "There was no joy in riding in the patrol car to the precinct. I didn't feel like yelling at the cops. They were just overworked guys, most younger than me, trying to do their jobs and get home to their families in one piece." She turned to Hirschman. "One of the demonstrators started everything. I think he provoked on purpose so he'd get on the news, one of those angry kids all hot to trot and thinking he knows everything." She looked out the window again. "Nothing's ever really black and white, is it?"

"You're not thinking of going back to Ronald, are you?"

"He's been calling."

"Perhaps resist?"

"Jason's been pushing for it."

"It's your life."

"Exactly."

~

The new arrangement, she told Hirschman, had conditions. Of course fidelity was required, as was asking for her forgiveness. Ronald swore he was through trying to punish all women for the behavior of his first wife. Therapy would be involved, not for Jason but for Ronald. Also, the car: he needed to be willing to share. And to stop simonizing and buffing. Three months trial. Then they'd reassess.

Jason, Wendy reported over her split pea soup, was overjoyed. He had grown attached to her, she said. The

282

feeling was mutual. He mattered to Wendy with a force that surprised her. At fifty, she didn't want to walk away from that.

"I'm happy for you," Hirschman said, wrapping up the other half of his salami sandwich. He too liked the boy. If the father had to come along, a package deal, he'd learn to live with it.

"Jason's become quite interested in famous Jewish criminals," Wendy said. "Ronald is worried but I tell him to chill, that it's age-appropriate. And a good sign, really. He's thinking big picture, right and wrong, developing a sense of justice."

Hirschman sipped his cream soda. The kid was a natural, a chip off the old, if purloined, block. He watched his daughter, whose sweater, he noticed, was an electric pink set off by a pair of enormous earrings in the shape of silverware.

"I'm telling you, Dad, the kid is on to something. A passion ignited," Wendy said, working the soup. "He also wants to hear more about your crooked ancestors." She looked up at him. "Assuming any of it's true."

Hirschman smiled. If she were an agnostic—and maybe she was; it was something they ought to discuss sometime—she'd know that whether the stories were provable or not was irrelevant. It was your choice whether or not to believe.

She bent over the soup, a miniature spoon dangling from her earlobe.

"Does it matter?" he said.

AFTER

· ◊ ·

My father, not long dead, warned me about this. He came to me in a dream, sitting in that chair he had, the one by the window with the lamp he never turned on, and said, Frannie, this is not a good situation. You're going to have to do something about it because you know it's not good.

That was it. No explanation, no blueprint for how to correct things. Just that steady tone of voice. Because, though you can't live other people's lives for them, sometimes you have to try to get them back on track.

~

When I was seventeen I ran away from home. I stayed out for two days until a policeman brought me back. We were very regular in our family, dinner together every night, and my not being home on time was cause for concern. It was a nice town, and the first thing my parents thought was that I'd been abducted. It happened every decade or so, a girl would disappear; years later someone would find her remains a mile from where she lived. It was October, and my sister Joanna was upstairs doing her homework and listening to the radio, my brother Robert on his way home from the Shaws, who lived around the block. My mother was in the kitchen but I hadn't come home so she called up to Joanna to ask her. Did Frannie say anything about staying late at school? Or about going to someone's house?

The way Joanna told it she didn't hear my mother the first time, too absorbed in the song on the radio, but when she finally heard what my mother said—maybe my mother repeated it or maybe Joanna just got alert and paid attention—Joanna's first thought was, Frannie's so selfish, she probably forgot to tell anyone she had something to do, God, sometimes I hate her.

This I heard after the policeman had brought me back and I'd been given a meal and a bath and was sitting on my bed. Joanna tiptoed in and started to tell me, confess really, that she'd had this terrible thought about me and how sorry she was and how she'd never think that way about me again, please Frannie, don't ever run away again, you scared everyone half to death.

Half to death? I thought. I was almost all the way to death. I glared at her and said nothing, though I was petrified, two days evaporated, no memory of them at all. But I made myself look closed off, so closed off that my jaw hurt from being clamped so tightly shut.

~

After the third flight that fall because I had to get away from what was going on inside my head, I was taken to a doctor, then a hospital. Over the months the medications changed and the diagnoses changed but not much else did. My mother drove me to day treatments and for programs—painting or ceramics; people tried to make me sing. My moods and tempers spiraled and fell and spiraled again. At home I'd break things—the piano bench, the framed pictures of my mother's grandparents because of how the foreign-looking man in it was staring at me—then afterward slump down and Joanna or my mother would try to comfort me. My brother pretty much checked out. He was twelve, then thirteen. He stayed out as late as he could until he was old enough to go away to a boarding school because he couldn't think straight in a household that contained me in it. No one could. But Robert, especially, had a lot to think about, it turned out, and he couldn't do it amid all the chaos and noise.

For the next ten years I smothered my family and battled them, living with my parents between hospitalizations, then coming apart. Finally, a person with wisdom and foresight—a doctor or social worker—had us all sign an agreement that I'd live somewhere else. A lawyer wrote it up so it would be all legal and watertight, and no one was allowed to break it, not me by begging nor my parents by feeling guilty. The idea was that if it were a contract, no one had to think it had anything to do with love.

And we all pretty much lived up to it. I can't entirely say where I lived all that time--halfway houses, supervised apartments. My parents and Joanna visited. They brought me pictures of Robert and his wife in Virginia.

Then my mother died. I killed her. My father said that wasn't true, but she was fifty-six and I'd worn her out. I didn't mourn her then because I couldn't concentrate very much, but I mourn her now. Joanna and her husband moved overseas to one of those oil rich countries in the Middle East. And then my father got sick. Cancer, early stage.

And I began to get well. Better, anyway. It can happen, Dr. Morrisey said. I was living on my own and had a job typing invoices at an insurance company. I was forty-two years old.

I can outgrow this? I asked Dr. Morrisey. After twenty-six years it can just stop?

He nodded. It can. Very nearly.

And it did.

Not all at once. But just like on the way down, bit by bit, that's how you come up. Like up out of an ocean. Fewer and fewer near-drownings. I saw my father more. We played chess and cards. I visited him when he had to go to the hospital. The tables are turned, Frannie, he said. You're in the visitor's chair now.

Joanna came back from overseas. I met her children.

My skin improved and my weight went back to normal and my hair, though gray, grew in softer. I took my first vacation in thirty years, two weeks on Martha's Vineyard with Joanna, Charles, and their boys. I went to the Greek Islands with a tour. Then, three days before my forty-sixth birthday and a month after his seventy-eighth, my father died.

And I got well.

~

And now there's Robert.

I get the call from Joanna. He's in a hospital in Washington, D.C. and needs a bone marrow transplant. Joanna is not a match.

Tell me what to do, I say. I'll go tomorrow, whatever you tell me.

A long pause, and I know before she starts what Joanna will say. He won't take it from you.

But it's not contagious! I say. I'm fine! Five years! I'm on such low doses I can go off and they'll be out of my system in a day! I'll get a letter from my doctor! Proof!

Joanna is sniffling. Is it his wife? I press. Maura? Is she the one who won't let me?

No, no, she'll do anything for a match.

I stare at the photos of Joanna's family on the fridge, Adam in braces and Charles and Todd with their dog. I don't know what Robert looks like. Joanna's last pictures of him were at his son's high school graduation but you can hardly see Robert, covered up with sunglasses and a captain's hat. Does he look like my mother? Like Joanna?

DISPLACED PERSONS ◊ WEST

Or the worst possibility: me.

Have you talked to him? I ask. A stupid question. Of course she has. How did he say it, I wonder. Harshly, in a rage? Or in measured tones, the way I imagine a physicist would talk. Controlled fury.

Yes, she says. He's made up his mind.

How sick is he? I say, my voice dropping, as if saying it too loud—*sick*—will make the worst happen. How much longer?

A few months. They're still searching the registries but it's not promising.

What about his children? I ask, then think: does a parent take life-giving marrow from a child?

They can't, Joanna says. The boy had childhood cancer and the girls are too young.

Childhood cancer? That happy boy at graduation? Why had no one told me?

Or maybe they had. Did you ever tell me that, Joanna? I whisper. About the boy's cancer?

We did, Frannie. Dad was there.

We're both weepy now. This happens often. I ask Joanna a question, a fact I'm supposed to know, and she answers. A cousin's child, a Presidential election. My missed life. I am like from a time warp, one of those Rip Van Winkles who wakes up after a long sleep and finds everyone she knew either old or dead, the world an alien place full of strange machines.

This is terrible, I say, and Joanna murmurs, Yes, but Robert is a grown man, entitled to have his wishes respected. We hang up and I look out the window. Snow covers the little yard out front, and I think about that first big snow five years ago when I went outside and wasn't afraid of the icy waves which once could have risen up off the green lawns and white pavement and swallowed me.

~

When I was ten and Robert six we were sent together to Maine to Orchard Beach where my Aunt May and her husband Lou rented a summer cottage. My mother was going to the hospital for "female troubles"—a hysterectomy—and Joanna had come down with chicken pox. My grandmother came to stay with Joanna so my father could go to work.

May and Lou were progressive types who believed in letting kids have free reign. They kept a key in a flowerpot by the front steps, showed us the refrigerator, told us to have fun, then took their towels and chairs off to Pine Point every morning. When it rained they read books on the screened porch; sometimes they took us to the movies. But mostly they left us alone.

Which was fine with us. We learned the short cut to the beach where we played elaborate games of two-person tag and jumped around in the water. Some days we found May and Lou on the sand and sat with them before moving on. We trekked home salty and hungry and made tomato sandwiches. We went through May's collection of jigsaw puzzles; even then Robert had a gift for seeing shapes and the vacuums they left behind. At night Robert let only me help him in the bath. He felt funny with May or Lou, he said, and I was just as capable as either of them

291

of washing his hair and getting the sand out of his ears. At bedtime we took turns reading aloud to each other. One night I was the grownup and Robert the baby; the next night it was the reverse. In this way we each got what we needed: to be both the nurtured and the nurturer, and no one had to be ashamed.

~

I fly to Washington a day after talking to Joanna. She offers to come with me but I say no; traveling by myself is one of my greatest pleasures because now I know I won't fall into a subterranean cavern during the cab ride or see myself outside the window of the plane, a mocking tooth-filled double. I like to hear the whoosh of the ascent, see the ant-like world below, accept the can of Coke from the smiling stewardess as if I've been flying this airline for years.

I know it's Maura in the corridor by the nurses' station though we've never met. I know too that I am risking their wrath by showing up uninvited. But I took the chicken's way out because what if he'd said I couldn't come? I wanted to see him. And there is my father to think of, and the dream.

Frannie, Maura says. Then she is hugging me and saying how good of me to make the trip, how wonderful that I'm well, Joanna has told them everything. Robert is having tests in another wing, she says, pulling herself away. Her hair is thick and shiny, dark reddish, like cherry wood. She wipes her eyes and takes me by the hand to a small room down the corridor. Family Lounge, it says on the

292

door. My parents spent long hours in rooms like these—a window with a view of the street, watercolors of sailboats, soft mauve couches meant to keep everyone calm and distracted from the fact that electric shock was taking place down the hall. I have a flood of questions: how is she managing, how long has he been ill, when might he go home.

Maura shakes her head. The prognosis is not good. A swiftly moving cancer, moving especially swiftly with Robert. A little fatigue, he wrote it off. You know how he is. Stiff upper lip.

Yes, I say. The boarding school. My father had been worried. It was strict, truly military, it could be rigid, racist, antisemitic. My mother, exhausted, waved off his objections. Give the boy some say here, God knows nothing else in his life is in his control.

Joanna told you about the transplant? Maura says.

I nod.

Maura's eyes fill. He won't accept you as a donor, she says.

I know, I say.

She takes my hand. I tried to convince him, Frannie. I know there's nothing wrong with you as a donor. No medical reason.

I lay my free hand on hers to stop her. She shouldn't have to say this. It's okay, Maura. Really. I wanted to come anyway.

Maura dabs at her eyes. It's late, she should go home, the children are old enough to manage by themselves but the ordeal has been awful. Why don't we talk more later, I say. I'll come back after dinner. The desk said visiting hours are until eight.

I'll tell Robert you were here and that you're coming back. That's fine.

Do you know where to go to eat? Are you okay in the city? I'm fine.

We stand, and Maura wraps her arms around me and I feel her crying before she speaks. We never came to see you, Frannie, she says into my sweater. We never came, and I'm so sorry.

I pat her softly on the back. Her hair smells like apples. It's okay, Maura. Outside the little window the sky is silver-gray. It's okay, I murmur again. I wouldn't have known the difference.

~

A light rain has begun to fall. In a coffee shop I order a ginger ale and a salad. My taste buds are gone, vanished with the worst of my sickness, and sometimes I miss the excitement of food. I eat out of obligation, to sustain the body, occasionally with appetite. But the food always disappoints.

The waitress brings the salad and a little basket of rolls and asks if I'd like anything else. Not right now, thank you, I say, and wonder: has Robert lost his taste buds too? Is the treatment he's receiving destroying that pleasure? Or had he lost that long ago when he watched me writhing on the kitchen floor, certain the linoleum was alive with bugs that wanted to consume me? Or when he heard me screaming about blood and babies? Joanna has been considerate, giving me only snatches of detail about the times I refused to use anything to soak up the monthly flow, letting it stain my pants and the kitchen chairs, terrified that if I stopped it up, it would come up into my throat and choke me. Sanitary napkins! my mother implored. They don't stop up anything, they'll just absorb, like cloths, like diapers, like the rags my great-grandmother used to use!

But that was terrifying too. They'd absorb the baby, suffocate it before it had the chance to turn from liquid to solid, a tiny floating egg. You couldn't see it but it was there, and no napkin, no diaper, no rag, was going to take away my baby. And there was Robert, watching and listening to me rant and seeing me bleed all over the furniture.

I finish my food, sip tasteless tea. Outside, the workday is ending. I've never been to Washington. Maybe tomorrow I'll take a tour, ride by the White House, the Washington Monument, the Lincoln Memorial. A free citizen. I could line up with all the other foreign nationals, all of us from alien nations grateful for the new country we're in. Long ago, when she still believed I could do anything about it, my mother once said that if I got well she'd take me to Paris and buy me whatever I wanted. Fancy clothes and scarves and French perfume, a trip to the Riviera if that's what I chose.

Dazed, in a Thorazine dream, I said to her in one of those hushed mauve Family Lounges, Can you buy me another Revolution? Liberty, Equality, Fraternity?

~

My brother is propped up on pillows, his bed cranked to sitting position. Beyond him the curtain is closed, the soft murmur of Spanish; his roommate has company.

Maura hugs me and I take a chair opposite hers, on the other side of Robert's bed. He turns to look at me, an oxygen tube in his nose. His eyes are blue, not like mine. He looks a little like my father, maybe more like my mother. But mostly he looks like himself. I'd recognize him anywhere.

I'm sorry you're ill, Robert, I say. This must be very difficult for you.

He looks away, then back at me. I'm not sure he's going to talk. He always had a stubborn streak, a defiance that said, *I can outlast you*, whether it was holding our breath underwater or a staring match across the kitchen table.

Well, it's hard for you, too, he says, turning and addressing the wall.

Yes, well, not really, I say. I knew I had to come see you. The day before I heard about your illness, I saw Dad in a dream, and he told me I needed to do something, that the situation was not good.

I hadn't planned to talk about the dream, it sounds so crazy, so typically Frannie to cite a visit from the dead as a precipitating factor for anything, but there it is, out there, the truth. And it is the truth. I don't know if I'd have had the courage to come without that dream.

Well, I'm glad you're still in touch with Dad, Robert says to the wall. You always did have a way of hearing and seeing what the rest of us couldn't.

A quick intake of breath from Maura. Robert's anger is right there, thirty years of it sitting on top of his head.

I don't think Frannie meant she saw Dad literally, Maura says. Sometimes dreams can be very helpful. They can point to unresolved conflicts.

Yeah, well, Frannie's dreams are no piece of cake, Maura, Robert says. Maura glances at me and I raise a palm to show her it's all right. Let me tell you, Maura, Robert says, Frannie had the most unhelpful dreams you can imagine, and we all heard them, didn't we, Frannie. We all had to hear them. His voice is charged, the power behind those words like a trillion tons of dammed up water.

You did, Robert, I say. They all did, but it fell hardest on him, the youngest, the most impressionable.

But Frannie's better now, Maura says. She's looking at Robert, who's looking at the wall. That's all that counts, Maura says. That Frannie's well and free of all that torment.

Poor Maura. That's not all that counts but I can't tell her that. She'll have to hear it for herself, from Robert.

But Robert's closing up, too restrained to give vent to whatever he's feeling. It falls to me and Maura to speak.

Where did you eat? Maura says.

A coffee shop. It was fine.

And the walk? Not too bad in the rain?

Oh no, it was nice. Maybe tomorrow I'll see some of the sights.

Maura nods and says, I brought pictures of the children. She fishes in a bag that holds her knitting, then reaches across the bed just as Robert shoots up an arm.

She can't look at these! he says, grabbing the pictures. Forget this pretend loving aunt business, this fake family reunion! I don't want her gazing at our children and saying how cute, how handsome. Let's stop all this pretense right now!

Robert! Maura says, horrified. Where's your decency!

297

Frannie was sick! She was no more able to help herself back then than you can help yourself now! What's the matter with you!

What's the matter with me? He looks at Maura. I look at my hands. You want to know what's the matter with me? I've spent my whole life trying to get out from under the damage she did in our family, and I finally succeeded. I've got you and the kids and our life here. But first she wrecked my life for a long, long time. You don't know the half of it. My mother, my father, Joanna, you think any of them weren't destroyed by her?

Maura puts a hand over her mouth. I look at the foot of the bed. The hum of Spanish behind me has stopped; someone on the other side of the curtain coughs. Robert has put together a life on a shaky foundation, a fragile house of cards. Because anyone who grows up with someone like me knows that any second it can crumble, your world a heap of nothing at your feet. And now here I've come to rattle the floorboards.

A chair scrapes the linoleum behind the curtain. Maura has her face in her hands. I pick up my coat from my lap and quietly walk around the bed, pat Maura on the shoulder on my way out. Robert's eyes are closed. Maura's footsteps trail me to the corridor.

~

The last time I saw Robert, he was home from boarding school for Christmas vacation. He was sixteen; I was twenty; Joanna was a senior at the local high school. I was getting outpatient treatment and supposed to be studying

298

for the GED. I hadn't been a bad student before but now I could hardly concentrate. I had no friends, no life. I wasn't fat yet from the meds and spent a lot of time looking in the mirror, not sure what I was seeing but still wanting to look. To kill time I'd put on makeup and constantly change my clothes. The pills I was on kept me barely within the lines.

It was snowing, predictions of a big storm coming, and Joanna and my mother had gone out for groceries. Robert and I were home alone, and I knew my mother had told him to watch me. I'd been in the hospital again that fall, on a floor with a lot of girls who were suicidal. My mother was terrified I might try something though it wasn't in my profile.

I was in the bathroom playing with Joanna's makeup when I heard the car pull out of the driveway. Joanna had started to date that year. My parents wanted her to have a normal life and go out and have fun. But she never brought anyone home. Instead she was making out in cars and in other people's basements, which upset my parents but which they felt powerless to change because they couldn't tell her to bring her dates to our house. She wouldn't do it.

Robert was downstairs. He'd been home for two days and had hardly talked to me. He couldn't even look at me. He had a crew cut like some army guy. This was the 1974, Vietnam. I thought the army were pigs.

I'm bored, I said, walking up behind Robert at the kitchen table. I put my hands on his head. His scalp was like peach fuzz. He was reading the newspaper, the remains of his lunch in front of him. A glass of milk, two sandwiches, cookies. He'd gotten big, six feet, and worked out every day. He looked a lot older than sixteen. I tapped my foot fast, a rhythm only I could hear. The new meds had a way of revving me, I was hyped all the time. I fished in my pants pocket for a joint and pulled it out.

What are you doing with that stuff, Frannie, Robert said. It's bad for you, it's bad for everyone. But you especially, with all those pills you have to take.

Oh Robert, Robert, I said. You're such a straight arrow. I lit the joint and he pulled it from my mouth and stubbed it out on his plate.

Don't do it, he said, angry. Or do it somewhere else if you have to, but not here.

Not on your watch? I said. I put my hand up in mock salute. Yessir! No dope on your watch, sir!

He turned back to the paper and made a disgusted sound. I paced around the kitchen. My whole body was racing. I'd have to tell them at the hospital about it. I thought I might get a heart attack.

I went upstairs to my room and opened the closet. I didn't like the pants I had on, they were dull. Everything was dull. I couldn't eat, couldn't taste, couldn't sleep, and my pants were dull. I took off all my clothes and swished through the hangers, then went, naked, to Joanna's room, to her closet and pulled out a black skirt. A mini for Joanna, who was four inches shorter than I was. Making it a handkerchief for me.

I put it on and checked myself in the mirror. I had a headache like the Grand Canyon and couldn't stop tapping. I pulled out a blouse, a see-through number Joanna wore with a pale blue shell she thought brought out her eyes and put it on and looked in the glass. You could see everything through it. I went downstairs to the kitchen, back to Robert's chair, and twirled around in Joanna's skirt. Robert was on the sports section.

Why don't you dance with me?

He shrugged my hands off his shoulders, kept his eyes on the paper.

C'mon, Robert. I'll put on some music.

I don't want to, Frannie. Leave me alone.

C'mon, it'll be fun.

I don't like this, Frannie. He kept his head down, as if he were really reading. You're out of control, you're weird, and you don't even know who I am.

I know who you are. You're little Robby two-shoes, little goody two-shoes. Har-rup! I saluted him and gave him the finger but he wasn't looking. I put my hands on his peach fuzz head and started to massage.

Get off! He shook off my hands and turned around in the chair. What the hell is the matter with you? You don't do this with your brother!

No? I said. What's the matter, little brother, no sex drive? No girlies yet?

Leave me be, Frannie! He got up, walked to the living room.

I followed him. He was on the couch, moving magazines on the coffee table, trying to find something to look at so he wouldn't have to look at me. Ah ah ah! I said, sing-song, a finger in the air. Mom said not to leave me alone.

I'm not going to be your fucking babysitter, he said. He pulled out a magazine and pretended to read. He'd got-

301

ten a lot bigger since the summer. Maybe he was older than sixteen and I didn't remember.

Ooh! Fucking babysitter! I said, prancing over to him, Joanna's skirt flapping around me. Fucking is the operative word! I opened my mouth, swept my lips with my tongue and flipped up the skirt, stuck my crotch in his face.

Agh! Go away! he yelled, getting up and storming out of the living room. I followed him, flipping the skirt like a burlesque, up and down, up and down. Jesus, Frannie, stop it! We were in the hall. Stop it! he yelled, me trailing him, fanning the skirt like an apron. Stop, or I'm going out that door!

No, you're not, I said, singsong again. Mother put you in charge. Now you're the grownup and I'm the baby. Baby needs patting. You're the grownup and you have to stay with me and do everything I say!

He went into the den and slammed the door. I heard the TV go on.

Open up, I yelled, or I'll hurt myself.

Shut up!

Open up, or I'll do it, I swear!

Shut up, Frannie! Go take a bath or a cold shower, or go smoke your dope, whatever you want! Just leave me alone!

All ri-ight! That singsong voice.

Silence.

The bath filling.

More silence.

Then Robert running up the stairs, banging on the door. He'd heard what girls of a certain type were capable of.

Let me in, Frannie, open the door!

Silence.

Let me in, goddamit!

He jimmied the lock, crappy doors to begin with, got in with a screwdriver and a pair of pliers.

The water was pink. I was underneath, head underwater, everything underwater.

Frannie! Frannie! He pulled at my arm, dead weight on the bottom. I was naked and he couldn't stand it, reached with his free hand for a towel.

Then I exploded out of the water, laughing and spitting spray at him and waving a little bottle of food coloring, shrieking and laughing and waving the bottle.

He ran out and slammed the door. Fucking lunatic! he screamed on his way down the stairs and out of the house, where he stood in the cold, the snow coming down, until the car came back, Joanna and my mother pulling into the driveway. Home with the groceries in case there was a storm.

~

Robert's room is crowded. Work people. They've brought special gifts to cheer him up. Stick-on stars and planets, a mobile of the solar system. I give Maura a little wave and motion that I'll be down the hall. Robert is out of view. After yesterday's visit Maura asked me to come back, to not give up, to give Robert time.

The Family Lounge is empty. I watch the corridor half expecting my former self to come wandering in in a checkered hospital gown, the pink slippers I refused to give up even after all the food and coffee stains had turned them brown. Five years ago, after Dr. Morrisey showed me the scans, the tests, the corroborating opinion from his associate, Dr. Pell, I put those slippers in a box along with my three bathrobes, a stuffed baby dragon and hundreds of drawings, and taped it all up and put it in the back of a closet.

A man is walking toward the Family Lounge. I perk up, sit up straight in case I'm drifting, a habitual worry, uncertainty over how much drift is normal. He comes in and I smile politely and keep looking at the door, the way you would in an elevator. I should have picked up a magazine but it's too late.

He sits in a chair catty-corner from me. Excuse me, but are you Frannie Stern?

I look at him, a flash fear that he's here to take me to the other side, evict me from the Family Lounge and bundle me off to the fifth floor, Psychiatry, Acute.

Yes? I say.

I thought so, he says and smiles. I've been visiting Robert, I heard you were here. I'm Kenny Rhodes. From Patchogue.

The name of my hometown sends a vibration to my knees.

I knew you when we were kids, he says. I lived on Red Rock Road.

Red Rock Road. Cheryl Feinstein lived there. When I was fourteen I babysat for the Cullens.

Your sister is Elaine? I say.

Yes, she's the oldest. I also have a brother, Stuart. Do you remember him?

I nod. Mostly, though, I remember Elaine. Small, pretty. In fourth grade she wore ruffled socks.

Elaine lives in Wisconsin now, Kenny says.

How did you find Robert? I say. Do you live in Washington?

An amazing coincidence, he says, and inches up on his chair. We're both astronomers and work for the same institute. I just moved here from Albuquerque. When I saw the phone list I had to call immediately, ask if he was Robert Stern from Patchogue. How many Robert Sterns could there be? He laughs. Actually, there could be quite a few. But sure enough. I hadn't seen Robert since eighth grade.

I don't know what to say. So, you have kids, a family? I ask.

Two girls, twelve and eight. My wife is a musician. She teaches, gives concerts. But, you know, with kids, it's hard. How about you?

Me? Does that mean he doesn't know? Rumors had spread at the high school, Joanna had her share of humiliation. No kids, I say. No husband either.

He folds his hands.

I've been ill, I say. But I'm better now.

So I've heard.

Oh? From who?

Robert. He said you were sick for a long time but that you've recovered. That it was a miracle.

He said that?

Oh yes. We were talking in his room just now. He said everyone had nearly given up hope, but that it was wonderful and that you were still young and could make a life.

He told you that?

A nod.

A shaft of light brightens the window. After a while, Kenny gets up and says, It's good to see you, Frannie, and leaves the room.

~

The summer before I ran away I worked as a counselor at the municipal day camp. Robert, who was twelve, went to a science program in town for smart kids like him.

Every night after dinner I sat outside on the curb with my friends sipping Cokes and watching the younger kids play tag and stickball until it got dark. One night a boy who'd just moved in, whose troubled family would move away within the year, shoved Robert hard, knocking him onto a neighbor's lawn, then put his foot on Robert's chest and said he played like a girl, even looked like a girl, probably was a girl under those fruity shorts he had on. I hustled over and told the kid to get lost, and when he didn't move and called me a bad name, I punched him in the jaw and said if he didn't play fair he couldn't play at all. The boy went home, but every night after that, I sat on the curb, and when the boy came back, he hung on the sidelines while Robert and his friends had their game in the street, Robert waving at me each time he ran past, and me waving back.

~

Maura has come to the Family Lounge to say that the visitors are leaving and that I should come to Robert's room.

Are you sure he isn't too tired? I say.

No, it's important for him to see you. I know he's sorry about yesterday. The medicine, the pain, it sets him off.

It's okay, I say. I understand.

No, it'll pass, the anger, Maura says, urgent. It has to, he doesn't have time for that anymore, everything has to happen quickly now.

In Robert's room, Maura takes her place next to the bed. She gestures to the chair opposite, where I sat the evening before.

Mr. Sanchez is taking a walk, Maura says, nodding at the open curtain. He's doing much better. She takes out her knitting, blue yarn the color of sky.

I turn to Robert. He's looking at the wall.

I saw Kenny Rhodes, I say. What a surprise.

Did you remember him? Robert says, then turns to look at me. It seems easier for him to talk if he's looking away.

A little. Mostly I remember Elaine, his sister. Do you remember her?

I didn't know Elaine, Robert says, back to the wall. She was older, your age, I guess.

Yes, I say. She and Patti Sands on the corner, we walked to school together. Patti had a younger sister, I don't remember her name.

Tina, Robert says.

Oh yes. Tina.

Someone is in the doorway. Mr. Sanchez. He shuffles in with a nurse, an I-V pole rolling beside him.

Mr. Sanchez, Maura says, putting her knitting in her

lap. This is Robert's sister, Frannie, she's visiting from New York.

Mr. Sanchez nods, and I say, I hope you'll be getting better soon. He and the nurse inch on, the curtain behind me sliding on the rod, the bed creaking. Robert's eyes are closed. Maura picks up her needles, says, Have you gotten out some, Frannie?

I went to the Smithsonian. Quite a place.

It can take weeks to see it all.

I think I'll go back later, or tomorrow.

The nurse stops at the foot of the bed on the way out. Need anything? she asks.

We're fine, Denise, thank you, Maura says.

Have a good visit, the nurse says to me.

I thank her and watch her go.

I think Joanna is coming down over the weekend, Robert says, eyes still closed.

I think so, I say. No school on Monday.

Presidents Day, is it? Robert says.

That's the one, I answer.

Robert nods. Maura's needles click softly.

~

I visit Robert twice a day for an hour each time. Each visit gets a little better. We talk about Maine. After that first summer, we went back again a few more times, all three of us. We talk about Dad and his regret that he never learned to swim, and the time Robert's ride home from boarding school broke down and how our mother panicked and called everyone she knew and thought of abductions, and then of me, and couldn't decide which would be worse.

In between visits I go to the Smithsonian again and look at the brains of the famous in their display cases. I buy souvenirs for Joanna's boys. We don't tell Robert, but Maura and I arrange for a bone marrow screening for me. I am not a match.

After the week, I went home. Six days later, a matching donor was found. A transplant was performed but within a week it began to fail.

Robert went home after that. There was no second donor and soon it got too late to do another transplant. We talked on the phone each day. Maura began to arrange for hospice care. On the Monday it was to begin, while Joanna and I were at the airport waiting to board our flight to D.C., Robert died.

He was glad we were coming, Maura told us afterward. He had been, she said, expecting us.

ACKNOWLEDGEMENTS

Many of the stories in this book would never have come about were it not for the extraordinary opportunity given me to live and work in Israel from 2007 to 2013. I thank the Shaindy Rudoff Graduate Program in Creative Writing at Bar-Ilan University for inviting me to be visiting writer those years, with special thanks to Michael Kramer, Allen Hoffman, Linda Zisquit, Marcela Sulak, Judy Labensohn, and Evan Fallenberg. I am indebted to Jackie Stein of the American Center in Jerusalem and Risa Levy of the U.S. Embassy branch in Tel Aviv for sending me out to offer cultural programming in sectors of the country I would otherwise not have visited, enriching my experience immeasurably. Gratitude as well to the African Refugee Development Center in south Tel Aviv for accepting me as a volunteer ESL instructor and to the valorous refugees and asylum seekers I had the privilege of teaching. In each of these remarkable settings, I learned as much from my students as they did from me.

For support during the writing of these stories I thank the MacDowell Colony and the Virginia Center for the Creative Arts for the gift of artist residencies; Hugo House in Seattle, which appointed me writer-in-residence and for two years provided me with a workspace in the heart of the city along with a welcoming literary community; and the Hadassah-Brandeis Institute, which generously offered me a writing room during one Boston winter when it was especially needed.

My gratitude to the editors of the publications where many of these stories first appeared, with additional thanks to the judges who awarded them individual prizes: Ron Carlson for the Nelligan Prize from *Colorado Review*; Walter Mosley and Andre Aciman for two *Moment Magazine* Karma Short Fiction Prizes; and Jane Smiley for Honorable Mention in the Goldenberg Fiction Prize from *Bellevue Literary Review*.

Last, my heartfelt thanks to Weike Wang, judge for the 2022 New American Fiction Prize, for choosing this collection as the winner, and to David Bowen and all the staff at New American Press for bringing this book into the world.

JOAN LEEGANT'S first book of stories, *An Hour in Paradise: Stories*, won the 2003 PEN/New England Book Award and the Edward Lewis Wallant Award, and was a Finalist for the National Jewish Book Award and a Barnes & Noble Discover Great New Writers pick. She is also the author of a novel, *Wherever You Go.* Her prize-winning fiction has appeared in over two dozen literary magazines and anthologies. Formerly an attorney, she has taught at Harvard, Oklahoma State, and Cornish College of the Arts in Seattle where she was also the writer-in-residence at Hugo House. For five years she was the visiting writer at Bar-Ilan University in Tel Aviv where she also spoke at Israeli schools on American literature and culture under the auspices of the U.S. Embassy, and taught English to African refugees and asylum seekers. She lives in Newton, Massachusetts, with her family.